D1598400

Heather

Heather

Cordia Byers

FAWCETT GOLD MEDAL • NEW YORK

HEATHER

© 1979 Cordia J. Byers

Published by Fawcett Gold Medal Books, a unit of CBS Publications, the Consumer Publishing Division of CBS Inc.

ISBN: 0-449-14272-8

First Fawcett printing: November 1979

Printed in the United States of America

10 9 8 7 6 5 4 3 2 1

With love to my husband, family and friends who gave me encouragement and support.

Bearing up under harsh conditions the small heather aways blossoms again in the spring as a delicate and beautiful flower.

Chapter One

In the early spring of 1650, in a small cottage near the village of Romsey, Heather Cromwell was born.

It was a lovely day even though the second civil war during the last ten years was raging. Nearly a year and a half had passed since Parliament had tried Charles I for being a traitor and executed him. A threat now came from Charles II in Scotland, where he had been proclaimed King.

Heather was not to know who her father was because of the brutality of war and the lust of soldiers. Her mother had taken Cromwell for the child's last name because it had been his troops that had marched through their small village that hot July of the previous summer.

Holding her child, Ellen tried to forget how savagely it had been conceived. She had left the cottage in the afternoon with her spirits soaring. Tom Crawley, the young blacksmith, had proposed marriage. He had spoken to her father that same afternoon, and their wedding was to take place after the fall harvesting.

Ellen could hardly believe her good fortune in finding a man as fine as Tom to love her. In his mid-twenties, he was tall and muscular with large brown eyes and coppery red hair, which fell boyishly over his brow.

They had met for the first time when her father had taken her to the smithy to have his plow mended.

Tom was a good man and wanted a home to raise strong, fine sons. He loved Ellen, for unlike the village trollops who flirted shamelessly with all, she was chaste. She would make him a good wife and be a fine mother for his children.

On that hot afternoon, Ellen's thoughts were only of her future. She did not hear the blue jays singing in the tall oaks, or see the troops camped in the nearby meadow.

Ellen loved this part of the day best, for it was hers alone. Earlier there had been more taxing chores around the cottage and on the farm. And she had had little privacy. But gathering the sheep was a solitary task, a task that allowed for dreaming.

Slowly Ellen walked up the heath and pulled together her now small flock. Her people, like others in the village, had suffered the ravages of war. As things went, they were luckier than most, for many of the farms lay barren.

She watched the setting sun paint the sky in vivid red, gold and purple. It was so peaceful that she stayed longer than usual. Glancing into the valley below she became aware of the oncoming darkness. Candles already glowed in the cottage windows.

Angry with herself for having taken so much time, she scurried the sheep down the heath. As she passed along the edge of the meadow path she met three soldiers coming from the direction of the village. She started to pass them when one spoke up. "Ay there, missy, where ye going in such a hurry? My, ain't she a nice one?"

Ellen froze. The man was tall and skinny and looked

8

as if he had never taken a bath. His hair, cut in the short choppy style of the Roundheads, was black and greasy, and when he smiled he showed decaying teeth.

"Well now, me pretty, we thought for a minute ye were a star with that golden hair," he said as he came closer. Ellen could smell the alcohol on his breath and knew that they had been to the Wild Boar Tavern in the village.

"You're the nicest piece we've come across in a long time," the greasy one laughed. Ellen was too shocked to notice that the other two had made a circle around her and she jumped as a voice came from behind her. "Sure 'tis, mate. What say, missy, lost yer tongue?" Glancing around Ellen saw a short, fat man with a red pockmarked face. Over one eye he wore a black patch and his lips were curled into a sardonic grin. He was slightly shorter than Ellen and breathed as if a heavy weight rested on his chest. And when he spoke it sounded labored.

Before Ellen could say a word the third man spoke. "Sure would like to have a piece o' that, wouldn't ye?" The one with the patch turned a leering dirty-toothed grin on Ellen and said, "That's the best idea I believe ye've ever had, mate." And before Ellen could move, a dirty hand clasped her hard by the shoulder, spinning her into fat, odorous arms, and slimy lips pressed down on hers.

As Ellen tried to free herself and scream for help, one clamped a hand over her mouth to stifle her screams and dragged her behind a clump of hay. The greasy man pulled a dirty rag from his pocket and tied it over Ellen's mouth, while the other two held her hands and feet.

Ellen saw the third man for the first time as he bent over her to tear her clothing from her. He was as gruesome as the other two, but a scar disfigured the right side of his face. He was not as old as the others, and she knew he could not be much older than her own eighteen years. However, by the cold, hard look in

9

his eyes as he stared at Ellen's nakedness, one could tell that he had never known kindness in his life. And by the smirking grin that appeared when her bodice was torn away and her small white breasts were exposed, she knew she could expect no mercy from him.

Ellen struggled to escape but she was held firmly. "My, ain't them nice ones though, mate," the greasy one said as he fondled one of her small breasts. "Which un should be first to taste this bit o' white pears?" the man with the patch asked as he looked greedily at Ellen's exposed flesh. "Me, mate. 'Twas me that first saw her," the greasy one said as he pinched Ellen's nipple, making her wince in pain. "All right then, have a go at her," scar face said and grinned as he walked to the other side of Ellen so he could get a better view.

Ellen felt a searing pain rip through her breast as he bit into her flesh. She fainted, but came back to consciousness, her face tingling from the brutal slaps. "What ye doing that for?" asked the greasy man. "'Cause when I take a woman, I want her to know it. And enjoy it." The man with the patch laughed.

Ellen's eyes had started to swell and her senses were numb. Yet she was aware that her skirt had been ripped from her and her body exposed. "Now, I knew it would be worth waiting for," scar face said. But before he could decide to attack, he was pushed roughly aside. "I didn't wake her up for nothing, you bastard. On this I get first choice. Before she faints again, I want to see her enjoy it," the one with the patch growled, showing black decaying teeth.

Ellen could smell the putrid odor of his body as he threw himself upon her. Bile filled her throat. The fat clammy hands explored her secret parts roughly and then the pain seared through her body, ripping and tearing greedily. Mercifully Ellen fainted once more.

Hours later she awoke. Battered beyond belief, Ellen somehow crawled home. She was almost unrecognizable. Her face and lips were swollen and bruised. Dried blood crusted her battered body. Teeth and claw marks ran down her breasts, stomach and thighs. She burned with fever. At the slightest touch she moaned in pain. She could not speak.

Ellen's mother sent for the leech and he bled her. She was delirious for days.

After a week, Ellen finally regained consciousness. She didn't remember anything of her ordeal until she asked her father if Tom had come to visit. Her father hesitated to tell Ellen that Tom had already been there. Upon learning what had happened, he had exploded with anger and stormed from the cottage, saying only that the marriage was off. Finally her father spoke, and the horrifying night returned in full clarity. And when she learned, a month later that she was with child, Ellen nearly went mad. Her parents watched her cautiously, afraid that she might do herself harm. She had not mentioned anything of that night to them, but when she had been delirious, she had screamed and raved until they had pieced together what had happened.

Ellen remained in a dazed state, most of the time sitting before the fire and reliving the terrible night that had destroyed her future.

Ellen didn't realize when the summer turned into autumn. Nor did she see the leaves turn from green to yellow, then to gold, and finally disappear. The cold winds from the north began to blow, bringing the freezing rain of winter.

Then on a midwinter morning when soft light snow covered the ground she felt the babe quicken in her womb. It was strange, Ellen thought as she placed her hand on her swollen belly, she should hate it but she could not hate an innocent child no matter who the father might be. And with that thought in mind she seemed to come back to reality.

If not the same happy girl that she had once been she was not half as troubled as before. Ellen wept for her lost love but realized that his love had not been strong enough to overcome what had happened to her. She knew, too, that any man would want his own son and not one so foully begotten.

Ellen knew that a man's love had passed her by and that she would never marry. All the love that she had felt for Tom was now transferred to the coming child. Raising it to be respected became an obsession with Ellen.

During the rest of the long months of winter Ellen made plans for her and the child's future. Sitting before the fire, she would knit small clothing for it and dream of their future together.

Ellen decided that she would leave the small village, where the circumstances of the child's birth were known to everyone. She would go to London, where she and her child might have a fresh start.

As the warm sun thawed the frozen earth and the small spring flowers poked their blossoms toward the clear blue sky, Ellen's time came. With the pains of labor she began to relive the horrid past. With each pain that ripped through her she seemed to feel the weight of the fat man once again upon her and even to smell his sweaty body. Her own sweat-drenched body seemed to be attempting to cleanse itself of the evil. But as the pain continued, the menacing faces leered at her until there was nothing but agony.

Yet at the first cry of life and the sight of her child's small pink face, she was able to put aside the past and dwell only on her child.

When Ellen regained her strength, she gathered her few meager possessions and said farewell to her family. She hated to leave them, for she loved them deeply. However, she knew that it was her only chance to make a life for herself and Heather. When she announced her plans, her family had tried to persuade her to give up her dream and remain at home. But after much discussion they realized she was determined and would not change her mind. They kissed her goodbye and gave her a few shillings for her journey.

Catching the coach in Romsey on an early summer morn, she and her child started toward London. It was an uncomfortable journey. The coach was packed tightly with passengers, and the air reeked of human sweat. Anyone with less determination might have turned back.

Ellen avoided the other passengers, pretending sometimes to doze or ignoring their attempts at conversation. She had heard many frightening tales of what could happen to young women journeying alone.

After five days of tedious travel the coach came within sight of the small forts that protected the city. Soon the gates of London appeared. The wheels of the coach turned swiftly into the crowded streets. Ellen gasped. She had expected London to be larger than her village but never dreamed it would be so huge and chaotic.

Ellen could not draw her eyes from the masses of people. She could see women with baskets trudging down the street with their daily shopping. Others hawked merchandise to passersby. Mixed with the shoppers and merchants was an assortment of beggars. Street urchins dashed in and out of the crowd, pushing and shoving. If a purse happened to come within reach, it was snatched. Soldiers also crowded the streets, even though the civil war had come no closer to London than Brentwood, twenty miles away. Though Ellen didn't know it, the bustling city was even more active than usual this day. Preparations were being made to honor Cromwell for his many victories.

Ellen had thought that her anxieties would diminish when she reached London, but as her eyes took in the city she felt overwhelmed.

Her money was almost gone, the trip had cost more than she realized. One thing she did know, she had to find work as quickly as possible and find a place where she and the child could live.

The coach stopped on one of the crowded streets and Ellen stepped down, cradling Heather in her arms.

She was tired and dirty. Collecting her small reticule, which contained all her possessions, she started her search for a place to stay.

Ellen walked the streets for most of the day. Finally she found a room for rent at Goodlinger's Inn. As she entered the inn she realized that a tavern occupied the lower half of the building. The rooms were located above it, and the kitchen adjoined the tavern.

It was the first time in Ellen's short life that she had ever entered a tavern and she was apprehensive. Through the dimness she saw a gruff-looking man standing behind a large oak bar.

As she approached he looked up. Thinking it was one of the street urchins, he said, "Be gone with ye, 'fore I box yer ears so hard that ye'll look like a peddler's cart!" Ellen started to leave but as she did Heather whimpered. Looking harder at the small figure still shadowed by the light that came from the street, the landlord said, "Wait, what ye got there? What ye doing with someone's bairn?"

Ellen looked at the man for a moment and then replied, "Sir, this is my babe." The man walked from behind the bar and looked Ellen over. "Beg yer pardon, miss, I thought ye were one of them little varmints that run in and out if ye don't stop 'em. Ye being so small and all." And with a smile he said, "What can I do for ye?"

Ellen looked up into the face, which held gentle blue eyes and a jovial smile. And she automatically returned the first true smile that she had seen since she had begun her journey. "I'm looking for a room for me and my babe."

"Well, ye've come to the right place. Ma has the last room left in all London," he said.

"May I ask, sir, how much the room will let?" Ellen asked, knowing that she probably would not have enough money.

" 'Tis a shilling a week without meals," he said, and Ellen's features fell.

"Sir, I'm sorry to have caused ye trouble, but I cannot afford that." And she turned to leave.

The landlord watched Ellen as she walked to the door and knew by her clothes that she had just arrived in London. He had noticed that the babe could not have been over a few weeks old at most. She did not seem to be one of the camp followers that always accompanied the army's arrival. By her actions he knew that she did not have any money and needed a place to stay. And besides, the tavern needed a new barmaid. "Wait a minute, miss," he called. Ellen turned once more toward the man and he continued, "Do ye need work?"

Ellen could see from the light that filtered into the room the concern in the man's eyes and said, "Yes sir, I do."

Motioning Ellen back into the room, he said, "Well, if ye be looking for a position, there's one open here as a barmaid. It don't pay much but there's a room in the back that goes with it. It would be room enough for the babe and yerself," he said.

Ellen did not hesitate in accepting the offer and said, "Thank ye, I'd be glad for it."

"Well, come with me to meet Ma, for she's the one with the final say," he said as he turned and led Ellen through the door at the back of the tavern. As she entered the small room, she saw a fat, short woman sitting in a corner behind a small table littered with paper. If the woman had not had gray hair, she would have passed for the man's twin even though he was taller and not as stoutly built. As they approached the table the man said, "This is me ma and she owns the inn. And I'm George Goodlinger, her son." With this he gave Ellen a small smile, which was noted by the woman who sat at the table. "Ma, this girl is looking for work and I told her we needed a barmaid. She said she'd like to have the work so I brought her to ye to have the final say."

The woman rose to her feet and walked around the

table, eyeing Ellen. Her gaze rested on the bundle in Ellen's arms and she said, "And what do ye plan to do with the bairn while ye be working? It's too small to stay by itself."

Ellen glanced down at Heather sleeping peacefully and realized for the first time that what the woman said was the truth, but before she could answer the man said, "Tilly can keep it in the kitchen while she's at her duties. We do need a girl 'cause the soldiers keep the place packed since Cromwell arrived last week. I can't do all the work meself."

" 'Tis right ye be, me son," Ma said. "But before I say, I have to know, are ye a camp follower?"

Ellen gave the woman a shocked look. "A camp follower? No, for I've no use for soldiers," Ellen answered, shaking her head.

"Well, I just had to make sure. I can't have ye traipsing off when I need ye," Ma said, and then continued, "If ye are willing to work hard, ye have the job, me girl. And ye can start tonight at the supper hour."

Ellen's face brightened with a smile as she said, "Thank ye, ma'am."

As Ellen turned to leave, the old woman said, "What's yer name, girl?"

Ellen said, "Ellen Cromwell."

"Well, ye can call me Mrs. Goodlinger, and have Tilly show ye to yer room in the back. Ye'll find her in the kitchen."

George showed Ellen to the kitchen and then returned to the barroom. As Ellen stepped into the kitchen she could see that it was a large room as was everything in it, including the fireplace and even the beef that sizzled over the fire. To Ellen it smelled like heaven, for now she noticed the gnawing hunger in her stomach. Her child, too, was hungry as she nuzzled at her breast.

Before the fireplace was a plump little woman with round pink cheeks, bending over a pot which sat on the hearth. She wore a big apron which was greasy, as

16

if she wiped her hands often on the dark material. Her dark blue dress clung damply to her plump figure, for the kitchen was boiling hot. Despite the uncomfortable heat of the room her face wore a cheerful expression.

Hearing Heather's whimper, the woman turned and saw Ellen and her child standing in the doorway. "Well, what ye be wanting, girl?" she asked.

"I'm the new barmaid and Mrs. Goodlinger said ye would show me to my room."

Ellen's voice was faint, for hunger had begun to weaken her. Tilly noticed how the young woman's gaze traveled back to the beef over the fire and said, "Well, 'fore I do, I want to know, have ye eaten?"

Ellen shook her head and said, "No, ma'am, not all day."

A smile crinkled Tilly's face and she said, "Well, what are ye standing there for? Come and get yerself something before ye faint. Give me the babe and I'll care for it while ye eat."

Ellen walked over to Tilly and gratefully handed Heather to her. "Well, my oh my, it ain't a month old yet. Is it?" Tilly said. "And look at them eyes, I ain't never seen that color afore. Does it take them after the father?" she asked.

Ellen shivered and thought, *I hope not!* but said, "Yes, she does, but he was killed in the battle of Oxfordshire." Ellen was shocked at how easily she lied. She had thought it would be much harder to do than that. However, if it was that easy, she didn't have to worry.

After having a good meal and feeding Heather, Ellen was shown to a small dirty room at the back of the inn. The room was nearly as filthy as her father's pigsty at home. The only furniture the room contained was an old cot with a straw mattress, with one tattered blanket lying on it.

A sigh escaped Ellen's lips as she looked around. She could nearly smell the clean sheets from her bed at home and the lavender that her mother always used when putting the linen away. And see the patchwork quilt which her mother had made especially for her.

Tilly turned to Ellen and said, "It ain't much but it's better than sleeping in the streets like the gutter rats do."

Ellen smiled at Tilly and nodded her head. "Yes, you're right, and at least it will look better once some of the filth has been cleaned out." Walking over to the cot, Ellen jerked the mouse-eaten blanket from the bed and threw it to the floor. "Do ye think I might use a tub from the kitchen to wash the blanket before I put Heather to bed?" Ellen asked as the dust filled the air.

"I'll ask Ma if she hasn't a better one than that to warm yer bed," Tilly said as she left.

Once Ellen was alone, she sat down on the rickety old cot and clutched Heather to her. As the full meaning of her predicament hit her, tears cascaded down her cheeks. So much had happened in such a short time. Now she cried for all the misery of the last year. After a while, Ellen wiped her eyes and said to herself, "Well, it may be dirty but at least it's mine and Heather's."

Ellen rose to her feet and spreading her shawl onto the cot, laid Heather on it. She then began to clean. After a few minutes she heard a slight tap at the door and then Tilly entered, carrying two clean blankets. "Here, Ma said ye would be needing these for yerself and the bairn," Tilly said, handing the blankets to Ellen.

"Oh, thank ye so much, and I'll be thanking Mrs. Goodlinger," Ellen said, smiling at the old woman as she held the blankets in her arms.

After Tilly had gone back to the kitchen to prepare for the evening customers, Ellen smiled to herself and thought, *My luck is already turned for the better.* She bent and kissed Heather, who was lying on the clean bed, and said, "My little love, our future has already begun to look brighter."

A few hours later, Ellen left Heather in the kitchen

by the hearth with Tilly and began her duties in the tavern.

As she walked into the tavern, Ellen was stunned by the din and the crowd of people that packed the large room. Most were soldiers, who had come for their evening ale. Looking at their uniforms made a tremor run up her spine, for they brought back painful memories.

Ellen looked about the room and realized that it would be the same every night with the dirty men and their pawing hands. But she was determined not to let this hinder her. She knew that she could stand anything for Heather.

Ellen worked hard and long hours in the tavern, and with George's help and friendship managed to conquer some of her fear of the customers. She had come to rely on George's protection; he had rescued her on several occasions when some of the men had become obnoxious. And he had also taken instantly to Heather and was always bringing her something special to nibble on or to play with. George would play with Heather for hours, making her laugh and giggle at his antics. And this made Ellen happy, for the only bright spot in her life was Heather.

At first Ellen thought that time had stood still, but after adjusting to her new environment the months seemed to slip by without much notice. Except in the way in which Heather grew.

Now two years old, she had big soft blue eyes, which changed with her moods. When she was happy, her eyes would shine like clear pools of rainwater after a spring shower. When she was angry, they would turn dark as the thunderclouds of a summer storm. When she smiled, her cheeks dimpled. She had a small pink mouth and her hair lay in golden ringlets around her face.

Studying her child, Ellen knew that she had inherited her coloring. As for her other features, she could not say. It was strange to think that such animals could beget something as sweet and charming as Heather.

She was a gentle child and would play quietly for hours by the hearth in the kitchen. Tilly adored her and had nicknamed her Sylphie. For she was like an imaginary being and seemed to glow with a mysterious charm that would follow her throughout her life.

On a night about two weeks after Heather's second birthday, Ellen left her in the kitchen with Tilly and went to her duties. When she reached the tavern she saw Ma serving customers at the bar. Ma motioned for Ellen to come to her. With some puzzlement Ellen asked her where George was, since it was he who usually tended the bar.

Ma finished with her customers and turned to Ellen. "George's ill, so I want ye to run down to me brother's on Kearney Street and ask if he would come to help out till me boy is on his feet again," she said.

Ellen nodded her head as she said, "Sure I'll do as ye ask."

Ma knew Ellen would do anything she asked of her if it was for George. There had been something between them that she really didn't like. This was the first time in his life that someone besides his mother had mattered to him and it infuriated her.

Ellen went up to her room for her shawl and wrapped it snugly around her, for the weather had a slight chill. As she left the inn, she passed the kitchen and looked in to see Heather asleep on a pallet by the fire. Seeing the warm pink glow of Heather's cheeks, Ellen could not resist tiptoeing across to her for a goodbye kiss.

After one last glance at her sleeping child Ellen stepped out into the mist-shrouded streets. She pulled the shawl closer about her head and tucked her hair beneath to keep the dampness from soaking it. This year the spring rains had been hard. Now they had slacked off into a heavy mist and the fog was so thick it was hard to see even the torches that burned outside the many pubs that littered the sides of the street.

Ellen hurried to her destination and after delivering

the message from Ma, she started back to the tavern. She walked as fast as the fog would allow. And as she turned the corner to the street on which the inn was located, she saw that a brawl had begun in front of the Yellow Hen Tavern. Ellen knew that it would take time if she were caught in the rabble that surrounded the fight, so she stepped into the cobbled street. In her hurry, she did not see the black coach with its gold coat of arms and the sleek black mares coming at full speed down the foggy street. Nor did the coachman see Ellen as she stepped into their path.

Ellen turned as she heard the rumble of the horses behind her but only had time to give one terrible scream before she was trampled beneath their hooves.

The coachman quickly pulled the horses to a stop, but it was too late to be of any help to Ellen. Jumping down from the coach, he hurried to her. He felt for a sign of a pulse but found none; he could feel no breath as he passed his hand near her mouth and nose.

Getting to his feet, he looked down at the crumpled body of a once beautiful young woman. Then he hurriedly walked back to the coach to tell his master what damage had been done. Opening the door, he looked into the velvet-lined interior and said, "I think she's dead, sir."

A gruff voice replied, "Find out if anyone knows her and I'll send her family a couple of pounds."

The coachman returned to where a crowd had gathered around the battered body of the young woman. Looking at the rough faces, he asked, "Does anyone know who this girl is?"

A small girl with stringy hair and a dirty apron came forward. "I think she's Ellen, the barmaid from Goodlinger's Inn down the street, sir." Tossing her a coin, he turned and went back to the coach.

"She's a barmaid from the inn down the street, sir," the coachman said.

"All right, Jess, take this to the inn and tell them to deliver it to the family," the Marquis de le Dunhan

21

said as he tossed a bag of coins to the coachman. "Tell them you'll be back to assure that the family received it or they'll pocket it for themselves. There's nothing except scum in this part of the city," the Marquis said, showing his face for the first time.

It was a face of a stern man edging toward middle age. It was neither a handsome nor an ugly face, but a face that had character. In his manner he seemed to be a cruel man, but only because he had dealt with this type of human refuse before. During the early days of the revolution when the feelings of all ran high with their loyalties, it was this scum that took advantage of the situation and the Marquis had been the one appointed to see that they were kept in line. He had learned from experience how this part of London's population lived. One more or less didn't matter to him, for they were all alike. They'd sell themselves, their children and their souls for a shilling. He knew well enough that two pounds covered the death in any family on this side of the city.

Jess took the bag of coins and hurried down the street to Goodlinger's Inn. He entered the tavern and walked up to the bar, where an old woman was pouring ale. Glancing up, she asked, "Now, what will ye have?"

"Nothing except some information," Jess said.

A sly gleam came into Ma's eyes as she looked at the fancy livery of the coachman. "Now what can that be, fine sir?" she asked.

"Does a barmaid of the name of Ellen work here?" Jess asked.

"And why would ye be wanting her?" Ma questioned as she smiled at Jess.

"I don't want her. I want to find her family and notify them of her death," he said.

Ma gasped and turned a little pale. She had thought a lot of Ellen even though she didn't really care for anyone deeply except her son and herself. Her jealousy had not stopped her appreciation of Ellen's hard work.

She would miss her but wondered how George would take the news. He had taken a fancy to her the first time he had seen her and her bairn come through the door. Ma knew that if Ellen had lived they would probably have married. At that thought, Ma shivered with relief that Ellen was no longer a part of the inn's inhabitants.

Jess interrupted Ma's train of thought as he said, "I've two pounds here for her family from the Marquis."

At the mention of money Ma's eyes glowed with greed but another thought crossed her mind. If it was the Marquis' coach that did the girl in, then she would make the Marquis take the bairn. Then it would be off her hands. For she could not be expected to bring it up. "Wait here a minute, fine sir," Ma said as she slipped out of the room.

In the kitchen Tilly was preparing the evening meal. Ma spoke as she came near. "Ellen's been done in by a Marquis' coach."

Shocked, Tilly looked at Ma, glanced at Heather, then asked in a weak voice, "What's going to happen to little Sylphie?"

Ma looked at the child and then turned to Tilly with smug satisfaction. "That's what I've come to tell ye. The Marquis sent his man in to buy us off but I'm going to make him take the bairn with him. Then it'll be off me hands."

Tears started in Tilly's eyes at the thought of losing her little blue-eyed fairy. "But Ma, I could keep her and raise her as me own," Tilly said.

Ma looked at her with contempt. "Now, how would ye do that if ye ain't got a job, me girl? 'Cause if ye keep her, you're out on yer ear. Ye better think of the old man that ye are keeping in gin before ye decide to do anything rash," Ma said with a smirk on her face, and turned and walked back to the bar, where the coachman waited.

"Now, fine sir, I've seen to it that ye will find Ellen's family in the kitchen, and it's through that door."

"Thank you for your help," Jess said and laid a shilling on the bar.

As Jess entered the kitchen, he could smell the aroma of fresh-baked bread and roasting meat. He saw Tilly basting a huge roast over the fire. Walking over to her, he said, "The innkeeper told me I would find the barmaid's family here. Are you part of her family?"

Tilly gave him a curious glance and laughed. "No sir, there's her family." And she pointed to Heather, who sat playing with a kitten by the hearth.

Jess, seeing the small child for the first time, said, "You mean that's all of her family?"

Tilly nodded her head and said, "Aye, that'll be it, I reckon. Well, all I know of anyway; her ma never spoke of having any kin." Tilly bent and picked Heather up into her plump arms. "Now, what do ye want with them anyway?" she asked, already knowing the answer.

"The barmaid died a while ago," Jess said, looking at the golden-haired little girl.

"How'd it happen?" Tilly asked.

"In front of a coach," Jess said, remembering her scream and the sound of her body as it hit the cobbled street beneath the coach.

Handing the bag that contained the money from the Marquis to Tilly, Jess said, "Here's two pounds from the Marquis de le Dunhan for the child. It was his coach that hit her mother."

"What do ye want me to do with it? She ain't no kin of mine," Tilly said, suddenly handing Heather to Jess. "Take her to the Marquis. He took her ma so he can take her too."

Jess looked down at the child in bewilderment. He did not know what to do until she looked up and smiled at him. The golden ringlets that clustered around the plump face and the pale blue eyes combined with the dimples of her smile made his heart ache. Thinking of how unfair life was and how it could be so cruel to such a small, sweet thing, Jess made up his mind. He would take her back to the Marquis. This child would make a fine playmate for the Marquis' five-year-old son—if he could only convince his master. *And my Kate would love to take such a little beauty to her heart.*

Jess turned his attention once more to Tilly, and said, "Would you please gather her things together?"

Tilly looked at him in disbelief. "She's got her things. This bairn ain't no princess, mister."

With that, Jess picked up the rough blanket on which Heather had been playing and wrapped it around her. As he opened the door, he stopped and asked, "By the way, what is her name?"

"Heather Cromwell," Tilly said as she turned away to wipe her eyes. She sniffed and blew her nose loudly.

Impatient for his coachman's return, the Marquis had left the comfort of his carriage. He could barely see Jess as he came down the street, but as the servant drew near he could discern, through the lifting fog, that Jess carried a bundle in his arms. As for Jess, he imagined his master's reprimand and, for a brief moment, he had the urge to turn and flee back to the inn. But he knew that was impossible. He knew they would send the child to a foundling home, or worse, she would end up in the streets, begging. One could hardly want either alternative for such a beautiful little angel.

Studying the child in his arms with the small earnest face that looked up into his, Jess thought, *Those eyes reach into my very soul.*

When Jess looked up, he was only a few feet from the coach and it was too late to turn around. He had to go through with his plan now and try to convince the Marquis that it would be for the best.

"What have you there?" the Marquis asked.

Jess folded back the rough blanket. The puzzled look on the Marquis' face turned to one of surprise, then to one of disbelief. "This, sir, is Ellen Cromwell's family," Jess said hesitantly.

"Well, why on earth, man, did you bring her back with you?" asked the Marquis. Jess shifted uneasily. "Why didn't you leave her where she belonged? Did they think by sending the child they'd get more money? Well, they're wrong!" the Marquis said caustically.

With each word the Marquis uttered, Jess was more uncertain of what to say or do, or how to explain about the child. Waving his arm in the direction of the inn, the Marquis said, "Take her back and tell them two pounds was enough for any of this scum." When Jess did not move the Marquis shouted, "Didn't you hear me, man! I said, take her back!"

Jess stood his ground. "Sir, I can't," he said firmly.

The look of puzzlement returned to the Marquis' face as he said, "What in the devil do you mean, you can't?"

"Well, it's like this, sir. The child is Ellen Cromwell's family and that's it. No other at all. The people at the inn said they wouldn't keep her. And even if they did keep her it wouldn't be for long. They'd send her to a foundling home or more likely the streets."

The Marquis still looked puzzled as he asked, "But what's this all got to do with me? I sent two pounds for her upkeep. What more do you want me to do?"

That was the question Jess had been waiting to hear. "Sir, I thought that since you hate the people of the street, you wouldn't want to be responsible for adding to their number. Maybe you could take this child and let her become a playmate for young David. I know my Kate would love to take her to raise since we have no children. She's a beautiful child, and bright too, it seems. Sir, if you would just look at her."

With that Jess abruptly placed Heather in the Marquis' arms. As the Marquis looked down at the small child, she returned his gaze and with dimples deepening, smiled. The Marquis being more kindhearted than he would have liked, looked at the golden hair and the blue eyes that said thank you.

She could have been his child had his wife not died giving birth to their son. His wife too had been golden-haired and blue-eyed.

His heart ached at the thought of his wife. He had loved Gwendolynn more than life itself. If it had not been for David, his son, he didn't know what he would have done. Many of his friends urged him to remarry, but the thought of another woman taking Gwendolynn's place repulsed him.

He had his son and that was all he wanted. But this child might be good for David. The boy needed a companion and this little girl might fill that need—for a few years anyway, until she was old enough to go into service.

"All right, Jess, but she'll be reared in the kitchen with the rest of the servants," the Marquis said as he placed the small bundle next to him in the coach.

With a smile on his lips, Jess climbed up to the driver's seat of the coach and started back to Dunhan, the Marquis' home in the country.

Jess thought as they rumbled down the dark cobbled streets, *The Marquis only came to London to see his old friend Cromwell; now he's taking a small Cromwell with bright blue eyes home with him.* Jess was pleased. Tragedy had perhaps given the child a better life than she might otherwise have had. Heather would have an education and maybe even be learned as a lady. Smiling once again, Jess whipped the horses to a faster pace.

❧ Chapter Two ❧

1664

A cold drizzle dampened Heather's back as she watched the last of the dirt put into the black hole. She wept as the only two people who loved her were put beneath the wet sod.

Standing beside her was David. But Heather neither felt the comfortintg arm that rested around her shoulder nor heard the words of sympathy intoned by the minister. Her only thought was for those two dear people with whom she could no longer share life. Jess and Kate had been her adopted parents and she had loved them as if she were of their blood.

When she had been old enough they had told her the truth about her parentage, as far as they knew. Jess had told her of the accident that had taken her mother's life; he had even told her that he had been the driver of the coach. Tears slid down the roughened cheeks as he asked Heather's forgiveness.

Heather had thrown her arms around his neck and

kissed him. "Dear Jess, I do not remember having any mother besides Kate. And you have been my father. If you had kept it from me, I would never have thought that you were not my true parents. I thank you for telling me for my true mother's memory. Yet that does not change the feeling I have for you in the least, dear Jess."

Fresh tears cascaded down Heather's cheeks and mingled with the raindrops as she realized she would never again kiss those sweet old cheeks or hug her dear Kate.

But tragedy was not Heather's alone, for the plague raged throughout England and Europe, sparing no one, neither peasant nor nobility.

Until Jess had gone to London on business for the Marquis, the sickness had not touched them. But after Jess's return, first he had become sick and then two of the stable hands. As Kate nursed the fevered Jess, she also had been stricken.

Jess died and within a few hours Kate had joined him. She had been rational enough to realize that her beloved husband was gone and seemed to give herself up to death so they might be together through eternity.

As the last of the dirt was thrown into the grave, Heather looked up to see David's dark eyes filled with pity. "Come, Heather, you can do no more for them. No need to make yourself sick. You know that would not please them," David said as he pulled her away from the grave and led her from the cemetery.

"But David, I can't go back to the cottage; it holds too many memories," Heather said.

Rubbing a slender hand across his smooth square chin, David considered the problem. "Well, I can fix that. You can have one of the rooms in the manor. There's a small one in the servants' quarters that would be suitable to your needs. Does that meet with your approval?"

Heather nodded her head. "Yes, David, and I would be closer to my work," she said, unable to keep the resentful tone from her voice. Even in her grief for her parents, her pride was hurt when she was reminded of her status.

"Heather, you know I did not mean it that way," David said, sensing that he had said the wrong thing. He did not want to add to her hurt on such a day.

"Well, it would be convenient," Heather said as she turned, leaving David standing alone outside the gates of the cemetery.

Heather settled into her new surroundings and then returned to her duties as a serving girl. She worked all morning in the kitchen helping prepare the meals and in the afternoons she had her lessons. Through the years she had been schooled with David, but now that he was attending a college at Oxford, she studied alone.

Heather's education had been one of the promises that Jess had made when he first adopted her and now that Jess was gone the old Marquis had taken over the responsibility.

It was the bright spot in Heather's life, for she enjoyed her lessons, especially the singing and dancing. She excelled in these two so much that her tutor told the old Marquis that she would do well in the theater. But the Marquis shook his head and told the tutor not to be putting ideas into the girl's head, for she was going to make him an excellent housekeeper one day. That was why she was getting all the education.

One afternoon while David was home on vacation, he met Heather as she started to the schoolroom. "Heather, I am going to be the one to give you your lessons this afternoon," he said.

Heather looked up to find an impish grin on his handsome face. "Now what could that be?" she asked.

"I've come to give you riding lessons," David said, but when he saw the look on Heather's face his smile dissolved. "What's wrong? Every young lady needs to know how to ride. You've had all the lessons of a lady so you must have this one also."

"No, I will not have riding lessons," Heather exclaimed, her eyes darkening. "You know that horses frighten me."

David stepped closer to Heather and said in a determined voice, "Yes you will, for I am going to give you riding lessons whether you like it or nor. You are still my servant." Grabbing Heather around her small waist, he carried her screaming into the courtyard, where the horses waited. Throwing her onto the saddle of a small chestnut-colored mare, he then mounted his sleek gray. Taking the reins of Heather's horse, he trotted off with Heather clinging to the saddle, tears rolling down her cheeks.

David looked back at Heather and winced. The girl was obviously petrified. But he was convinced that the only way to conquer fear was to meet it head on. Besides, he liked forcing her to do as he ordered. There was a power in it, and on some level he enjoyed watching her squirm.

After leading her through the courtyard and then into the meadow he noticed how silent Heather had become. Glancing back he saw that she had her eyes tightly closed. Tauntingly he asked, "Heather, aren't you going to say anything to me?" She did not reply.

After riding for about half an hour, David decided that he might have made a mistake in forcing Heather to ride. He led the horses back to the courtyard, then slipped expertly from his so he might help Heather from the saddle. But she had already scrambled to the ground and run into the house. He handed the reins of both horses to the groom and hurried in search of her.

David found Heather in the kitchen, standing in front of the fireplace. Her small figure shimmered in the firelight. Her golden hair hung to her waist and he could not see the smoldering anger in her eyes as she gazed into the leaping fire nor read the thoughts that whirled through her mind. *David has been cruel before but this is the worst thing he has ever done. During the past it had been only childish mischief, today he was merciless.*

She both loved and hated him. His moods were unreliable. There were times when he was gentle as a brother and other times, as today, when he acted as though she were no more than a subservient fool. If only he had asked her instead of insisting that she obey his orders. Surely she would have tried to please him. She would do anything for him.

Heather knew her place, but she had a proud bearing, a bearing that said I'm as good as anyone. She did not believe that the accident of birth made you either inferior or superior. Heather was fourteen, but she already had a sense of the world and its people and how she wanted to be treated.

Hearing a sound, Heather turned to find David standing by the corner of the hearth. Still churning inside, she said, "What do you want, sir?" Before he had time to reply, she continued, "Don't you know these are the servants' quarters?"

Seeing anger blazing from Heather's eyes, David's apology was stifled and replaced by laughter. "You honestly do think you are special, don't you?" he said scornfully.

"What do you mean?" Heather asked defiantly. "I'm in my place. I belong in the kitchen, where the servants' children are supposed to stay. But what are you doing here? I thought you were too good to humble yourself to enter the kitchen."

Heather hadn't meant to say so much but anger overcame her. She could see the change come over David as her words sank in. His laughter was replaced by anger, and before she had time to avoid his wrath, he had drawn back his hand and slapped her across the face, sending her sprawling to the floor. "Yes, I am the future Marquis and you are my servant, so I advise you to hold your tongue," David said.

Tears of frustration and pain welled up in Heather's eyes as she choked to contain her words. David had never struck her before. And they were both amazed at what had transpired between them.

David turned and strode from the kitchen. Once out in the corridor, he leaned against the wall and put his hand over his eyes. What on earth had come over him? To strike a servant, and Heather, of all people. He loved her as a sister, for they had been reared together and had played and fought since he could remember. Yet today had been the first time he ever laid a hand on her.

It seemed that she had always been able to bring out the best or the worst in him, even when they were children together and would romp around the nursery.

Slowly he lowered his hands from his eyes and looked around to see if anyone had observed him. Seeing no one, he opened the door leading to his mother's flower garden. The scent of roses assailed his nostrils as he seated himself under an elm. He thought of Heather and the effect she had on him. As he contemplated these strange emotions that she had been able to arouse, he realized with a start that the spark came from her eyes. So many emotions could play in the soft blueness of them that one was forced almost against one's will to respond. David thought, *If she ever realizes her power, no man will be safe.*

Once again he remembered the fear that he had seen in her eyes as he had thrown her into the saddle on the mare. And again he wanted to apologize to Heather but his pride and the awareness of his darker nature held him back. *Damn it,* he thought, *after all I am the future Marquis and can't run and apologize every time I hurt a servant's feelings.*

The weeks passed and David's time at home grew short. He and Heather had not spoken since their argument in the kitchen and he was determined that she would be the one to apologize. If he did so, it would be the same as admitting that he was wrong and he would not have that.

Heather missed David's companionship more than

34

she wanted to admit. She wanted to be near him even though he had hurt her pride. She also wanted to make amends, but the time never seemed right. Soon David's vacation ended and he returned to Oxford.

Heather continued to work in the kitchen and also continued with her education. Her tutor reported her progress monthly to the Marquis. All reports proved that Heather was an exceptionally bright student.

When home on holiday, David would always check with Heather's tutor to see how she progressed and when he found that she was an excellent student and excelled in the social graces, it pleased him tremendously.

In her free time, Heather would practice for hours on her singing. Her voice was soft and clear, and astounded her tutor. As he had once remarked to the old Marquis and now told David, "The young lady, sir, has a voice to enchant a king. She would do well to think of a career in the theater. With her voice she would have all London begging her favors." Hearing of this didn't make David at all happy. He knew he should be pleased that Heather was so accomplished, but the news had only brought clouded thoughts, which he did not completely understand.

One evening on a cold and dreary winter day, Heather sat cleaning silver in the china closet, and as she worked, she hummed a soft tune from her childhood. The door was partially open and as the Marquis passed he heard Heather.

He was a lonely man, and his interest in life was centered around his son. After all these years he still missed his wife and sometimes he regretted his decision not to remarry. But he knew that he could never love another woman as much as he had loved Gwendolynn and felt that it would not be right to marry just for companionship. David had filled the void in his life until he went away to school, and now the Marquis was lonelier than ever.

The Marquis entered the small closet and asked, "Where did you learn that song?"

Heather looked up with a warm smile brightening her face. "From your son, David, sir. He used to teach me songs when we were small and that was his favorite."

"Well, young lady, come into the drawing room. I want you to sing it for me."

When Heather entered the drawing room she found the Marquis intently studying the flames in the fireplace. He smiled as she came forward and Heather caught a glimpse of David in him. "Please have a seat, Heather," the Marquis said as he indicated a small chair directly across from his own.

The Marquis walked to his favorite chair and sat down, relaxing deep into the plump softness. He then propped up his feet on a large ottoman and with his face in the shadows, he said, "Now, Heather, sing the song that David taught you." Heather responded. The song was of war and love and death. Her thoughts drifted back to her childhood with David and she did not look at the Marquis until she finished singing. Then it was to find tears in the old man's eyes.

Heather, thinking that he might be ill, placed her small hand on his sleeve. "My lord, what ails you? Is there something I can do?" she asked.

Surprised, the Marquis looked down into clear blue eyes that held much concern and replied, "No, my child, it is only that I miss my son. The song brought back many memories—the beautiful lady who was David's mother and the way in which she gave her life to give me a son." Then, realizing to whom he spoke, he cleared his voice and said, "But no matter. This is none of your concern, girl."

Heather removed her hand from his arm and lowered her eyes. "I'm sorry, my lord, I thought I might be of some help."

Staring into the small innocent face, the Marquis realized that she was sincere and not just one of the gossipy servants. He then said in a much kinder voice, "You have been; you have helped my evening considerably. Yes, my girl; you have helped more than you know. So I'll expect you to sing for me each evening henceforth."

Heather's face brightened and she rose from her chair and curtsied to the Marquis, and with dimples deepening said, "Yes, my lord."

Each evening after that Heather would go to the drawing room, take her place in front of the fire and sing for the Marquis.

Gradually he began to talk to Heather as a friend and they would discuss the day's happenings. At the end of each evening the subject usually turned to David. Heather enjoyed that part the most. She loved to hear the Marquis reminisce about David's childhood and of the enjoyment which the two had shared.

Between the two men a great understanding existed, unusual for a father and son. On many evenings when David was home on holiday, instead of going with other young blades to the club or gambling houses, he would stay with his father.

They would spend their evenings quietly playing chess or sitting in front of the fire, discussing matters of the estate, which they both loved. Each was addicted to fine wines and fine horses and they always found ways of enjoying these together.

Sometimes Heather was asked to join them in the drawing room to sing. She enjoyed the rapport which existed between the two men, but at times such as these she felt a small nagging loneliness for Jess and Kate. They too had spent happy hours sitting before the fire in their cottage.

When David was home, the Marquis forgot about his friendship with Heather and treated her as a servant. At first this treatment hurt Heather's feelings, but then she realized that when David was with the Marquis, no one else in the world existed for him.

At times she felt David's eyes on her. But when she

looked toward him he would turn back to the fire and resume the conversation with his father. Often Heather wondered if her presence irritated him since he considered her beneath him.

Time passed quickly and soon David was ready to leave Oxford. After a short stay at home, he would embark upon a grand tour of the Continent, as all young gentlemen did. Upon his return, he would take over the management of the estate.

David was a man now, Heather realized. He was tall and slender with dark hair and eyes. There was an elegance about him that hid any flaw in his character. He knew that one day he would be master of his estate and this gave him a haughty bearing which commanded respect.

Heather, nearly seventeen, was turning into a lovely young woman. Her hair was still the color of wheat and her pale blue eyes were alluringly fringed with dark lashes. Her complexion was smooth and clear like fine alabaster with a delicate tint of rose that colored her cheeks. Heather's brows arched provocatively over her beautiful eyes and there was a sensual quality to her smile. She had even white teeth, and dimples that accented her lovely mouth.

Heather's angelic face was a mirror to her emotions. She had yet to learn that one must conceal certain feelings so as not to be quite so vulnerable. This air of innocence that surrounded her would remain always, no matter the evil she was to experience.

The most noticeable change in the young woman in recent years was in her figure, which though trim was developing soft full curves. The few frocks that she had now tightly pressed her full firm breast until it appeared as if the seams would split. Her waistline had not changed but her hips had developed and the skirts clung to their roundness. As Heather went about her duties at the manor, one could see a slim delicate ankle beneath the hem of her frock, which had become too short. This attracted the attention of the young gentlemen who called at the manor, or came for the hunts, for which the Marquis was famous.

One afternoon as Heather was about to enter the drawing room with a tray for tea, a young gentleman collided with her. The tray with its contents crashed to the floor. As she bent to pick up the broken china, he also bent and they again collided. To steady himself and Heather, he reached out and drew her into his arms.

"Are you all right?" the young man questioned.

"Yes, thank you, sir," Heather said as she looked up for the first time.

The man whose arms encircled her was young, dark and handsome. His eyes were so dark that they seemed nearly black to Heather. Dark lashes as black as his hair curled around them. As she gazed into his eyes, she saw a gleam of humor, as though he were laughing at himself and the world.

His complexion was deeply tanned as if he spent a great deal of time in the sun. And he towered over Heather. She could feel, even through the uniform he wore, the well-muscled strength of the arms that held her.

Though David was dark and tall, this man made him seem of smaller stature. David was slender and commanded from his haughty bearing where this man would command through the strength that radiated from him. Heather had never come upon anyone that made her feel so small and helpless and she blushed under his intent gaze.

The breath caught in his throat as she looked up at him. *She is lovely,* he thought. Such beauty was rare. Certainly there were beautiful women at court but cosmetics made them seem so. This young girl had a natural beauty that could not be found easily. Her sweet, innocent face with those captivating eyes and that golden hair. It was an unusual combination and this made her seem all the more breathtaking.

Sir Nicholas Guyon's thoughts went to the many

women he had collected, as so many objects on a chain. *None can compare with the exquisite creature that is now before me,* he thought. *Every eye at court would be on me with envy if ever I should take such a lovely creature there.*

"Let me introduce myself. I am Sir Nicholas Guyon, captain of the King's Guard. And may I ask your name, fair damsel?" he said lightly as he gave a slight bow without releasing his hold on Heather.

"Heather Cromwell, sir," she replied as the color deepened in her cheeks, showing the embarrassment that she felt.

"And what may I ask is such a lovely maiden doing carrying a tray for tea?" he inquired, raising one eyebrow slightly with mock concern while an impish smile played on his full lips.

"I'm the serving girl, sir," Heather answered.

As Captain Guyon started to speak again, they heard a sound behind them. Releasing Heather's arms, he turned to find David watching.

David had entered the hall right after hearing the crash of the tray. And had observed the two. He could see Heather was embarrassed and that Guyon was taken with the young girl. Guyon was always in search of lovely ladies and David could see that his friend thought he had found a rare prize.

"Well, David, I often wondered why you stayed on your estate so much instead of in town. Now I know the reason. If I had a wench as comely as this piece, I'd never enter the gaming rooms." Captain Guyon laughed.

Heather blanched at the last statement. By lowering her eyes to hide the resentment, she did not see the dark flush that spread over David's face.

"Nay, my friend, she is no more than a servant. Come now, let's return to our game of chess." At that David turned to Heather and said, "Get back to your duties, girl."

David didn't see the anger in Heather's eyes or the

piercing look that she gave him as he and his friend returned to the drawing room.

Heather gathered up the tray and its contents, then hurried back to the kitchen. Once inside, she threw the tray down, breaking the remaining china, and ran out of the house. Crossing the garden, she ran down the hill into the clover-covered meadow.

She found her favorite place under an old oak, its limbs draped to the ground, giving it the illusion of a secluded cave. Heather threw herself down into the soft clover and sobbed. Why was he so cruel to her? Couldn't he see that she cared for him.

Rolling onto her back, she looked up into the clear blue of the sky and thought, *That's the second time I've cried over David's cruelty.* As the soft clouds passed, she decided that she would never again succumb to such wretched behavior. Exhausted, she turned on her side and dozed.

When Heather awoke the sun had set and the mist from the moor had brought chill to the air. She rose and suddenly sensed someone near. Looking back, she saw Captain Guyon.

Leaning against the trunk of the oak, he gazed down at her. Guyon had changed from his military uniform and was now wearing elegant evening clothes. To Heather he seemed even more handsome and sardonic than when she had first laid eyes on him. He took off his hat and gave an exaggerated bow.

"What are you doing here?" Heather asked.

"After our game of chess, I decided to take a walk and keep a beautiful lady company. And here I find her sleeping like a babe." He laughed, exposing white gleaming teeth. "What more could a man ask than a lovely maiden in a bed of sweet-smelling clover? And," he added teasingly, "secluded in the arms of an old oak."

"How did you know where to find me?"

"I saw you run from the garden into the meadow. From there I could follow your path easily. And after the game I excused myself and came in search of the maiden with the golden hair. I had hoped to rescue her from the old dragon of loneliness." He laughed once again and his dark eyes twinkled with humor.

Heather's temper had begun to rise and now as he spoke it crested. "How dare you follow me. If I had wanted company, I would have asked," she said venomously.

Nicholas Guyon could not quite believe that the angelic-looking Heather was truly David's mistress. And yet, there did seem something between them. How could one miss David's look when he saw them standing in the hall together.

"Ah, the lightning flashes in the starry eyes. The maiden has a temper," he said as he casually seated himself next to Heather. He propped one strong arm on his knees as he observed Heather's expression. With her small chin held so high and eyes dark with anger, she was even more beautiful.

As the night settled, a cool breeze stirred and sent a shiver of apprehension down Heather's spine.

Far over the hill a nightingale's lonely song was the only sound to be heard. All was still as darkness approached. Heather decided it was much too late to be about, especially unchaperoned and in the company of a man like Captain Guyon.

The eyes that met hers carried a meaning even a young and inexperienced maiden could read. "I have to get back now before I'm missed. Cook will already be mad because I haven't helped to serve the evening meal," Heather said and started to get to her feet. As she did so Captain Guyon reached out and grasped her by the hand, pulling her toward him.

Unbalanced, she fell into his arms. "My, aren't we the eager one, though." He laughed as he pulled her closer.

"Let me go, you lout!" Heather said through her teeth, writhing in an attempt to break his hold on her.

"I'm a lout, am I?" he said with all trace of humor gone from his voice. "I'll show you, my little vixen."

Heather fought violently as he drew her into his arms. A hard, fiery kiss was pressed on her lips and she was pushed to the ground.

Heather still tried to escape but could no longer move with his weight on her. His hands were large enough so that he held both of hers in one of his without any trouble while the other explored the soft maturing curves of her body. With one quick move, Captain Guyon put his hand inside her bodice, exposing a while silky breast. He caressed the young soft flesh and as his fingers found hidden places his desire began to mount.

When he had first arrived under the large oak and found Heather sleeping, he had planned only to steal a kiss. But now, as he saw the blue fire in those dazzling eyes and felt the warm softness of her flesh, he realized a kiss was not enough. Only to have her would ease the ache in his loins. There was no turning back; she might be David's mistress but his hunger had to be satisfied. As Heather tried to escape, her movements only heightened his desire.

She tried to bite the greedy mouth that possessed hers but the attempt failed and his kiss deepened. Turning her head quickly she managed to escape his hungry lips and find that they were moving slowly down the side of her cheek and onto the smooth skin of her neck and shoulders.

Captain Guyon's hand left the warm softness of her breast, to be replaced by his lips. He explored the rest of her body, unlacing her bodice, with adeptness.

He caressed Heather's hips through the thick material of her skirt, then, becoming annoyed with it, pulled it up out of his way till he came in contact with a warm thigh. The musk smell of her young body filled his senses. Intoxicated by the feel of her, he worked at his own clothing, trying to let his aroused manhood escape from its tight prison so it could feel the warmth of the beauty's flower.

As she moved trying to avoid contact with his hands, Heather automatically aroused him further by the touch of bare white thighs against his now bare chest and midriff.

Releasing himself from the tight restraint of his britches, Captain Guyon's swollen organ throbbed with want of fulfillment. As he came on top of Heather, she could feel the curly hair that matted his chest prick sharply at her nipples.

So intent was he upon his purpose, Captain Guyon did not hear the grass rustle. And as he spread her thighs with his hand so he might at last possess her, Heather suddenly stopped moving. Looking down at her for a moment, Captain Guyon thought she had acquiesced to his demands. Yet something in her eyes made him look in the direction in which she was staring. At the same moment a streak of pain slashed across his face. He released his grip on Heather, and fell to his side.

He was stunned by the blow, and it took a moment or so before he came to his senses. Then he saw a tall, slender silhouette against the moon. Recognizing David instantly, Captain Guyon said, "What the hell did you do that for?"

David stood facing Guyon with a riding crop in one hand, the other resting on the butt of a pistol at his waist. "Sir, you are my guest and as so you have certain privileges, but molesting my serving girls is not one." David's voice was filled with restrained fury.

Getting to his feet a little unsteadily and touching his lace-edged handkerchief to his cheek where the crop had drawn blood, Guyon bitterly replied, "So, David, I was right in the first place. A serving wench, aye, what she serves you is better than tea; am I right?"

David's fingers tightened on the butt of the gun and his eyes became hard and glittering. His voice was harsh as he replied, "Sir, this girl is a mere child of seventeen. And as holder of this estate I have a responsibility to take care of my servants. As I have told you once this afternoon, she is only a servant to me. But no matter; I do not have to explain things to you. As for your actions tonight, I will expect you to be gone from my house by mid-meal tomorrow." As he finished speaking, he picked up Guyon's hat and handed it to him.

Captain Guyon glanced once more at Heather, readjusted his clothes, then took his hat and left David and Heather.

David turned to where Heather had stumbled against the trunk of the giant oak; he for the first time took full note of her disheveled appearance. Far from distracting from her beauty, it seemed to enhance it.

Her face was flushed. Her big blue eyes brimmed with tears. The golden hair cascaded down onto her white shoulders, drawing attention to the open bodice and the firm young breast that peaked through.

At the sight of her, David's pulse began racing and a small ache spread through his loins. "Are you all right?" he asked as he walked up to her.

"Yes," Heather meekly replied, looking into David's face.

At the same moment David felt an overwhelming temptation as he stared into those trusting innocent eyes. He forced himself to turn away. A sob broke from Heather and she fell into his arms. "Oh, David!"

David's arms automatically encircled her, pressing her closer to him. He stroked her hair and then placed his hand under her chin, raising it. And as their eyes met he lowered his lips onto hers.

Soft, tender lips responded to his kiss. Desire, which before had been only a small spark, now exploded into flames, making his body tremble. His loins throbbed with passion. But David resisted. Abruptly releasing Heather, he walked away. One more kiss and he would not have been able to leave.

Heather, stunned by her emotions, stared at David

45

as he walked from the shadows of the oak into the moonlight. "David," she whispered, and her voice trembled with tears.

At the sound of her voice, he turned once again to her. "Please don't go," she said pleadingly.

"Heather, I must," David said in a choked voice.

"But why, David?" she asked.

"Can't you see? If I stay, I would be like Nicholas. Don't you realize that a man can't keep his hands off someone as tempting as you?"

Heather walked over to where David stood staring with troubled eyes out over the moonlit meadow. A cool breeze ruffled his dark hair. Placing her hand on his arm, she looked up into his face to find his mouth set in a hard line. "David, please, can't we be as close as we once were?"

David, trying with all his power to resist her closeness, removed her hand roughly and replied in a strained voice. "No, Heather. Never! My feelings for you aren't those of a brother. Can't you understand? Since we were children I have cared for you, thinking it was a feeling a brother would have for a sister. Then I went away to school and each time I returned you became more beautiful. And still I thought I loved you as a sister; not until today did I realize differently. I can't stand it. Oh, Heather!" he said as he turned and crushed her in his arms. "See what you do to me; here I am raving like a bumbling youth."

Holding her once more, David's willpower dwindled and his lips searched hers. When Heather returned his kiss desire seared through his body.

His hand gently traveled to her firm, round breasts and fondled the tips of her pink nipples. Heather trembled and pressed closer to him, molding her body against his. "David, I love you so much," she said with passion and pressed her lips once more to his.

Fire fed by the fuel of desire surged through their bodies. Gently laying Heather down in the soft clover, David started to remove her clothing. Her milky-white breasts were exposed to the pale moonlight; he kissed each tenderly. Raising up on one elbow, he stared at her loveliness, absorbing every inch of her. But as his gaze traveled to her eyes, which sparkled in reflected moonbeams, he thought, *Oh God! I can't!*

Brusquely getting to his feet, David returned to the manor, leaving Heather lying bewildered. Heather watched the dark silhouette disappear through the garden gate. With trembling hands, she smoothed her clothing and then also returned to the manor. Without lighting a candle, she found her way to bed, where she tossed and turned for hours. New feelings stirred within her this night and she found it difficult to sleep.

Heather awoke early the next morning and watched the first rays of the sun come gently through the window.

She now had a better perspective on last evening's events. The complicated emotions were gone. She realized that David did care for her, otherwise he would have taken his pleasure. Not many men would have found as willing a playmate as Heather had been. At that thought a blush rose and brightened her cheeks.

Heather decided to find David and thank him for his consideration of her and tell him that she loved him that much more for it. With that thought in mind, she brushed her hair until it shone and pulled on a new frock. Then she rushed down to the kitchen to help serve breakfast.

When she entered the dining room, she noticed that the Marquis was the only one present. Heather served his favorite breakfast of kidney and eggs, with hot tea. Wanting to find out David's whereabouts without raising anyone's curiosity, she asked the Marquis, "Shall I await your son, sir?"

"No," the Marquis replied, intent upon his eggs. "He won't be dining; as a matter of fact, he won't be dining here for quite some time. He left at dawn for his tour."

Should the Marquis have looked up then he would

47

have seen Heather pale and her hands begin to tremble. However, he did hear the tray crash to the floor, and to his amazement, found Heather lying beside it.

When Heather regained consciousness, she was being carried up the stairs in strong arms. Looking up, her eyes met the same black eyes that had frightened her so terribly the night before.

To Heather it seemed an eternity before they reached her room. Captain Guyon kicked the door open and walked in without hesitation. He moved toward the bed but made no effort to release her.

Heather's anger mounted and could clearly be seen in her eyes as she looked up at Guyon and said, "Put me down." At her request he gently placed Heather on the bed and she slid away from him.

Captain Guyon looked down at Heather and a sardonic smile crossed his handsome face. "Don't worry, fair maiden, I am here to rescue a damsel in distress, not to attack her virtue. I'm sure you shall be in better condition once you recover from your lost love." He laughed. "And remember, I don't have time. I have to be gone before luncheon today," he said as he ran a finger down the bandage on his cheek.

For the first time Heather noticed that he once more wore his military uniform. The red velvet coat made just the right contrast between his dark eyes and black hair to impress upon Heather once more how handsome the man was.

However, looking into his knowing eyes made Heather shudder. "Please just go away and leave me be," she said as tears splattered down her cheeks and fell onto her hand, resting in her lap. She reached up to wipe them away but before she had the chance, Guyon had already done so.

"So he told you he loved you, did he?" Captain Guyon said gently. "And then ran off without so much as an au revoir." He looked at the tearstained face and thought, *My Lord! She looks so much a child*. He was touched by her vulnerability.

He was a connoisseur of beauty who had never before been affected by a woman's tears. He was puzzled that this serving girl should so disturb him, when none of the women at court had ever made the slightest ripple in his emotions.

He still didn't know what to make of last night. He had never before taken the offensive. Usually it was the women that made the first advances to the captain.

Why, does she affect me this way? he pondered as he gazed into the misty blue eyes. *And to top it off she is a servant and cannot help advance me in any way*. It was ridiculous. Besides, a woman was decorative, to be displayed on your arm and flaunted at your friends. Certainly not to be taken seriously.

Trying to lighten the mood and to avoid further play upon his emotions, he said, "My poor little beauty, let me mend your broken heart."

Jumping to her feet and slapping his hand away, she cried, "No, no, no!—no to you on all counts, Captain Guyon. Now please be good enough to leave my room this instant!"

Captain Guyon looked at Heather, all his tenderness and laughter gone. "Well, the fair maiden talks as if she were a lady instead of a serving wench, good for a roll in the hay, or should I say meadow!"

Anger surged through Heather at the remembrance of last night's escapade. She tossed her golden hair back from her shoulders and marched to the door. Opening it, she said, "Sir, would you please leave or shall I go to the Marquis and tell him of your little episode last night!"

Heather stepped back as Guyon approached the door. With lightning flashing in his black eyes, he looked as if he might strike her. Captain Guyon had never been defied by a woman before and if he longed to possess her previously, he now was determined to have her. "Well now, fair maiden, it seems that the

49

game has changed hands for the moment, but before I go, I want you to remember this: for now I shall bide my time, but I shall have you. Just remember those last words, I shall have you!" He laughed and gave Heather a low exaggerated bow, and the last words she heard him say as he walked away were "Remember, little vixen." They made Heather tremble and she fastened the door quickly.

The scene with Captain Guyon had once more exhausted Heather, and she sat down on the bed. Her eyes glittered but there were no tears. All her troubles had started with Captain Guyon and a tea tray. The only good thing to come of it was the apparent certainty of David's caring. Yet she was again assailed by doubts. If he really cared why would he have gone on tour? He could have at least said goodbye instead of leaving it to the Marquis to break the news to her. But why had he said he cared for her, unless, as he said, "Desire drives a man mad."

Heather studied the small room that had been her home for so many years. She knew every nook and cranny of it, yet it helped soothe her troubled thoughts. So much had happened since that first day after Kate and Jess's funeral, when she had come to live at the manor house. She had loved David then and still loved him. Slowly the thoughts stopped whirling and she drifted into a troubled sleep.

For miles and miles there was nothing except hot burning sand and she struggled to climb a huge mountain of the searing grit. With each step she would fall, yet something kept her climbing until she reached the summit. Looking into the valley below, she could see a cool refreshing oasis and under a large palm stood David, holding out his arms to her. Heather's mouth felt dry and she was drenched in perspiration. Exerting all the strength left in her exhausted body, she tried to run to him but something held her back. A pair of strong hands gripped at her waist and turning she saw an evil smiling face—a face unknown to her.

Heather rose from her bed trembling. She was awake, but the dream lingered. Going to the window, she stared out at the meadow. What horror she had found there but also what joy.

Now she had to decide what she was going to do. Should she stay at Dunhan Manor and become the housekeeper for which she had been trained or should she leave and seek employment elsewhere?

She could most certainly find a position with nearly any household she chose. If she left she wouldn't see David again and she couldn't bear that thought. Perhaps when he returned things would right themselves. If not, she could then leave.

✍ *Chapter Three* ✌

Several weeks had passed since David had left for the Continent. He had planned to go to Italy first and then proceed back through the various countries to complete his tour.

David was not happy about the trip, despite having made a hasty departure from his beloved estate. He had agreed to the obligatory grand tour only to please his father. And, as it turned out, to escape Heather.

As he looked out over the shimmering blue water of the Atlantic and felt the surge of the ship beneath him, David remembered what had happened during the past few weeks. Again and again he relived his moments with Heather. His mind conjured up her big blue eyes, the golden hair that caressed her soft white shoulders, the soft luscious curves that so snugly molded themselves to his body. And as her image filled his mind he could almost touch her, feel the warmth of her body as vividly as he felt the warmth of the setting sun. Wouldn't she be the delight of any man?

Why had he not taken her when he had the chance?

David asked himself as his hands tightened on the rail. *While I'm away someone will probably possess her anyway,* he thought irritably. But as he remembered the look in her eyes he knew the reason for not taking her, and also the reason for his leaving so abruptly when his tour had not been scheduled for more than a month.

He had packed up and run, without even a goodbye. He had fled like the coward he knew he was. If he had stayed at Dunhan, he would have had to face his feelings.

David knew he could never make Heather lady of the manor, despite her graces. His father would insist he marry a woman of equal status in society. While he loved Heather, he knew loyalty and duty forbade him from making her his wife. Only the love he felt for her kept him from making her his mistress.

The sun was setting and David looked up as the evening breeze ruffled the white sails.

Turning to go back to his cabin, David saw Captain Whittier approaching. "Ah, Lord Montclair, I see you are taking your evening constitutional. Are you enjoying the voyage?" Whittier asked as he stopped beside David and looked out over the blue water. "Fine, sir. I have always enjoyed the ocean."

Captain Whittier gazed at the water and then at the red sky. "Aye, we've been lucky so far and by the looks of it the good weather will continue tomorrow. As they say, red sky in the morning, sailor take warning, red sky at night, sailor's delight. Aye, that statement holds true. By watching the sky we know how to navigate the next day."

David looked at the squat frame of the captain. For such a stocky man he was built powerfully, with a broad chest and muscular arms. His gray beard and weather-beaten face made him seem ageless, but for the small paunch beginning to form around his middle. Yet he carried himself well, and commanded his ship with complete efficiency. In the eyes of his crew he was a giant. He knew all there was about sailing and they felt safe with him as their commander.

"Lord Montclair, would you join me for dinner tonight in my cabin?" Whittier asked.

"Sir, it would be a pleasure," David replied.

"Well, good; now if you will excuse me, I have some business below," the captain said, leaving David to make his way back to his cabin.

Arriving at the appointed time, David was admitted to the captain's cabin by the first mate. "Good evening, sir. The captain will be detained for a few minutes and he asked that I extend to you his apologies and tell you to help yourself to some wine."

"Very well. I hope it is nothing serious," David said as he gazed around the comfortable cabin.

To one side of the cabin stood a desk cluttered with maps and other paraphernalia pertaining to sailing. The other side of the room contained the captain's bunk, which was neatly made, showing the strict discipline of the man's character.

In the center of the room was the dining table, where a tempting dinner had been placed. A bottle of Madeira stood on a side table with fruit and cheese for dessert. Two glasses were set for the wine and this surprised David. He thought that the first mate would be joining them for dinner as was the usual custom.

David turned to the first mate and asked, "Will you not be joining us?"

"No sir, the captain stipulates either he or his first mate should be present on deck at all times after we leave the outline of the coast." With that the cabin door opened and the captain came in.

"Will that be all, sir?" the first mate queried.

"Aye, John. However, you had better be on the alert, for there is a full moon tonight. I don't expect to have any trouble before we hit the Strait but you can never be sure." As the first mate left the captain removed his hat and threw it on the peg behind the door.

"If you will excuse me for a moment I'll change into something more comfortable," the captain said, stepping behind a screen made of painted Oriental silk. "I'm sorry I wasn't here when you arrived but some matters kept me busy all afternoon. Take a seat and have some wine. I shan't be much longer."

David poured himself a glass of wine and seated himself in one of the leather chairs. It was unusual for a cabin, even a captain's cabin, to contain such luxurious furnishings. David commented on it as he sipped his wine.

The captain stepped from behind the screen wearing a velvet dinner jacket. "Yes, I like it that way. You see, this ship is my home and I like my few small amenities. Won't you join me, sir?"

David seated himself across from the captain at the small dining table. The conversation continued with the usual small talk until dessert had been served, and then David asked, "Sir, I heard before I left London that pirates had been reported of late in this area. Was that your cause of concern?"

Nonplussed by the question, the captain looked up from his coffee. "Yes, I had heard from other captains that had been lucky enough to survive that pirates had been attacking unescorted ships. But I don't think we will have any trouble right now. If at all, it will happen when we enter the Mediterranean."

"Why so then?" David asked.

"Because that is where the pickings are greater. Ships by then are more likely to be loaded with cargo. And it is also closer to their havens, thereby making escape easier."

Pouring David and himself a glass of brandy, the captain glanced out of the porthole. "Yes, there is a full moon tonight, yet I still think we are too far from the Strait to be in any real danger. We have made good time and it should not be more than a day or so before we see it."

David watched the captain with interest. "Sir, I also

56

heard they were burning the ships and taking captives. Is this true?"

The captain looked at David, trying to discern whether the questions that he asked came from fear. If they did he couldn't tell him the truth. He might panic and that would mean disaster for his ship. Gambling on his perception of David as a secure young man, the captain went on, "Yes, that is true. Most pirates just loot ships. But of late they have been taking captives to sell in Constantinople. I hear whites are bringing a high price as slaves from the Saracens," Whittier said truthfully.

David contemplated the captain's words as he sipped his brandy. "Sir," the captain continued, "I would appreciate it if you would not mention this to any of the other passengers or the crew. I don't want panic among them. I have seen most of the passengers and I believe it would be best not to mention it."

David smiled at the captain, trying to reassure him that he would be discreet. "Of course, I would not think of saying anything." Finishing his brandy, he said, "If you don't mind, sir, I think I shall retire. I thank you for the evening, it has been enjoyable. And you can put your trust in me, sir, I shall not repeat what you have confided to me this night." The captain returned David's smile and then shook his hand. "I shall appreciate that."

Stopping by the rail, David looked out over the water. It shimmered in the moonlight. The stars looked close enough to touch but David's thoughts were not on the beauty of the night. He was thinking once again of home and Heather. It would be awful if something happened to prevent him from returning to the place he loved so much. At that thought he shuddered. As he looked up at the sky, a falling star seemed to him an ill omen. Even though David wasn't superstitious, a chill lingered within him as he walked swiftly back to his cabin.

On the following day all ominous thoughts had vanished and David enjoyed the warm balmy weather. He stayed on deck most of the time and read one of the books he had brought with him.

Something disturbed his train of thought and looking up David saw a gull sailing gracefully above the ship. Wondering why a gull would be so far from land, he rose to his feet to see that they were nearing the Strait.

David's attention was drawn from the huge piece of granite to another vessel bearing down on them. It had sleek lines and could move much faster than Captain Whittier's *Lyme*. As he glanced about he could see that the crew had already been alerted and Captain Whittier was shouting orders.

Soon the sleek ship was broadside and its flags visible. David could see the skull and crossbones hoisted above a red flag with the emblem of a serpent.

As David stood watching the other ship, he was nearly knocked off his feet by the blast of the *Lyme*'s guns. He recovered his balance and now saw that the explosion had fallen short of its target.

There was a second blast, but this one came from the pirate ship. David was knocked to the deck. Splinters flew in all directions, barely missing him. He heard a cry and looked up to see the mainmast fall and, before his eyes, pin the captain to the deck.

David stumbled to his feet, realizing with a sharp pain that the second blast had injured his leg. Dragging himself forward, he made his way over the dead and dying to reach the captain's side. But as he neared the body he could tell that it was useless to hurry; the captain was dead.

David turned and saw that the ship was in flames and that it was being boarded by the pirates. Bending over the dead captain, he retrieved his sword and rushed to the deck below. Automatically he had decided his course of action.

In the back of his mind a thought had been growing unconsciously since the captain had affirmed the story that he had heard in London. He would rather be dead than be taken captive. But before he died, he would take a few of these bloody bastards with him. Smiling at that thought, David charged into action.

During the fray, David saw the captain from the other ship boarding the *Lyme*. After slaying his opponent, David made his way to where the captain had just slain the first mate. Wiping the edge of his cutlass on the dead man's shirt, the captain turned to see David charging.

"Ah, matey, I see ye have blood in yer eyes. And I regret having to end yer youthful life but I see by yer look that is the only course left for me to take."

David, being an excellent swordsman, countered the thrust of the pirate's blade. "Ah, but I don't regret having to put an end to your roguish life," he said as he thrust his sword through the captain's defense. A bright stain of blood appeared along the sleeve of the pirate's shirt.

"Well, I see ye play a man's game. So ye must take it as a man," the captain said, as he thrust at David once more. David also countered and again put the pirate on the defensive.

Suddenly the captain rushed at David, throwing him off guard. His blade slashed the young man and almost forced him into the mass of ropes lying on deck. But then David countered automatically stepping backward. He tripped on the ropes and fell. Lying prone and helpless, David saw the sword coming toward him.

✑ Chapter Four ✑

Heather went about her duties as she had done since she had been old enough to go into service. No one could see the change that had come over her in the few weeks since David's departure. Heather buried herself in work but her loneliness was almost unbearable. Nothing seemed changed in the household until one afternoon at teatime.

She tapped lightly on the study door and then entered, to find the Marquis in deep discussion with two young men.

As Heather approached, the conversation stopped. Curtsying to the Marquis, she said, "Sir, would you have your tea served now?"

"Yes, Heather, we'll have it in here, and also tell Cook that we will be having guests for dinner."

Heather curtsied to the men and turned to go. As she did the Marquis spoke once more. "Heather, I would also appreciate your presence after dinner in the drawing room to sing for us. I know these young gentlemen would enjoy your entertainment." A smile lit Heather's face. She was pleased to be included in the evening's festivities.

This was the first time since David's departure that the Marquis had asked her to entertain him. Her spirits soared. Just to be with the old Marquis, she felt, brought her closer to David.

When the men were alone once more the conversation resumed. "My dear Sir Thomas," one of the young men said, "we don't ask you to join us, but we know from long standing that you were against Charles I and did not want his son on the throne. All we ask now is that you hear us out and then give us your advice on the situation."

The Marquis de le Dunhan looked at the young men standing by the fire. "Please, gentlemen, take a seat and rest yourselves." The men did as they were bid. They were indeed tired. The ride from London in the damp weather had been trying, but their mission was important to the cause.

For a few minutes no one said anything, and this gave the Marquis time to study the two men sitting in front of him. They were both dressed in traveling suits of quality. He could tell by the tailoring. Of course they would be, for he had known their fathers during the revolution and knew that no matter what happened they would always land on their feet. Others had forfeited everything for their beliefs. The Marquis himself had been fortunate. He could have lost everything he possessed because of his close association with Cromwell. Now here were Hastings' and Fairbanks' sons asking him to chance it all again—to plot as he had before against King and Catholic. He'd have had no qualms about it were it not for David. He had to manage things now so that his son would have an estate to inherit and not just an empty title like David's friend Nicholas Guyon. Guyon's father had gambled and lost and now his son was paying for it. The Marquis did not want the same to happen to his son.

The Marquis cleared his throat and said, "And why

do you want me in this at all?" One of the young men rose from his chair and looked out at the rolling heath. Then turning, he said, "Sir, you were one of Cromwell's most trusted men. You knew more about his strategy than anyone else. So we think you would be able to give us advice on how to achieve the information that we desire."

"And what, may I ask, is that?" the Marquis queried.

To this question young Fairbanks said, "To find out if the King is in league with the French to restore Catholicism to England. After all, James will be his heir if he and Catherine do not have any children."

A slight frown crossed the Marquis' brow as he thought over what the young man had said. "But he may make Monmouth his heir," the Marquis replied.

A knock interrupted further conversation, and Heather entered with the tea. She noticed that the Marquis seemed agitated as she served the tea and biscuits. And she observed that the two young visitors appeared as though caught with their hands in the pie. She could tell that they wished her gone so that they might continue with their business. Hurriedly she finished pouring their tea and left the study.

As young Hastings once more sat down, he said, "But sir, that would mean having to prove that he had married Monmouth's mother. And if he had wouldn't he have said so before this? He loves the young Duke."

The Marquis rose from his chair and went over to the fire. He studied the flames for a moment and then kicked a log with the toe of his boot. "Yes, I guess you're right, but I don't want to get involved in any more battles. I fought mine during the revolution and now have my son to think of."

"Well, sir, why don't you ask him how he feels about it? That can decide it," young Fairbanks said.

"I would but he has gone on tour. He left a month and a half ago," the Marquis said.

"Sir, it is your cause as much as it is ours. You have

devoted your life to fighting this kind of injustice. All we ask is that you find out the information that we need," Hastings said.

"Then what would you do with it? How do you plan to use that information?"

Hastings and Fairbanks looked at each other and then back at the Marquis. "If it is necessary we will find a way to rid ourselves of the King and then have it to look as if James had planned the assassination. Then there would be no chance for James to hold the throne or for England to have Catholic rule," Hastings said urgently.

The Marquis shook his head and said, "Young sirs, you are brave, but I am sorry, there is too much at stake for me to get involved."

As the Marquis and the young gentlemen carried on their conversation, they did not hear the coach that stopped in front of Dunhan Manor.

A footman, dressed in black and yellow livery, opened the door of the coach and a beautiful young woman gracefully descended from the coach. She was followed by a dark young man.

As the butler opened the door, he recognized Captain Guyon and the Countess Beaufort. "Is His Grace at home?" Captain Guyon asked the man.

"Yes sir, I will notify him of your arrival," the butler said as he proceeded to show them into the drawing room. The spring rains had chilled them both and they were grateful for the warm fire that burned in the grate.

Captain Guyon looked around at the familiar setting and, after seating the Countess, walked over to the window. As he looked at the meadow, now damp and dark lush green from the rain, he remembered the twilight evening of his last visit.

Why he should think of the serving girl still puzzled him. He'd only to glance back at the beauty who sat warming by the fire to realize he did not lack the company of suitable young women.

Guyon went over to the Countess and placed a kiss on her raven hair. She looked up and smiled at him. "Nicholas, what has come over you? I can't ever remember you being so affectionate before. If it's the country air, I believe I may move to the country."

Nicholas smiled at the Countess. But as he looked into the flashing sea-green eyes, he thought only of soft blue ones that looked like flowers.

Meg's beauty was renowned at court. But her beauty was cold and indifferent, whereas Heather's was natural and earthy and would not fade with age. Meg, now twenty-five, was at her height, but the strenuous living at court would take its toll, he had no doubt.

Captain Guyon brought his thoughts back into the room. "Ah, my dove, it's not the country but my lovely companion that inspires such feeling." He smiled and caressed the curve of her throat and then seated himself opposite Meg to await the Marquis.

Hearing the knock on the study door, the Marquis paused.

The butler entered and bowed to the gentlemen, then said, "Sir, the Countess Beaufort and Sir Nicholas Guyon have just arrived and await you in the drawing room."

"Well, tell them I will be with them presently, Hopkins."

As the butler withdrew from the study, the Marquis turned back to the two young men. "Well, it seems this is my day for unexpected guests. Would you prefer to meet them at dinner or join me now as I greet them?" he asked.

Both the young men seemed to speak at the same time. "Sir, we would prefer that you did not make our presence known at this time. If it does not offend you, we would prefer to come at some other time to finish our discussion."

"Well, sirs," the Marquis said, "I have already given my answer and my reason. But I do wish you all the luck in the world. Godspeed, my brave young gentlemen." As the Marquis left the study, he turned back to Hastings and Fairbanks and said, "You may leave by the servants' entrance if you wish not to be seen."

Fairbanks and Hastings took very little time in absenting themselves from Dunhan. For two people they were not prepared to meet were Sir Nicholas Guyon and the Countess. Both were too involved at court. The Countess alone was cause for apprehension. It was said that she would be the King's next favorite, if Barbara Villiers could be ousted from the position.

And Guyon was known to be one of the most devoted of Charles's subjects. It was rumored that he was to be granted a post for services rendered the King.

As careful as the two men were they were observed by the beautiful young woman. The Countess Beaufort recognized both of them. She knew of their cause, and wondered what they were doing at Dunhan. They had been friends in her younger years and they had gone to the same parties and balls. But while she had gone on to court and become a devoted servant to Charles, they had chosen to oppose the King.

Meg turned and considered their host. He was in his sixties and she knew that he would have been in the revolution. Considering his age, would he again be plotting against the King? Perhaps it was the son? She smiled to herself. This bit of information might be useful in bringing her closer to the King. It could provide tantalizing gossip over a candlelight dinner with Charles.

Meg would love to see Villiers' face when she found out that Margaret Beaufort had taken her place as the King's mistress. Lady Castlemaine, as she was known, had been his favorite far too long in Meg's opinion, and this little episode today might do exactly what she needed. And the time was precisely right. Castlemaine was again pregnant and it would be so much easier to push her aside in her condition. Meg was sure her slim form would be much more alluring than Castlemaine's rounding figure. Charles was always susceptible to a beautiful woman, and a woman who had information of traitors would be one he could hardly refuse.

She glanced at the handsome Captain Guyon and her heart ached. She loved him so much but knew if she showed any feeling at all she would be deprived of even the small amount of affection he showed her.

Meg had ambitions but if Nicholas Guyon would ask her to be his, she would do anything that he wanted her to. She would forget about trying to oust Villiers from her position at court and be content to raise a dozen little Guyons. Meg had always been able to melt any man's heart and was even succeeding with the King. But Nicholas still remained a puzzle to her. As far as she knew, no woman had ever been able to capture his heart or even bring any feeling at all to the surface. He was pursued by every woman at court but only she had won what few favors he was willing to dispense.

Meg pushed her thoughts aside and rejoined the two men just as the Marquis mentioned Captain Guyon's last visit to Dunhan Manor. "I'm so glad that your injury has cleared up so well," the Marquis said.

"Yes, it left only a slight scar, but it could have been worse. The thorns on the hedge are quite brutal, especially when you are thrown into them," Guyon laughed.

"Oh, so that's the truth about your mysterious scar, Nicholas. And we thought it was woman's scorn." Meg laughed.

"Ah now, sir, you have ruined my reputation with the fair sex," Nicholas said and grimaced. They all laughed at his jest.

The conversation soon turned to the Marquis' favorite subject: David. "Sir, have you heard from David?" Guyon asked as he sipped the fine wine that the Marquis had served.

"The last message I had from him was the day before he left port. I should receive word from him any day now."

"Well, sir, when you hear from him, tell him that I asked about him." Guyon wondered what reaction David would have to the message. Certainly their last meeting had been unpleasant because of the incident with the young servant girl. Luckily David had not told the Marquis of their quarrel. That would have been a little hard to explain, that they, friends since David's, early days at Oxford, would quarrel over a serving wench. "My, but the weather is bad out there," Nicholas said. "I do dread traveling on to Gloucester."

"But you can't possibly mean to travel on tonight. You must plan on staying with us for the night," the Marquis said absently as he looked into the flames.

The Marquis' mind had been on his son. He was beginning to worry about David. It was unlike him not to have notified his father before now of his arrival in Italy. But a storm could have delayed his message. As Guyon spoke the Marquis's thoughts were drawn back to his guests. "Now, I must insist. It's not fit weather out for man nor beast. Nicholas, you should think of your beautiful companion. She must be exhausted. And here I am being an inconsiderate host. My lady, would you like to be shown to your room?"

Meg had been gazing into the leaping flames and listening to the conversation between the two men. She had retained nothing of their discussion, for her thoughts kept straying back to the two men that she had seen depart so secretly from the manor. And she could not but ask herself, if nothing was to be thought of it, why hadn't the Marquis introduced his guests to them?

As the Marquis spoke to Meg, she had to give herself a mental shake to bring her mind back to what the gentleman had just said to her. She smiled, collecting her thoughts. "Yes, I think I could do with a little refreshing, sir."

"Well then, I'll have a girl show you upstairs," the Marquis said as he rang for a servant.

When Heather heard the bell, she thought that the

Marquis required her to clear the tea service, but then she realized that it came from the drawing room. As she hurried in the first person whose eyes met hers was Nicholas Guyon. She stopped abruptly. Regaining her composure, Heather gave a slight curtsy. "Sir?" she questioned as she looked at the Marquis and at the same time noticed the beautiful woman staring at her.

"Heather, would you show the Countess Beaufort to the blue room," the Marquis said, and then added, "And see to anything that she requires."

"Yes sir. If my lady will follow me," Heather said.

Guyon once more had taken Heather by surprise. She had not expected him to visit the manor again, nor did she think that he would be well received. But she realized that the Marquis did not know of his quarrel with David. Until David's return he would no doubt be warmly received as a guest.

Heather swallowed the lump in her throat as she showed the Countess to her room. "My lady, will there be anything else?" she asked.

"Yes, have hot water sent up for my bath and afterward have someone come to fix my gown for dinner. Also I will require someone to do my hair," the Countess said as she swept by Heather into a lovely blue brocaded room.

Heather curtsied and said, "My lady, I will come directly back after you bathe and help you dress." Then she picked up the Countess' gown to have it pressed and hurried away.

The Countess noticed that Heather had a beauty and grace that were unusual in servants. She had also observed that when Heather entered the drawing room, Captain Guyon's eyes did not leave the serving girl. People did not usually consider Meg an observant person and she was often glad of it. She noticed small things that most people did not see, such as the stricken look on the girl's face when she saw Guyon. Obviously she was surprised. *I wonder,* Meg thought, *what happened during Nicholas' last visit.*

Heather hurried down the stairs to do the Countess's bidding. Just as she turned toward the servants' wing, Captain Guyon stepped from the shadows and said, "Well, my little damsel, we meet again."

"Sir, I would have thought you would not have had the nerve to return to this house," Heather said through her teeth.

"But why not? I am David's friend, though we did quarrel over a wench. It will not be the first or the last time that friends squabble over the favors of the fairer sex."

Guyon could see that Heather was visibly upset by the encounter. *Oh, such loveliness to be wasted on a country estate. If only I could get her to London,* he thought.

"Please let me pass, sir, I have Madam's gown to press." To her surprise Captain Guyon stepped aside without any word. Hurriedly she made her way to the kitchen and to her relief she was not followed. *Maybe,* she thought, *he has only been playing a game and now that he has the Countess with him, he will let me be.*

But Captain Guyon's thoughts were on Heather as he returned to the drawing room and poured himself another glass of wine. There was a frown on his brow as he sipped the delicate bouquet and stared with dark brooding eyes into the leaping flames of the fire. After a second glass of wine he realized it was time for him to dress for dinner.

As he ascended the stairs to his room all he could think of was the golden serving girl. To his surprise, that was how he had begun to think of her: the golden girl. As he passed Meg's room he could not resist knocking. From the other side of the door he heard her say, "Enter."

Meg was sitting in front of the dressing table brushing her long raven tresses. She was wearing a thin robe and the dampness from her bath made it cling to her body. She made an alluring sight.

Seeing that it was Captain Guyon instead of the

maid, she smiled and said, "Well, what a pleasant surprise, Nicholas. I thought that you would probably still be drinking port with the Marquis."

Captain Guyon tangled his hands in her hair, then placed a kiss on her shoulder where the robe had slipped to reveal the smooth white skin. "No, my dove, you interest me more than any wine and your kiss is much more exciting than the Marquis' conversation." He pulled her around to face him and then kissed her deeply on the mouth.

The kiss was full of desire and it made her tremble. She responded and as she slipped her arms around his neck her robe fell to the floor, leaving her naked in his arms.

Guyon picked Meg up in his strong arms and carried her to the bed. As he started to disrobe with the Countess' help, the door opened and Heather came into the room carrying the Countess' gown.

The scene which met Heather's eyes shocked her and she was unable to speak for a few moments. When her voice returned she said, "Excuse me, my lady. Here is your gown." Then she turned and fled from the room. As she did so, she could hear the high-pitched laugh of the Countess Beaufort but could not see the scowl that crossed Captain Guyon's face.

"Now, my love, where did we leave off?" the Countess asked as she kissed Captain Guyon again and finished unfastening his shirt. But as her hand went to his shirt, it was stopped by his. "Well, we are lucky the maid came in, Meg, for you are such a temptation that if we had continued we would have been late for dinner and that would have been rude to our host."

Meg's frustration at the interruption had not begun to rise until she had kissed Nicholas and offered herself to him, only to be turned down. *Wait till I see that intruding little wench! I'll make sure she never enters a room without knocking again,* she thought. Something had gone on between them and she would find out

71

what. But to Captain Guyon she only smiled and said, "Of course, you're right, my love, I do have to dress."

Heather had run as fast as her feet would carry her to the kitchen. Her face was flushed and she was trembling from embarrassment. *I should have knocked,* she thought, *but I did think that she would be alone.*

Heather sat down in an old chair and stared into the flames of the huge fireplace. *Why should I have been surprised?* she asked herself. *Most ladies at court have their lovers. But the Countess seemed so refined. But she did arrive with Captain Guyon and might well be his mistress.* Just as that thought crossed Heather's mind, she heard the bell from Meg's room.

Guyon was leaving the room just as Heather was about to knock on the door. As he looked at Heather, he sensed her embarrassment and smiled.

Heather entered the Countess' room once again without knocking, since the door was already open. When the Countess saw her, she snapped, "Don't you ever knock before entering a room?"

Heather lowered her eyes and said, "I'm sorry, my lady, it will never happen again."

The Countess looked at Heather, furious. "But it just has. You entered just now without knocking! Now leave this room and then return but be sure that you knock this time! Now get out and try to obey orders. Damn you!"

Meg's rage grew as she watched Heather walk out of the door. She seemed to be a perfect servant but her obvious pride infuriated Meg.

When Heather reentered the room according to instructions Meg was only partially mollified. "Now, you imbecile, help me dress and be sure that you do not wrinkle my gown!"

Heather performed the task with ease, though she had never been trained as a ladies' maid. Her fingers worked with dispatch on the intricate fastenings and ties of the Countess' gown. As she finished, the Countess said, "Now do my hair and don't pull it."

Putting the finishing touches to a beautifully arranged coiffure, Heather accidentally pulled a strand of hair. "Oh! You clumsy bitch!" Meg hissed and slapped Heather.

Heather's temper flared, but she controlled herself. "I'm sorry, my lady," she said, gritting her teeth, and vowed silently that in the future she would not be at the mercy and whim of those who presumed themselves her betters. "Is that all you require, my lady?" Heather asked, without a trace of the rancor she was feeling.

"No, but you had better remember what I told you!" the Countess answered. Heather turned and walked gracefully from the room, her head high.

Meg hated the serving girl, but admired her beauty and courage. Most servants would have fled at Meg's first outburst, but not this one. Even when Meg slapped her she held herself with dignity. For some reason Meg wanted to break the girl's spirit, as she would break one of her mares. *Now this is a change,* she thought. *Here I am trying to break the pride of a servant when I'm more apt to break the heart of a man. I have more important things to worry about. Besides, Nicholas would do no more than bed down the wench. And I've the King to think of.* At that, Meg smiled and then went down to dinner.

As she entered the drawing room Nicholas and the Marquis were sitting in front of the fire, enjoying their wine. Both came to their feet. The Marquis gave a slight bow and then offered Meg his arm to escort her to her seat. "My, how beautiful you are tonight, my lady," he said. "May I offer you a cordial before we dine?"

"Yes, I think I will have a small sherry," Meg said. Sitting down, she smoothed her emerald brocade gown.

The Marquis appreciated Meg's beauty and it showed in his manner as he handed her the small crystal glass containing the ruby liquid. "Everything has been done, I hope, for your comfort."

"Yes, now everything is just fine. You do have a beautiful home here. I do wish that the weather was better so I might be able to see the grounds.

"Yes, we love it, David and I. We have a beautiful garden which I am quite fond of—it was my wife's. And past that is a meadow with large oaks and a small stream. It's a wonderful place to have your rides. Don't you agree, Nicholas?"

Captain Guyon had paid scant attention to the conversation until the mention of the meadow and the oaks. At once he could nearly smell the clover and feel the soft flesh of his golden girl. "Um, yes, it is a wonderful place to take a gallop," he said, rousing himself from his reverie.

Dinner was announced and Captain Guyon was preceded by the Countess and the Marquis into the dining room. To his surprise they were not served by Heather as he had expected and hoped. "I see that you have added to your staff, sir," Captain Guyon said casually so that no one would suspect his intention.

"Yes, I thought I needed someone to take Heather's place in serving the meals since she already does so much. In fact, it was one of David's suggestions just before he left." The Marquis was a little surprised that Guyon noticed so insignificant a change in his household.

"Sir, I did not mean to sound as if I were prying into your personal affairs," Captain Guyon offered, trying to cover up his rude question.

"But you did, darling. You could not help but sound prying." Meg laughed. "My, but this Heather must be one of the true finds, sir."

"Yes, she's quite remarkable. She will also sing for us this evening. Her voice is so fine that she might well perform in the King's theater. And if she were not such a good servant, that is where I would send her."

While the Marquis went on about Heather both of his guests had their own thoughts on the young serving girl.

Guyon's was one of desire. The Countess'—though she talked favorably of Heather—was one of resentment. She wasn't worried that Heather would ever be anything but a servant, but she was irritated that the Marquis and Nicholas were not devoting their total attention to her.

As the three finished their dessert, a delicious mousse au chocolat, the Marquis suggested that they have their coffee and brandy in the drawing room. He also announced he would send for Heather to entertain them.

"Yes, do that," the Countess replied. "We would love to hear your treasure of a servant sing for us. It will be amusing to see that one not of royal blood can be so gifted." At this last remark Captain Guyon gave Meg a puzzled glance. He had caught a bit of venom in her speech, and could not understand why she should feel that way about Heather. Could she suspect there was something between Heather and himself? But then, nothing had actually happened, so he dismissed the thought.

While dinner was being served, Heather changed from her regular housekeeper's frock to a pale blue dress which was her finest attire. Standing in front of her small cracked mirror, she brushed her long blond hair until it glistened in the candlelight.

All her thoughts had been centered on the Marquis' guests, particularly Captain Guyon's mistress, the beautiful Countess. *How can anyone as beautiful as she be so cruel? I don't understnd, but maybe the contrast between the beauty and the wickedness is what makes men love her. I, too, can have her fancy airs,* Heather thought. *And I shall use them tonight. I won't be insulting, but I will be just haughty enough to annoy her ladyship.* At that thought an impish smile played on Heather's delicately full lips and she brushed her hair back from her face. She placed a small blue ribbon around her hair so that the curls fell over her shoulders, and drew attention to the whiteness of her skin.

Inspecting herself in the mirror, Heather smiled again, pleased. The bell rang and she glanced once more at herself in the mirror for confidence.

Approaching the drawing room, Heather could hear the conversation and the Countess' high-pitched giggle. As she opened the door the discourse halted and all eyes were on her.

"Oh, Heather, I'm glad you're here. Now you can prove to my guests that I'm not one to tell lies, and that you can sing like an angel."

Heather smiled at the Marquis and his guests and gave a slight curtsy. Meg's eyes were fastened on Heather. There was a mock smile on her lips, which, were she alone, would have been a sneer. Captain Guyon was also gazing at Heather but the look in his eyes was one of expectancy and ill-concealed desire.

Heather took her place beside the harp and then started to sing. The room was filled with soft music which had a relaxing effect on the Marquis. He leaned back in his chair and closed his eyes, letting the song soothe his troubled mind. The song did not have the same effect on Captain Guyon and the Countess. Their minds were otherwise occupied.

Meg was watching Nicholas, who in turn stared at Heather with more interest than a servant deserved, she thought. For the first time since Heather had been asleep under the oak, Captain Guyon could look upon her without being reproached for it. All his senses were full of her. He remembered her sweet fragrance, and he could almost feel her softness with his fingertips.

His only surprise was her air of gentility. She had entered the room with as much or maybe just a touch more grace than Meg. She could fool the highest nobility. It seemed his golden girl would always have a surprise in store for him. *God,* he thought, *if only there was a way to possess her.* To be able to unleash the fire that he knew lay dormant beneath the cool facade. Suddenly his thoughts came back to his companion and at once he looked at Meg. His eyes met hers and he only hoped that his face did not betray his thoughts.

Meg could not totally fathom the emotions that played on Guyon's face. But what she did see convinced her that there was something between Heather and Nicholas. She had never seen such an expression on his face—even when he made love to her.

When Heather finished her recital, the Marquis gave her permission to retire to her quarters. Once she had closed the door of her room behind her, she collapsed onto the bed. As far as she could remember she had never had to endure so much tension. The air seemed to tingle with the electricity.

The only person in the room who did not realize it was the old Marquis. His mind had not been with them but far away with his son. Meg's hatred had been apparent from the moment she had entered the room. And once Meg realized Captain Guyon's attention was not completely on her, it had intensified.

Heather had thought that with the Countess at his side, Captain Guyon would cease pursuing her, but tonight she realized differently. He had virtually devoured her with his eyes. One thing was certain, she would have to do her best to avoid any further contact with him.

Heather dressed for bed and was just starting to blow out the candle when she heard a commotion coming from the front of the house. It was unusual for any noise to come from that section of the manor all the way into the servants' quarters. Getting out of bed, she dressed once more in her housekeeper's frock and went into the kitchen to await a summons.

After the entertainment for his guests had ended the Marquis offered them a nightcap, but both Captain Guyon and the Countess declined and asked if the Marquis would excuse them so they might retire. "Yes, of course. I should have thought of your tiring journey myself. And I believe that I too shall retire."

The Marquis was in the process of getting into bed

when he heard the banging on the front door and then the sound of raised voices. He slipped on his robe and went downstairs. "Hopkins, what's all this commotion? And who in the blue devil has come at this time of night?" he blazed from the bottom of the stairs.

"Sir," the young man stepped forward and bowed, "I have news of your son."

"Well," the Marquis said, "out with it, man!"

The young messenger asked, "Sir, could we go into the drawing room where we may sit down?"

"Well, of course, but I assure you, sir, I cannot wait much longer for your news. If you have information concerning my son, then out with it. Because it must be important for you to come at so late an hour and disturb my household."

The messenger's voice was constricted by nervousness and it took all his courage to relay the message that had brought him in the dead of night to Dunhan Manor. "Sir, I'm afraid my news is unpleasant." At the look on the Marquis' face, he blurted out, "Your son, we have been notified, was lost at sea and is presumed dead. The *Lyme* was attacked and sunk by pirates off the Strait two weeks ago. The verification came from the War Office in London."

The Marquis' face reddened and sweat broke out on his forehead. As he gasped for breath a sudden pain attacked his heart, and he felt himself falling into darkness.

Seeing the effect of his message, the young man rushed to the bell cord to ring for help.

Hopkins, the butler, being just outside the drawing room, was the first at the Marquis' side. Then Heather appeared.

Seeing the Marquis lying on the floor gasping for breath terrified Heather. She did not have any experience in a situation like this and did not know how to handle it.

Captain Guyon, on hearing the disturbance, came downstairs. Taking in the situation at a glance, he im-

mediately took control. And for the first time since
Heather had met the man, she was relieved to see him.
Guyon ordered the servants to carry the Marquis to his
bed and then sent for the physician.

Meg descended the stairs just as Captain Guyon was
giving the orders. She had not come at the first sounds
of the disturbance because she needed a maid to help
her dress, and couldn't seem to summon the servants'
quarters. Finally she realized no one was coming,
slipped into her dressing gown and went downstairs.

As the servants passed with the Marquis, Captain
Guyon and Heather were close behind. Meg reached
out and touched Captain Guyon's arm. "Nicholas, can't
you let the servants handle this distasteful task and
wait with me until the physician comes?"

Captain Guyon gazed coolly at Meg and said
bluntly, "No, and I suggest that you return to your bed
before you catch cold. Heather and I shall handle this.
Thank you."

Meg's eyes flashed with fire as she watched
Heather's small trim figure ascend the stairs.

Heather stayed with the Marquis until the physician
arrived, then returned to the kitchen to await word of
his condition.

It seemed like hours since Heather had come to the
kitchen but it had only been a matter of forty-five
minutes before the bell rang once more.

Gathering her courage, Heather went to the drawing
room with a heavy heart. To her surprise, there were
four men waiting for her: Captain Guyon, the messenger, the physician and Hopkins.

"Please come in, Heather," Captain Guyon said.

Heather walked into the room, glancing uncertainly
at the somber expressions the men wore.

"Well, good physician, should I tell them or should
you?" Captain Guyon asked.

The physician, sipping his wine, made no reply but
nodded to Guyon to continue. "First I would like to
tell you that the Marquis is in a state of shock but he

79

has been bled and with rest should recover in a few weeks."

Heather couldn't understand what could have caused the Marquis to have such a seizure. And her curiosity could be contained no longer. "Sir, may I ask what was the cause of the seizure?"

Nicholas had been dreading that question. Still he knew that he had to tell Heather and Hopkins about the situation. Normally no one would tell the servants any of their master's business but this was a different affair. Having no living relatives, the Marquis had to have someone manage the estate while he was ill. These two were his most trusted servants.

Clearing his throat, Nicholas began once again, hoping to be able to break the news without upsetting them any more than was necessary. "Tonight, your master had a visitor, a messenger from London. The news he brought was a great shock to the Marquis. I thought it best to notify you both. Hopkins, you will know how best to direct the other servants so that work on the grounds of the estate will go on. Heather, you will be in charge of the household affairs. I will be unable to stay and see to these things, but I expect you to see that they do not fall into disrepair. Is that understood?"

Both Heather and Hopkins nodded.

"Well, I'm glad that you understand. Now you may return to your quarters. The physician is staying the night with the Marquis, so you will not be needed any further." Captain Guyon then turned his back to them and stared into the fire. He had dismissed them in the hope that they understood there would be no more answers for them. In this way he would avoid having to tell them about David. He did not turn from the fire until he had heard the doors of the drawing room close. With a sigh of relief he resumed his conversation with the physician.

Heather knew that she had been dismissed but was determined if at all possible to find out what news the messenger had brought. She knew Captain Guyon had information, and if he would not answer her questions with other people present, she would wait for him in the hall outside his bedchamber.

Heather sat on the window seat at the end of the hall, just in the shadows. She leaned back against the window and listened to the rain splattering against the glass. The day had been tiring and the sound of the rain gradually lulled her into a light slumber.

A slight shake of the shoulder roused her. She looked up to see Captain Guyon's dark eyes staring into hers. "Heather, what on earth are you doing here?"

Wiping the sleep from her eyes with her slender hand, she replied, "I was waiting for you and accidentally fell asleep."

With a smile starting to form at the corners of his mouth, he said, "My, isn't that a change?"

Immediately Heather's anger began to rise as he knew it would. It gave him a few moments' reprieve. He turned and went into his room, leaving Heather in the hall.

Thinking this slight maneuver would save him from her questions, he turned to find to his dismay that she had followed him inside. "Sir, I know you dismissed me, nevertheless I must know what caused the Marquis' collapse."

"I've already told you that it was a message from London," Captain Guyon said as he removed his coat and started to undo his cravat, hoping his actions would make Heather take flight.

To his amazement, she did not move. "Sir, what was in the message?" Heather asked point-blank.

It seemed there was no way of avoiding it now. He must tell her, even though he knew it would break her heart. "You know, Heather, that I know how close you are to the Marquis, but you are still a servant," he said, trying one last desperate evasion of her question.

81

Captain Guyon lounged against the mantel. Looking up at him, Heather asked, "Sir, please, I must know, if I am to be of any help to him."

Well, damn me! If that's the only way, I will tell her, he thought as he watched tears brim in her eyes.

Her face was full of emotion. "All right, Heather, the message was about David." He could see the muscles in her face and neck tense at the mention of his name.

And suddenly forgetting that she was the servant and he a lord, she said in a brusque manner, "Well, out with it, tell me! Is something wrong? Is David sick?"

To Captain Guyon's surprise he answered without placing her in her proper position. "Heather, David is dead." As soon as the words left his lips, he could see her begin to pale. He reached out and caught her as she began to slip to the floor.

Lifting her gently into his arms, Captain Guyon placed her on his bed. *What loveliness,* he thought. *She really loved David.* He had surmised as much, and that was the main reason he had dreaded telling her. He hated the dissension between himself and David; they had been friends for so many years. Now he would not have to confront David again. He'd never know whether David would have forgiven him. But looking down at Heather, he thought, *The field is clear. Maybe I can persuade her to come to London with me.*

Heather stirred slightly and slowly opened her eyes, to be met by a black piercing stare. Captain Guyon had been thinking of persuasive arguments to sway Heather and it was a moment before he realized she had regained consciousness.

Now fully conscious, Heather remembered what had made her faint, and tears began cascading down her soft pale cheeks.

Guyon could barely keep his arms from enfolding her. She seemed a creature of some other world, a spirit floating through the night. So pale, so ethereal, like a sylph, he thought.

Heather did not try to hide her tears or wipe them away. She let them flow freely for the first time in her life. Fate had again taken someone she deeply loved.

Now she was truly alone. Realization of this seemed to have destroyed a part of her, smashed it like a crystal glass into a million pieces.

Nicholas Guyon was more affected than he would admit. No woman had ever touched him so. He had never seen anyone cry so, as if the last person on earth had died. For Heather, he had.

❧ Chapter Five ❧

The evening sun cast shadows across the garden as Heather draped a lap robe over the Marquis' legs. Slowly he had been recovering from his illness during the past few months. It had been a while before Heather was able to cope with the tragedy of David's death, but now she was the Marquis' constant companion. The two seemed to be drawn together in their mutual grief, even though the Marquis did not know of Heather's deep love for his son.

The softness that had been present in the Marquis, and his peaceful attitude, seemed to have disappeared upon his son's death. And as he gained more strength, he became more restive and ill-tempered.

He was quarrelsome and complained about everything. When speaking to a servant he would no longer talk gently as he once had. Now his manner was hard and brusque. If an order was not carried out to his exact specifications, he would yell and storm until he was out of breath.

None of the staff could do anything for him personally, except Heather. The only other person allowed to serve him was his valet, for tasks of a more personal nature.

Heather alone was spared the old Marquis' wrath. Several of his friends tried to visit but he had refused to see them. The only people that he had seen were the two young men that had visited him on the day he was notified of David's death—Phillip Hastings and Millard Fairbanks.

After their first visit, which the Marquis wanted in private, Heather was included in most of their conversations. She contributed much to the discussions, surprising Hastings and Fairbanks with her knowledge.

They talked of current government policies, war with the Dutch and the defeats that the British had sustained in their recent battles. The Dutch had wreaked havoc on the British fleet. And the finances of the country were in the worst condition that they had been in since Charles I. Hastings and Fairbanks were careful never to mention their first visit in front of Heather. Nor did they speak of the cause, to which the Marquis now subscribed.

After she gave the Marquis his robe and served him tea, Heather was summoned by Hopkins into the house. She noticed the agitated state of the butler and, moving toward the study, asked what was the matter.

"There is a gentleman to see the Marquis."

"Who is it?" she queried, noting her own annoyance at the intrusion. Heather's agitation grew from the fact that it was she who attempted to elicit from visitors their business with the Marquis. This request was usually refused, for while the Marquis put great faith in Heather, his peers saw no reason to take into their confidence a young woman of low status.

Hopkins looked at Heather and then said, "It's Captain Guyon. He has asked permission to visit with the Marquis."

"Well, I shall ask the Marquis if he will see him.

Would you show Captain Guyon into the drawing room, Hopkins."

The Marquis was enjoying the afternoon sun as Heather approached.

"Sir, you have a visitor. Captain Guyon would like permission to see you."

Not looking up but staring at the roses in the garden, he replied absently, "Well, show him in. You know how close Nicholas and David were. Good friends, you know. Yes, show him in."

Heather went back to the house, her thoughts on the Marquis' words. *Yes, real good friends, so good in fact that David ordered him to leave the last time they were together. But you don't know that, do you, sir? No. And I won't tell you because you have had enough hurt. And I'll do my best to protect you from any more for David's sake.*

When Heather entered the drawing room Nicholas looked up and smiled. "My dear Heather, you seem to be yourself again, and I hope the Marquis is making the same progress. I hear from many of his friends in London that he has refused to see them. I hope he will allow me a short visit."

"Yes, he has agreed to see you, Captain Guyon," Heather said and returned his smile in a gracious if impersonal manner. "If you will follow me; he awaits you in the garden," Heather said.

Captain Guyon's eyes were on Heather as they walked toward the garden. He was admiring her petite figure, the provocative, natural sway of her hips. He did not try to speak with her but silently enjoyed her presence.

Once in the garden, he went directly to the Marquis and said, "Sir, I'm so glad to see that you are feeling better."

"Yes, I'm feeling much better, thanks to the care that Heather has been giving me. I've been meaning to write you, to thank you for your help during my attack. Heather told me that it was you who took charge of the situation."

At the mention of Heather, Captain Guyon glanced in her direction, surprised that she had even mentioned his name, much less given him the credit for taking command.

She was sitting slightly in the shade of an old lilac bush, knitting a scarf. Her gown was of a much richer material than when Nicholas had last seen her. Sitting there with her fingers working swiftly with the needles, she looked every inch a noble lady. *She has the same air about her now as she had when she entertained us on that eventful night,* Nicholas thought. *I wish I could put my plan into action now but I can't until I get back from this blasted war.* Remembering what he had come to talk to the Marquis about, he continued with his conversation.

"Sir, I have come to say goodbye for the time being. I'm going on maneuvers with the King's soldiers to protect one of the small towns on the Thames. We've had several attacks on some of the more important port towns." Nicholas glanced once more at Heather, who was now openly listening to the two men.

"Nicholas, you know I shall regret that you will not be with us, but I would regret it all the more if you did not come back to us once the flare-up is over. You are the closest thing I now have to a son." The Marquis' face constricted in pain and his eyes glistened with unshed tears.

"Thank you, sir. I appreciate the high regard in which you place me. And I would like to say that I have high regard for you also, sir. It should not take us long to defeat the Dutch, so do not concern yourself for my safety. I should not see much of the actual fighting, since I'm only going to be an adviser by the King's order.

As Captain Guyon was speaking with the old Marquis, Heather listened carefully, and formed her own conclusions. The Marquis sounded as if he were a true loyalist but Heather realized his true feelings, though he had never discussed with her his political beliefs. She could discern in his conversations with Hastings and Fairbanks that he did not support the King. Nothing had actually been said within her hearing but the visits were always secretive, it seemed, and were never mentioned to anyone except Heather.

Both the Marquis and Captain Guyon were showing different colors, it seemed.

The Marquis appeared the true loyalist and Captain Guyon the true friend. It was nearly a laughable situation, to see two men trying to deceive each other. And seemingly doing it. Only Heather as an observer could see what was going on.

"Blast those Dutch!" the Marquis stormed. "If I was only younger I would go and join up to help our new King." At this remark Heather could not help but smile. "What are you laughing at, young lady?" the Marquis asked. "You think I wouldn't make a good soldier, is that it?"

"No sir, I'm sure you would make a grand soldier," Heather replied.

"Yes, sir," Captain Guyon said, "I'm sure you would make one of the best soldiers in the King's army."

"But age has prevailed just as it always will. I can't go with you in person, Nicholas, but know that my spirit goes with you."

"Thank you, sir. And I now must go." Captain Guyon bade farewell to the Marquis and turned to Heather. "Watch over your master for all of his friends," he said warmly.

The Marquis took Captain Guyon's young strong hand into his old wrinkled one and shook it. "May God watch over you, Nicholas."

The farewells over, the Marquis asked Heather to help him back into the manor so he might rest. His interview with Captain Guyon had tired him and brought many memories rushing back. He wished to be alone so he might have his grief in private.

When Heather returned to the garden she found that Captain Guyon had not gone. She resumed her knitting, ignoring him completely.

Nicholas realized that Heather was not going to acknowledge his presence. "Heather," he began, "you have done a marvelous job for your master."

"Thank you, sir," she said, continuing to knit.

He reached down to still her hands and said, "Heather, what are your plans for the future now that David's gone?"

The color drained from Heather's face at the mention of David's name. No one at Dunhan Manor ever talked of the young master for fear of upsetting the Marquis. After a moment Heather found her voice. "Sir, my plans are as they have always been, to serve the Marquis."

Guyon yielded to the temptation of hinting at his own plans for her. And with a soft coaxing voice he said, "Don't you think a lovely young maiden could find something better to do than serve an old man? You could serve a far more pleasing purpose in London. Just think of all the young men who would vie for your favors."

Heather kept her gaze level with that of Captain Guyon. She was embarrassed, but refused to succumb to the feeling. She knew exactly what he was referring to. "No sir, I don't think that would be so. Are you not forgetting that I cannot pick and choose my suitors as do the young ladies of rank. I would just as soon stay and make the Marquis' last days happy than end up in the streets of London."

Guyon moved closer and began to caress Heather's cheek. "But would you consider London if you have a position waiting for you with a promising future?"

Heather looked into Guyon's dark eyes and said, with a firmness that seemed to close off further conversation, "No sir."

He could no longer restrain himself. Guyon took hold of Heather's hands and pulled her to her feet.

Looking into her eyes, he gently stroked the soft curve of her neck, then pressed his lips to hers. Heather stood motionless. Sensing her rejection, Nicholas stepped back, but did not release her. "Heather, you are much too beautiful to stay in the country. Why not come to London with me?"

Heather stared coldly at Guyon, a stinging remark ready, when Hastings and Fairbanks walked into the garden.

Releasing Heather, Guyon exclaimed in surprise, "I haven't seen the two of you for quite a few years. I thought you had moved to the Continent, where your opinions were more favorably accepted."

Guyon's surprise was no pretense. These were the last two people in the world he would have expected to find at Dunhan. He knew the Marquis to be loyal to the crown, despite the fact that he fought with Cromwell during the revolution. Guyon had no doubts about the Marquis' loyalty to the King. But the question kept coming into his mind—why were these men here?

Hastings and Fairbanks were no less surprised at finding Guyon at Dunhan—and especially embracing Heather, the girl they had begun to trust. Had they seen Heather's face they would have realized she was as upset with her predicament as were they.

Hastings bowed to Captain Guyon. "What a surprise to see you as well. It is nice to renew old acquaintances. We have just returned to England and thought that we would pay our condolences to the Marquis. While we were in London we heard of David's death."

"Yes, I too am here to pay my condolences. But what brings you back to England?"

Fairbanks, who had remained silent through the first part of the conversation, answered Guyon's question. "A longing for the old sod. Both Hastings and I decided to come back and live the squire's life and forget about past grievances."

"Yes," Hastings quickly reaffirmed. "We're going back to take care of our estates. Our fathers are getting old and are no longer able to manage things."

Guyon laughed at his. "Oh, it must be nice to have an estate instead of an empty title such as mine."

At that remark Heather looked sharply at Guyon. She knew nothing of his past, but assumed he was wealthy. To hear him laugh about holding an empty title puzzled Heather.

"Well, sirs, I must bid you adieu, for I'm off to fight the Dutch." Captain Guyon laughed. "That shouldn't take us long."

In a lower voice so the other men could not hear, Nicholas said to Heather, "We shall finish our conversation when I return."

Sir Nicholas' parting words disturbed Heather, they were so like the ones he had used on the day David left for his tour. He had a way of making her apprehensive. She could not understand the cold hand that seemed to touch her as she thought of his parting words and the fear that they caused. *Why can't the man leave things alone?*

Heather put her thoughts aside and turned to Fairbanks and Hastings. "Won't you please be seated and I shall notify the Marquis of your arrival. He has retired but I'm sure he will be more than glad to see you."

As Heather left the two men, Hastings, raising a questioning eyebrow at Fairbanks, said, "What do you think? Do you trust her?"

Fairbanks looked around the garden with a suspicion of being overheard, then leaned back in his chair and casually wiped his brow. "I don't know. I didn't even know that she was acquainted with Guyon, much less on such intimate terms with him. She certainly is unsuitable. And he has always been attracted to women of substantial means—the Countess Beaufort, I hear, has been his latest fancy."

A smile crossed Hastings' face as he said, "Of course! You're right. She visited here with him the day we first approached the Marquis. And Heather was in service then."

"If there has been anything between them, I'm sure Heather realizes he is merely playing with her," Fairbanks said, more to himself than to Hastings.

Nevertheless, Hastings replied, "Yes, I thought she had her wits about her, but now I'm not certain. We must find out what is between them so as to protect ourselves and the Marquis."

Heather hurried up the stairs to the Marquis' bedchamber and informed him that he had guests, but not until she mentioned their names did he decide to see them. He dressed quickly with the valet's assistance while Heather waited in the anteroom to take him downstairs.

The two young men did not notice them as they entered the garden, for they were in deep conversation. Finally realizing that they were not alone, they jumped to their feet and gave the Marquis a flustered bow. "Be seated, gentlemen. Heather, would you bring us some tea?" the Marquis said as he made himself comfortable.

Once Heather was out of hearing, the Marquis turned to his guests and asked, "Now, my young sirs, what has brought you here? What is so urgent as to jeopardize everything that we have worked for?"

Already disturbed about what they had witnessed between Heather and Guyon, they could not at first answer. Their mission was indeed urgent. But the new turn of events had to be discussed before going on to anything else. While Hastings and Fairbanks collected their thoughts the Marquis commented, "If you had been a few minutes earlier, you would have met Captain Guyon."

Almost simultaneously the two men answered, "We did, sir. He was here when we entered the garden." At this the Marquis paled, leaned back into his chair and took a deep breath of air. "How did this happen? He said his goodbyes to me over an hour ago."

The two men had hoped the Marquis himself could explain why Guyon was still on the grounds while his host had gone off to bed. But when he didn't they decided to tell him what they did know. "When we arrived Guyon was speaking with Heather."

A puzzled expression creased the old man's face. "Now why would he be speaking with Heather?" he asked.

They had not heard Heather come into the garden nor her approach. The three men were startled when she spoke behind them, "Captain Guyon was offering me a position from a family in London, should I decide to leave my position here."

"Well, of all the nerve! How dare he come and try to steal my most valued servant," the Marquis said angrily.

The two men looked at the Marquis and Heather as they discussed the rights and wrongs of Guyon's actions and then at each other. Both were thinking that Guyon and Heather had not looked as if they were talking about a position for a housekeeper. And if they were not, why was Heather lying?

They looked at each other wondering whether they would ever again trust Heather. They did not know how they could protect the Marquis without telling him the full story. The two young rebels knew that it would hurt the old man to be disillusioned about Heather. It was going to be a hard choice. Would they let things go as they were and not impart further important information to the Marquis or would they tell him of their beliefs? They also knew they must explain to the Marquis why they had come. His opinion was crucial to their next action.

Heather watched the two men and could nearly read their thoughts and their suspicions. She did not blame

94

them, for who would not think the worst after seeing her in Sir Nicholas' arms. Sensing their desire for privacy, Heather asked to be excused.

As soon as she had left the garden, the Marquis looked to his guests and said, "Do you believe what Heather just told me?" But he knew they did not. The Marquis had seen the glances that passed between the two men while Heather had talked. They did not trust her. He himself did not believe that Captain Guyon was offering her a position as housekeeper. The Marquis had known Heather far too long and could read the emotions on her beautiful face. She had blushed slightly and her voice had had a slight edge to it as she had answered his questions. He knew that she had not told him the truth.

From this day on, he would be careful of what he told Heather and he'd keep a wary eye on her activities.

"Well, sirs, I can tell by your faces that you don't believe what you have just heard and I know your concern for me. But set your mind at ease, I will be on my guard from now on."

Relief showed on the men's faces instantly. They realized that the Marquis wasn't an ineffectual old man after all.

Hastings and Fairbanks quickly stated their business. They had a plan to do away with the King, but wanted to hear the Marquis' views before taking any action. "He fancies himself as strong as Cromwell," the Marquis said. "Clearly he isn't. The country is in danger, we've not been able to recuperate from the plague of '65, nor the fire of '66. And now this current action with the Dutch."

"I know," said Fairbanks. "It is Charles's foreign policy that has led us to war again."

"And among his other tolerances," added the Marquis, "is a strong inclination toward popish ideas. He will destroy us if he is allowed to go on."

By the time they had finished their talk, the Marquis was in full agreement with Fairbanks and Hastings.

Letting his gaze wander over the meadow that lay next to the garden, the Marquis asked, "When will you be returning to London?"

Fairbanks answered the Marquis' question as he rose from his chair and walked over to the small fountain bubbling nearby. "Today. We only came to consult with you."

Rubbing his hand wearily over his eyes, the Marquis said, "As soon as you get back to London, contact your associates and have them start the rumor that James is plotting against the King. He is scheduled to go on a hunt with Charles at the end of the month and it would be a perfect time for an accident."

Fairbanks smiled at the Marquis. "I had something similar in mind and have already taken steps to acquire an invitation to the hunt. It has not been easy, since most know where my loyalties lie. Fortunately, I do still have a few friends at court and hope they will help."

"Well, I'm glad that we see eye to eye and there will be no difficulties there. After everything is accomplished I will expect to see you immediately. Now I bid you good day and good luck," the Marquis said.

"My dear Nicholas, I wasn't expecting you back from the country so soon," Meg said as Captain Guyon walked into the room.

Bowing to the Countess, Captain Guyon said, "Nor was I expecting to be back so early."

Taking Meg into his arms, he said, "However, my darling Meg, I'm glad that there was no delay in my return. I would rather taste the sweetness of your luscious lips than talk of the Dutch." Meg needed no further urging to surrender to his kiss.

In Guyon's passionate embrace her plans for the evening were forgotten. Then Captain Guyon slowly released her and stepped back.

She was confused and hurt. A slow deliberate smile crossed Captain Guyon's face as he gave Meg a peck on the cheek. "My love, don't be upset, but I see that you are dressed to go out and I mustn't detain you."

Meg's cheeks burned with fury as she said through clenched teeth, "Damn you, Nicholas! Yet you are right. I am supposed to dine with His Majesty in his private apartments tonight."

Smiling once again at Meg, Captain Guyon said, "My love, you are finally getting your chance. Do you think you can oust Villiers?"

As Meg turned toward the mirror and began to touch up the fallen strands of hair, she said haughtily, "I'm going to try, my dear Nicholas. Why shouldn't I? There's no one that I'm in love with at the moment."

Meg could see reflected in the mirror Captain Guyon's changed expression. He walked up to her and resting his hands on her bare shoulders, kissed her neck. "You mean to say no one, my love?" he whispered. "Are you sure?"

Meg trembled from deep inside her. She let her head fall back on Guyon's shoulder. "I'm sure. Though I wouldn't be if someone were to love me," she said.

The game was beginning to bore Captain Guyon. He released Meg and went to stare out of the window at the foggy London streets. "I hope you will give my regards to His Majesty," he said offhandedly as his thoughts returned to that afternoon in the country.

Turning once more to Meg, he said, "Do you remember Phillip Hastings and Millard Fairbanks?"

Meg looked puzzled. "Yes, faintly," she said. "I haven't seen them in years." Deliberately she pretended not to have seen the two men during her visit to Dunhan. Perhaps she could gain further evidence so as to incriminate Hastings and Fairbanks in the eyes of the King. She would have long since imparted what knowledge she did have if she had seen the King during these past weeks. Obviously to inform Charles of treason on the part of any of his subjects would enhance her chances of becoming his mistress.

Pouring himself a glass of wine, Captain Guyon remarked, "I thought both of them were on the Continent until I met them at Dunhan this afternoon." Sipping the delicious ruby liquid, Guyon continued casually to discuss the two men. It of course had never occurred to him that Meg would go directly to the King with what she learned.

The Countess patted the last strands of her raven hair into place. Guyon remarked that Fairbanks and Hastings claimed that they had come to Dunhan to offer their condolences and she asked, "Were they close friends of David's?"

"Not that I know. I haven't ever heard their names mentioned by David. That's why I'm curious."

"But why should you be curious of someone's kindness?" Meg said in an attempt to dissuade him from examining the situation. She had to be the first to tell the King.

"Knowing their background and their feelings about the King, I do wonder why they would visit the home of so staunch a loyalist as the Marquis."

Meg gave Captain Guyon one of her charming smiles as she crossed the room to put on her black velvet cape. "But my darling Nicholas, can't two people of different beliefs like one another?"

"Yes, I guess you are right, my love," Captain Guyon said as he kissed her on the brow. "Now I must be going. I've got to meet some friends at the club. And you have the King."

But before he could reach the door, Meg was beside him, talking breathlessly. "Nicholas, you will come again before you leave for your post?"

"Why, of course, my love. Did you think that I could leave London without having the pleasure of your company for at least one night?" Guyon kissed her once more and left.

Meg's fingertips touched her lips and she sighed. She stood some moments in the same place before she summoned her carriage.

When Meg arrived at the palace, she was shown to the King's apartments by one of his pages. He told her that it would be a short while before the King would be able to join her. As she waited, she inspected the luxurious furnishings of the chamber.

The walls were hung in royal blue satin and trimmed with gold. Many of the furnishings, such as the large desk near the marble fireplace, were inlaid with mother-of-pearl. The baroque style was seen in every aspect of the room, from the intricate gold chandelier to the small cherubic figures that were carved into the wainscoting.

As the King entered the room, Meg's gown swished provocatively across the black and white marble floor. She made a deep curtsy, showing her décolleté to perfection. "How wonderful you look, my dear Countess," Charles said as he took Meg's hand and led her to a beautiful small table laid with fine china and silver. "I hope you don't mind, my dear, but I thought that we would dine here tonight. I love intimate dinners. Especially with somone as lovely as yourself," he said, gently caressing her white shoulder.

Meg smiled beguilingly. "Your Majesty, it is an honor to be with you."

"Well, my dear, let us drink to our mutual enjoyment, shall we," Charles said, handing her a glass of bubbling champagne.

"To you, my royal sovereign," said Meg, her eyes holding his.

"Now let us dine, then we can proceed with more important matters."

Meg made no reply as he seated her at the table, but the expression on her face was clear enough. She'd grant his every wish.

As the servants brought their dinner, Meg marveled at each delicacy they were served, beginning with caviar, then a delicious bouillabaisse, which was followed by broiled salmon served with Chablis. There were numerous other dishes and wines and then a simple dessert of fruit and cheese. As Meg nibbled at each course she began to wonder how she would drop her bit of news to the King. She could not just blurt it out but had to work her way into it casually. She was delighted when the King himself provided the opportunity.

"Now, my dear, you can entertain me with tidbits of gossip."

"But sir, I'm sure that would bore you. I know you have already heard all from other sources."

"Yes, my dear, I do have other sources. But often some aspect of the tale is missing. This is why I like more than one interpretation."

For a moment Meg lowered her eyes to the hand that now held hers. She felt a sense of mischief. "If you insist, Your Majesty."

After Meg had told the King of most of the usual gossip at court, she leaned back in her chair and said as an afterthought. "Oh, guess who Nicholas met today in the country?"

Sensing that this wasn't just the usual tidbit, the King leaned forward in his chair. "Who?" he asked.

"Two people I haven't seen in quite some time," Meg said, hoping to entice him a little further.

"My dear, must you torture me like this? Let's dispense with guessing games," Charles said anxiously.

A smile crossed Meg's lips as she said, "Your Majesty, I'm so sorry. I did not realize that I was torturing you or that you have the curiosity of a cat."

Both of them laughed. "You little minx, you know what I mean. Now tell me, vixen, before I strangle you."

"Very well, sire. If you threaten my life, I must tell. It was Phillip Hastings and Millard Fairbanks."

The smile that had been on Charles's lips was instantly gone and his dark eyes flashed with apprehension. "Where did he see them?"

Meg realized that their game was over and abandoned her flirtatious manner. "At the Marquis de le Dunhan's manor in the country. They had come to offer their condolences; his son died in a pirate raid."

At the thought of his old enemies, Charles forgot his amorous intentions. He rose from his seat beside Meg and walked over to the fireplace. Casually he kicked a log with his gleaming boot. It was a nervous habit, a habit he retained throughout his many wanderings. Why had they suddenly returned to England? Charles pondered. What were they planning? He knew the young men well. Their presence in England could only mean some political maneuverings were afoot.

Charles held out his hand to Meg. "Come, my beauty." Gently he led Meg into a lovely room which contained the most beautiful bed that she had ever seen. It had small elegant curves and delicate posters. It was white with gold inlaid in the carvings.

"Oh! Charles, what a beautiful room. Where did you get such a lovely bed? I have never seen anything so exquisite," Meg said as she sat down upon the down mattress.

"Louis sent it to me. I thought you might like it," Charles said. Then, as if it were an afterthought, he continued, "I think I shall give it to you, my love, for the news that you have brought me this evening." He picked up a small flat box that lay on a gilt table beside the bed, and handing it to Meg, he said softly, "And this is to complement you beauty while you rest in the bed."

Meg took the box from Charles's slender hand, as bejeweled as her own. She could scarcely speak as she opened the case to discover one of the most beautiful emerald necklaces she had ever seen. "Thank you so much, Your Majesty!" she finally managed.

"It is of small beauty compared to you, my lovely Meg," Charles said as he bent to kiss her lips. Meg responded to his kiss only to find him withdrawing.

She'd been twice rebuffed this day, first by Nicholas, and now, the King. This puzzled Meg, but she did not display her anger to Charles as she had with Nicholas.

"My darling Meg, you are so tempting, but I have to send for Captain Guyon so I can find out more about the mysterious visitors at Dunhan Manor. But I shall make this up to you as soon as I have everything in hand." He kissed her once more and then rang for his most trusted page.

Meg realized that she was being dismissed and tears of frustration welled in her eyes. After all her scheming to oust Barbara Villiers, all she had succeeded in doing was ousting herself from Charles's bedchamber.

After leaving the palace Meg rode back to her house in a depressed silence, tears sliding down her cheeks. If she had played it differently she would now be in Charles's arms instead of in this damp carriage. And he would be searching out the delights of her body instead of pursuing traitors.

As soon as Meg left, Charles's page arrived. "Send for Sir Nicholas Guyon at once. He will be at the Wild Stag. Notify him that I require his presence immediately."

"Yes, sire," the page replied as he retired in haste. He knew that something very important must be happening, for the King would not likely end an evening so early with a woman as lovely as the Countess.

It did not take him long to reach the Wild Stag. He knew the district well, for he had often visited the famed gaming house. He assumed he would easily locate Captain Guyon. The young rake might be found most any night at the tables with some sumptuous beauty at his side. It was a well-known fact that he was penniless and lived on the charity of an old uncle and a pittance from the King's Guard. But women seemed drawn to him. Many a young blade would give his fortune to attract the kind of women that Captain Guyon attracted with ease.

When the page entered the Wild Stag the rooms were packed, but the Cavalier Room seemed to be drawing the most spectators. *That,* he surmised, *is where I shall find him.*

Captain Guyon's reputation at whist, always brought forth a great many observers, most of them wishing to see him lose—though they were often disappointed.

Pushing his way into the room, he saw Captain Guyon at the table. And, as the King's messenger had imagined, a lovely lady sat by his side. As expected, there was a mound of chips in front of him. Everyone else had withdrawn from the game with the exception of Captain Guyon's opponent, the Earl of Clarendon.

A hush fell over the room as another pile of chips was pushed across the table to Guyon. Everyone in the room knew that more than money was at stake in the game. Of late the Earl's popularity had gone downhill in the eyes of King and Parliament. The Earl had been an adviser to Charles I and now was chief minister to Charles II, who had started to withdraw support from him. The Clarendon Code, which was named after the Earl, had earned him many enemies, especially in the House of Commons.

Guyon's influence had increased of late. To the old man sitting across the table from Guyon it seemed that more than a game of cards was at stake—it was his political future as well. He felt that if he won at the cards, he would win in other areas as well. He had already lost a huge sum to Guyon and could not afford to lose any more, but he was determined to show the young whelp that he was the power and could not be pushed out so easily. Besides, he was sure that his luck would change in the next hand.

The cards were dealt once more, and the expression

on the Earl's face told the story. The old man aged visibly as the crowd watched. Captain Guyon had won once more and the pile of chips grew larger.

Before the next hand was dealt the page made his presence known. Bending close to Guyon's ear so as not to be overheard, he relayed the King's message. Guyon frowned. *Just when I have the best winning streak of my life, I have to leave. Damn!* he thought.

"Tell your master I will be with him presently."

The Earl recognized the King's page and knew that Guyon had been summoned. He also knew that now he would have no chance of winning back his money.

"Sir," Guyon said, "I'm afraid we will have to continue our game at some later date. I have to attend to certain matters. If you will be kind enough to excuse me."

The old man knew that he could only accede to Guyon's plea and he did so graciously. "Not at all, sir. We can resume our game at a more opportune time."

Guyon bowed to the Earl and then told his valet to take care of his winnings. He then left the club and hastened to the King. He knew the matter must be urgent or the King would not have summoned him at this late hour, especially with Meg as his companion. She had made many stronger men forget themselves, and Charles had a weakness where beauty was concerned.

As his coach approached the palace, Guyon once again wondered what could be so urgent. He hoped that it was not the Dutch. But of late no one knew for sure what their next move would be. They had totally surprised the English fleet with their maneuvers on the Thames. That was why he was to be sent with his outfit to Gravesend.

The coach stopped at the main entrance of the palace. Guyon was met by the King's valet, who escorted him through the magnificent marble halls to the King's private chambers.

Charles was leaning against the mantel of the fireplace, so absorbed in his own thoughts that he did not hear Nicholas enter. "Sir Nicholas Guyon," the valet announced. Guyon bowed. With a wave of his bejeweled hand, Charles gestured for him to rise.

Charles seated himself comfortably behind a large desk. "Nicholas, I've had some disturbing news tonight and would like some further information on the subject. Please be seated."

Taking the chair opposite the King, Nicholas said, "Sire, I'm at your disposal."

"First let's dispense with the titles. You and I are friends, so let's speak as if we are. Now that is settled, I shall begin. Tonight I had a very interesting conversation with a mutual friend of ours, the Countess Beaufort. She mentioned that you had seen two of our acquaintances—Hastings and Fairbanks." Charles leaned back in his chair so he might observe Nicholas' reaction. But it was nil. No emotions played on his face as he spoke.

"Yes, I saw Hastings and Fairbanks at Dunhan Manor. And my curiosity was also stirred by the sight of them. Tomorrow morning before taking leave I was going to request an audience with you, to tell you just that."

"Nicholas, you should have notified me as soon as you returned to London. But I shall forget your lack of urgency. Now we must find out what is happening. Knowing those two, I'm sure there's a plot against the throne." Charles rose from his chair.

"I questioned them as much as was feasible without raising any suspicions. I could not discover anything other than the fact that they are returning to their land. But I'm sure this was just a ruse to satisfy me. I did not want them to suspect anything so I questioned them no further." Nicholas brought our his snuffbox.

"You were right to do so, Nicholas, for we must make sure they do not leave England again. I want

105

those two in the Tower. A leopard doesn't change his spots so easily," Charles said irritably.

"I agree, but the thing that puzzles me is, why were they at the old Marquis de le Dunhan's manor?"

"The same thought occurred to me, Nicholas. I don't believe for a moment that it was to offer their condolences to him. The Marquis was at one time a power with Cromwell. I remember it well. They had been great allies, but once Cromwell was dead, he swore allegiance to me. Mostly, I believe, for the sake of his son. Of course, now that his son is dead, he could have gone back to his old beliefs."

As the King spoke, Nicholas' thoughts returned to Dunhan Manor and the lovely Heather. If something happened to the Marquis, Heather would have to find other employment. And that might not be as easily done as one would think, if he had anything to do with it. Perhaps that wasn't the right way to get her, but he had to possess her. She had become an obsession with him, though he would be the last to admit it. "Yes, that could be true," was all he said in answer to the King's last statement.

"Nicholas, may I ask what makes you daydream when something as important as this is under discussion?"

Giving himself a mental shake, Nicholas brought his thoughts back to what Charles had asked. "Sire, please forgive my lapse, but I was thinking of Dunhan Manor."

"Well, arrest the old Marquis for me—for I still owe him a debt of vengeance on my father's honor—and it shall be yours. Once I have him in the Tower we can concentrate on Hastings and Fairbanks." Charles walked to the bell cord and rang for his valet. Instantly the huge doors opened. "Bring us wine." It was only a few moments before wine was served to them in crystal glasses. "Now let us drink to our success," Charles said.

Accepting the wine, Nicholas raised it in a toast to

his King. Simultaneously they smashed the glasses in the fire and laughed. Both had something to gain: Charles, his vengeance, and Nicholas, Dunhan and Heather.

⋅⊰ *Chapter Six* ⊱⋅

The morning fog shifted and birds began to chirp as Nicholas and the small troop of guards drew closer to Dunhan Manor.

Nicholas' thoughts were already there. He had set a relentless pace through the night so as to reach the Marquis' estate in the shortest possible time. His orders had been clear-cut, his mood decisive, upon setting out. But now he was in turmoil. There was his friendship for David to consider and his fondness for the Marquis. Suddenly he wished that he had not taken charge of the patrol. Yet, might it not be better that he, rather than a stranger, tell the Marquis of the charges of treason against him? As for Heather, he knew what her reaction would be and he was not looking forward to it.

She was a strange creature, so beautiful and seemingly so cold. He was certain that beneath the cold facade there was fire. Hadn't he seen it in her anger? How he longed to bring that fire to the surface.

Nicholas was roused from his thoughts as his sergeant rode up beside him. "Sir, we're almost at the gates."

"All right, Sergeant, you know my orders. And make sure that every courtesy is shown." Nicholas looked up the tree-lined drive. It had always been one of the most beautiful places that he had ever seen. And in his eyes, its beauty was no less because of his mission.

The manor house itself, built in the fourteenth century, was in the classic Gothic style. That was the most recent addition to the structure. The first of the buildings had gone up during the time of William the Conqueror. Surrounded by lovely gardens, the manor itself was a magnificent architectural structure.

As Nicholas rode up the drive he could see there were few servants about. He dismounted in front of the manor, and a sleepy-eyed footman opened the large double doors. Swiftly covering the small flight of steps leading up to the manor, he handed his hat to the footman. "Would you tell your master he is wanted," Nicholas said.

"Sir, the Marquis has not yet come down, and I dare not disturb him."

Nicholas gave the footman a hard look and said, "I did not ask for your opinion, but gave you an order. The responsibility of waking him is mine."

The footman, realizing that there was nothing he could do but face the wrath of the Marquis, bowed to Nicholas and then proceeded to do as he was told. Nicholas went into the study to await the Marquis.

As he entered the study he was once again aware that Dunhan Manor was as beautiful inside as it was outside. He had been to many elegant houses, but none had ever had the same effect on him. This room was paneled in rich dark mahogany and all the furnishings were masculine and made of leather and dark wood. A room in which a man could work or relax.

Over the mantel hung a portrait of a man on a huge black stallion. It was a painting of the first Marquis

110

de le Dunhan, who had been awarded his estate by the Conqueror in 1066.

Thinking of the heritage that spanned so many generations, Nicholas was again troubled. To have such a distinguished family line and now to be arrested for treason. He stared out at the meadow, still wet with morning dew, and his thoughts turned to Heather. Just then the study door opened and the Marquis entered.

"Sir," Nicholas said as he bowed to the Marquis.

The Marquis' face was flushed with anger as he walked swiftly into the room and blurted out, "What in the blue devil are you doing here so early in the morning?"

"I have come on the King's business," Nicholas said.

The Marquis turned pale as he sat down behind his desk. "And what may I ask is so urgent that it requires my attention at this hour?"

"The business, sir, is a matter of treason," Nicholas said as he sat down across from the Marquis.

The Marquis now turned a deep red as the blood rushed through his veins. "Now, sir, would you be so kind as to explain such an accusation?"

Nicholas stood and said, "Sir, I am here by the King's order to inform you that you are to be taken into custody on the charge of high treason against the crown."

At this the Marquis also rose from his chair, although a little unsteadily. "Sir, am I hearing you right? You are charging me with treason. I, who have sworn allegiance to the King. You must be joking."

"That I am not, I can assure you, sir. The King has information linking you with rebellious subjects of the crown. And you are also remembered for your friendship with Oliver Cromwell. That together with your meetings with these rebels automatically opens you to the charge of treason. The King has also ordered me to put his seal on your estate until you have been tried."

At this the Marquis sat down abruptly. "How dare you! To come here as a guest one day and the next inform me that you are going to arrest me and confiscate my estate!"

Nicholas flushed slightly and said, "Sir, I'm bound by the King's orders and our friendship cannot enter into this. Now, if you would be so kind as to prepare for your journey to London. For after I have escorted you back to London I have to report to Gravesend to be with my unit."

The Marquis looked at Nicholas in astonishment. "You expect me to go back to London with you to-day?"

"Sir, I do not expect it, I insist. And I hope you will come as a gentleman, but if necessary I will use force." The Marquis did not reply but only stared at Nicholas in amazement. "Now, shall I summon a servant so you may tell him of your departure?"

Neither man looked at the footman when he entered the study, but both continued to stare at each other with animosity. Finally the Marquis spoke. "Tell Heather that she is to come to my study immediately." With a sense of relief the young footman turned and withdrew.

Heather entered the study, then stopped abruptly when she saw Nicholas. "Come in, Heather," the Marquis said, "I have some disturbing news for you." Heather looked puzzled but did as the Marquis requested. She could see that he was upset and it seemed obvious that it had something to do with the captain. Glancing at Nicholas, she observed a complexity of emotions stirring on his face.

For a few moments no one spoke but then the Marquis said in a strained voice, "Heather, I'm to leave for London immediately."

Heather's fine brows arched in surprise. "Sir, are you sure that your health will not suffer from such a journey?"

"My dear Heather, I'm afraid that does not matter in this case. It's by the King's order. I'm being placed under arrest for treason against the crown."

112

Heather felt as if the breath had been knocked from her. She could not reply for a few moments. Only after regaining her composure was she able to look at Nicholas. Without asking consent to speak as was expected of a servant, she said, "And you're the one that has come to arrest the Marquis! A friend, supposedly, of his son and himself. How dare you!" By the time she had finished speaking, she was facing Nicholas, trembling with rage. She slapped him.

As the blow struck, Nicholas automatically reached for Heather, crushing her arms to her side. When he looked into her eyes the hatred was virtually palpable, and he physically drew back, though retaining his hold on her. He had expected a violent reaction but this was far in excess of anything he could have imagined.

His face stung from the slap but he would not have changed it. He had broken the icy barrier that Heather had erected around herself. Nicholas saw at last the fire that lay beneath her cool exterior. Someday she would be aflame with desire, that was a promise he made to himself as he held Heather in a firm grip. She struggled to free herself of him. "Stop it, Heather!" he exclaimed and shook her.

Just as suddenly as her rage had come, it left her. With tears streaming down her face, she looked at the Marquis, who sat with a stunned expression on his face because of the scene he had just witnessed.

The Marquis knew that Heather in the past months had become as one of his closest friends but he did not realize the devotion that accompanied that friendship. Now as he looked at Heather, he thought of the first time he had seen her in Jess's arms wrapped in an old woolen blanket. During all the years that had gone by he had never noticed her except when he needed something for himself. In the past months the only reason for his friendship was because of his need, but now he realized that she was more than a servant. He regretted his suspicions of the previous day and knew that Heather's loyalties would always lie with him. *Yes,* he thought, *just as a daughter's would*. And that was what she seemed, especially since David's death.

Holding out his arms, the Marquis said, "Heather, come here, child." Without a moment's hesitation, Heather ran into his arms. Stroking her hair as she wept on his chest, he said, "Heather, do not take on so. I will be all right. And as soon as I prove my innocence I will be back. After I talk to the King everything will be set right once again."

Sniffing back tears, Heather looked up at the Marquis' wrinkled old face. She knew that everything would not be all right. Hadn't she witnessed enough in the past months to convict the Marquis of the charges made against him? But that did not change her feelings for him, nor her will to protect him. He was the last link with her past. Were he found guilty, he would be executed, and she would be destitute, with neither friend nor family to protect and care for.

Holding Heather at arm's length, the Marquis looked into her shimmering tear-filled eyes. His throat constricted as he said, "Heather, would you see to it that everything is ready within the hour." With a sob Heather turned and ran from the study, realizing now there was nothing else that she could do.

Neither man spoke for a while. Then the Marquis turned to Nicholas and said, "Now, if you will excuse me I will go and prepare myself for our journey." Nicholas gave a slight bow to the Marquis as he left the room.

Nicholas walked over to a small table which contained a decanter of brandy. He poured himself a glass, then moved to the window. From there he had a view of the meadow. But his mind did not conjure up beautiful memories of the time he and Heather were there. Rather, he brooded over the scene he'd just witnessed. *So early for brandy,* he thought, but it seemed as though he'd already been through an endless day. Swirling the amber liquid in the glass and vacantly staring at it, he thought, *Damn me, this is the most unpleasant thing I've ever had to do. The rewards for this day's work will be great, but nothing can change the look in Heather's eyes. Hate. God, if it could only have been passion. I must see her alone before we leave.* As that thought crossed his mind he was already walking toward the door.

He did not find Heather upstairs as he had expected, preparing the Marquis' departure but found her instead staring out into the meadow, as he had done only minutes before.

Absorbed in thought, she did not hear him approach. He touched her shoulder, and when she saw him she trembled with anger. "What do you want now? Haven't you already done all the damage that you could do? Do you have to gloat over it?" She could not bear the sight of him and turned away.

"Heather," Nicholas said, as he reached out and turned her to face him once more, "I did not do this of my own accord. It was by the King's order." Heather glared at him but did not answer. "Come back to London with me. You have no place here now that the King holds the estate."

As Nicholas said this, a look of surprise crossed her face. "What do you mean, now that the King holds the estate?"

"I am ordered to put his seal on it until this is cleared up."

Heather's face showed the shock that she felt. She bit down hard on her lower lip.

"Heather, come to London. I'm sure you'll enjoy the position I will find for you."

Pulling herself free of Nicholas, Heather said, "No, I've told you before that I've no interest in what you can offer me. A cur like you! How dare you! To do as you have done and then to come and offer me a position. I would rather die first."

As Nicholas saw the anger flare in Heather's eyes he could not resist taking her into his arms and kissing her. She fought violently but her strength was no

115

match for his. He held her firmly and then threw back his head and laughed. "You are a tiger. I know that I can never explain that I could make you happy in London but someday you will know. As I have told you, Heather, you will be mine. But now I have to finish with my work here so I may return to my unit."

Heather pushed herself out of his arms and stood glaring at him. "You are wrong. Never, never will I have anything to do with you. You have brought nothing but trouble to me and I hate you. First David and now his father. For as long as I live, I will hate you!" She turned and fled into the house as though demons pursued her.

Her pace did not slow as she ran up the stairs to find the Marquis. Bursting into his bedchamber, she ran to him and threw herself into his arms. Grasping the front of his jacket, she looked up into his eyes. With an effort she regained control of her voice and between sobs asked, "Sir, is it true that the King has confiscated your estate and that we have no place here? What are we to do?"

Patting her gently on the back, the Marquis said, "Heather, don't upset yourself so. Yes, it's true, but it won't be for long. And in the meantime I plan to provide you and the other servants with your regular income so you won't have to look for other positions. Think of it as a holiday." Stepping back and readjusting his jacket, the Marquis then continued with his packing.

Heather was in turmoil. What was she to do? All the other servants lived and had families in the village, but she had no one. Where would she go? All these thoughts ran through her mind as she watched the Marquis preparing to leave.

"Heather, come here," he said. "This is for a comfortable stay in London. I know you have no family and will probably have to stay there for a while until all this is settled." He hugged Heather to him in a fa-

116

therly embrace and kissed her on the forehead. The Marquis then went to join Nicholas and the soldiers.

Heather watched from the window of the Marquis' room and a sob broke from her throat as she collapsed to the floor and wept. When the Marquis rode away with Nicholas, he looked as she imagined David would have looked at the Marquis' age. All the pain of losing David came rushing back as she watched his proud father disappear down the drive of Dunhan Manor. As long as the Marquis had been here she had felt that she was still close to David, but now she was bereft. It was as though she had lost him for the second time.

Tears streamed down her face as she looked around the richly furnished room. It was the master bedroom, the one in which David had been born. She moved slowly around the room touching each piece of heavily carved furniture. She wanted to remember it always. As she left the room, she glanced at it once more and closed the door. She knew she had closed the door on the past.

✥ Chapter Seven ✥

The weather was hot and humid and the dust clung to the dark green foliage of the trees as the coach jolted its way toward London.

Inside the coach the air reeked with the stench of human sweat. Several of the passengers had tried to cool themselves by making crude fans but this only made them all the more uncomfortable by stirring up the dust that drifted in through the open windows.

The coach was packed so tightly with passengers that it was impossible to move without disturbing the person next to you.

Heather did her best to sit as still as possible. However, with each bump or curve in the road, she would find herself thrown against one of the other passengers.

For a good part of the time, Heather had been so absorbed in her own thoughts that she had paid slight attention to the discomfort of the trip and the lewd glances of some of the male passengers.

Over the past week she had made plans. Once in London she would look for work as a housekeeper or

119

seamstress. She knew with her qualifications it would not be hard to find such a position.

She also knew that with her education she was qualified to be a governess or companion. But she was aware that such positions were usually given to the daughters of clergymen, or young ladies of class with neither fortunes nor dowries.

Late in the afternoon of the second day Heather wearily looked out of the window of the coach and realized that they were approaching London. As the coach jostled over the bumpy streets, Heather was amazed at the crowds. There was an air of excitement as the people moved about buying and selling their wares. Heather was to find this an everyday occurrence in the shopping district of London.

Like her mother years before, she felt the same mystification on her arrival.

As the coach finally jolted to a halt in front of the station, Heather climbed down and wiped the dust and sweat from her face. She collected her bags and set out to find a place to stay and something to eat.

She was tired and hungry, not having eaten anything since she had taken the coach at Dunstableham. The food that they had received in the hostelries along the way was so unappetizing that she was unable even to bring herself to taste it.

Heather looked around the street in bewilderment. She had no idea of where to find a room. Seeing an inn a short distance from the station, she picked up her bags and began to work her way through the crowds. Not being a Londoner, she did not know that she needed to guard her purse. Within a few feet of the inn, a small dirty imp snatched it and was out of sight before Heather realized what had happened.

Nine of the eleven gold sovereigns which the Marquis had given her were gone with the cutpurse. The last of the sovereigns was in her bag, where, for some reason she could not have explained, she'd hidden it.

120

Heather's spirits sank. The one sovereign would have to last until she found work. Heather entered the inn.

An old woman sat behind a long oak bar. She was stoutly built and had wispy gray hair. Her skin was mottled and had the look of coarse wrinkled leather. Heather came forward and asked for a room. The bright blue eyes seemed to flicker with recognition as they looked at her. But as quickly as the look had come, it disappeared. Heather could see yellow broken teeth as the woman answered, "Aye, I got a room for a shilling a week be that it suit ye."

Heather paid what had been asked and was shown in a tiny room at the back of the inn. She looked around the room and a fleeting memory stirred deep in her. Since the moment she had entered the inn, she had a strange sensation of having been there before. But, of course, that was impossible, she thought.

She knew the story of old Jess but also knew that she had only been a baby when he had taken her with him to Dunhan. She could remember nothing except her life at Dunhan. However, the familiar feeling the inn evoked made her uneasy.

Well, I've other worries, Heather thought, shaking off the discomfort. Slowly she unpacked her bag. Surely she'd get control of things. But the sight of her few possessions brought tears of frustration. With an angry swipe, she wiped them away. *I must find a position as soon as possible, or I'll be begging in the streets.*

Heather went downstairs to the inn's public room and ordered a simple meal. As she ate the tasteless food she remembered the delicious meals served at Dunhan Manor. She had only been away from the manor for two days and she already missed it bitterly.

Finishing her meal, she went back to her room to rest, but sleep did not come easily to her in this strange city with all the sounds of the night.

Heather awoke early the next morning and rushed downstairs to get the notices that were posted each day for employment. There were several positions open for

121

housekeepers and seamstresses. She decided to do without breakfast so as to save time and money, and went in search of work.

The morning slipped by and Heather had been to several interviews. All had progressed smoothly until she was asked for references. She had been honest and told them that she had none in written form; however, she had worked for the Marquis de le Dunhan. At this, each person to whom she talked seemed to withdraw and the interview ended without explanation.

As she walked back to the inn from her last interview of the morning, she puzzled over the reason for the abrupt dismissals. Everything had gone perfectly well until she had mentioned the Marquis. *But why?* she asked herself.

After she had lunched on pasties and cheese, Heather set out once more. This time she covered seamstress openings. This group of positions, she discovered, were either filled or she was once more turned away when she mentioned the Marquis.

After a grueling afternoon Heather went back to the inn, tired and dirty. She went directly to the public room and ordered a simple repast, which she eagerly consumed.

Heather did not notice when the old woman came and sat down across from her. "Enjoying yer meal?" she asked as she watched Heather take the last bite on her plate.

"Yes," was all Heather said as she swallowed her food.

"I see ye were out looking for work today. Did ye find it?"

Heather was startled to know that the old lady had been so interested in her comings and goings. "No," Heather answered. "There was nothing left open for me but I shall try again tomorrow."

The old woman inspected Heather with her shrewd gaze and said, "Me girl, it won't be as easy as ye may think. Girls like ye flock to London by the hundreds in

122

search of work all the time. And many of them hoping as ye are to find it. But most end up on the streets, begging."

Heather was shocked at this bit of information and also to think that she had not even considered this in her plans. She looked at the old woman for a few moments and then said, "But most don't have the qualifications that I do. I've been in the service of the Marquis de le Dunhan for the past few years."

Surprise showed on the aged face and Heather's hopes rose a little only to be dashed to the ground once more. "Well, ye may have the qualifications but the reference will not get ye in the back door."

"What do you mean?" Heather asked.

"Well, it's none of me concern, but I will tell ye since ye seem to be a nice lass. The old Marquis that ye worked for has been charged with treason, it's said, and none of them highborn folks will hire anyone that has anything to do with him." The old woman had a knowing smirk on her face.

Heather was stunned by the information but now she understood what had gone wrong in all her interviews. "Well, what am I supposed to do?" Heather asked, and for the first time let the despair that she had been feeling come into her voice.

"Well, the answer to that I don't know, but many a less-fine-looking lass has gone into the theater. It's better than begging in the streets," the old woman said.

Looking at the old woman, Heather remembered the conversation that she had overheard between her tutor and David: "She would do well in the theater with her voice." There was a glimmer of hope. "How do you go about getting into the theater? I've never acted before."

Again the cunning look came over the old leathery face. "I've friends that might be of some assistance to ye for a price."

With this Heather felt her hopes diminish. The corners of her beautiful mouth drooped and it seemed that some of the twinkle had left her pale blue eyes. "But

I've no money. It was stolen just before I reached here yesterday."

"Well now, maybe something can be arranged for ye."

"But how?"

"Leave that to me. Now ye go and get yer beauty sleep, me girl, and we'll talk again in the morning," the woman said as she hobbled away.

The old woman watched Heather leave the room and then smiled to herself. She had found out what she had wanted to know and now she could probably make a pretty tidy sum with the information. *Yes, I thought I recognized the girl. She's Ellen's bairn. She couldn't have been anyone else by the look of her, just like her ma, and just as dumb. But now I will have my revenge for her taking my son.* Once more she smiled to herself. *Yes, I'll have my revenge once and for all.* Calling out to one of the barmaids, she said, "Go and get Pierre. I've work for him."

As Heather lay in her small bed she thought of all that had happened to her in the past few weeks and tears once more began to run down her cheeks.

When she made her plans, she had thought that her association with the Marquis would be of help to her. Now to her great surprise it was a hindrance. She did not know what would happen if the old woman was unable to help her. *Funny,* she thought, *I did not even ask her name, but she seemed to know me without ever asking mine.*

This puzzled Heather, but then it was just one more thing that didn't fit into place. All her plans for her safe and secure future had gone awry. *Wouldn't Captain Guyon laugh now if he knew of my predicament.* Finally, she fell into a restless sleep.

Heather awoke early the next morning and, as she dressed, looked out of the dirty window to the bustling streets below. She could see the shop owners preparing for the day and the fishwives setting up their counters. Beggars were already selecting their spots on the street.

Many had small children with them covered in sores. Heather shuddered as she looked at them. If she were not successful today she might soon be in their ranks. She stepped back from the window, not wanting to look at the sorrow written on their faces.

After Heather finished dressing she went downstairs in search of the old woman. She found her dozing behind the bar. Several of her customers were also there sleeping off the effects of the night before.

As she approached, the shrewd blue eyes were instantly alert. It was as though she had only been pretending to sleep. "Good morning," Heather said.

"And a good morn to ye, me girl. Did ye sleep well?" the crone queried.

"Yes, thank you," Heather said not wishing to mention the dream-filled, restless night she had spent.

"Well, I've some news for ye, me girl. You're to go to the Globe at noon this day. There ye shall find a man named Pierre and he will see if he can be of help to ye."

A smile brightened Heather's face. "Thank you," she said. "How can I ever repay you?"

"No need to worry, me girl. I like to be of service to decent folk. And ye seem like a right nice girl, not like the trollops here about."

Heather blushed at the reference the old woman had made and said, "I'd rather die than make my living like that. I've only loved once, and we never could have married because of the difference in our social standing. He was too much the gentleman to make me his mistress. Now that he is gone, I know that I will never give myself to anyone." Pain showed in Heather's face as she spoke and then she said, "I'm sorry. I didn't mean to sound so righteous or burden you with my misfortunes. I guess it's because you've been so kind, Mrs? Forgive me, but I don't even know your name."

"Ah, yes, it's Mrs. Goodlinger, but everyone just calls me Ma."

Heather waited a few momnts, expecting Ma to ask

125

her name, but when the question was not forthcoming she said, "I'm Heather Cromwell." Ma accepted the information as though she had known it. Heather noticed this but did not let it bother her. She had a friend now.

After Heather had finished her conversation with Ma, she ordered a meager breakfast and then went to her room. Later she would go to the Globe, as Ma had instructed her. She changed into her best frock, the same one that she had worn when she entertained the Marquis and Captain Guyon. As she slipped into it the memory of that night was vivid in her mind.

So many awful things had happened since then. Heather hoped that her luck was about to change. Perhaps the man called Pierre held the key to her future. She hurriedly finished dressing and set out on the London streets.

As Heather walked along trying her best to maneuver in the crowded streets, she could see many new buildings being constructed. It had been nearly two years since the fire, which supposedly started in Pudding Lane on September 2, 1666. In many places you could still see the charred ruins of buildings. Where St. Paul's Cathedral had once been, the cobbles were still covered with the melted lead of its roof. It would be a long time before London forgot and rebuilt what the disastrous plague of '65 and the fire of '66 had done to the city.

After about half an hour, Heather managed to make her way to the street on which the Globe was located. It was sheer luck that she was not covered from head to foot in dirt. Walking was not the way to travel the streets of London. Filth ran in the gutters and streets and as the carriages passed they splattered anyone who happened to be walking along.

When Heather approached the theater she could see that it was closed. But she suspected that the actors had a rear entrance and walked down the alley beside the Globe. She had been right, there was a rear entrance. However, it too looked deserted. She knocked on the door but there was no answer. *Maybe I'm too early*, she thought and decided that she would wait awhile.

She sat down on some empty cartons that had been dumped in the alley. A rat scurried out of hiding and Heather shivered. Better to move about, she thought, and paced the cramped space of the alley.

More than an hour had passed and Heather decided that she would return to the inn. *Maybe I misunderstood the time, or the place.*

She had nearly reached the street, when she was startled by a man who came out of the shadows. He was a tall man, dressed in the flamboyant clothes of a rake. But it seemed to Heather that his dress was extravagant even for the young roués she had passed on the streets.

He wore a tightly fitted velvet jacket over his slim figure, and satin breeches, also tight. The cravat was tied in many ruffles, but seemed unkempt. The lace-edged sleeves which protruded from his jacket were as exaggerated as his cravat. Still further marring his appearance were his mud-splattered hose and stained slippers. To Heather he looked ridiculous.

Heather stood still, awaiting his approach. As he came closer she could see that he had a thin face with small beady eyes. His lips were thin and he had a small mustache.

He was only a few feet from Heather when he gave her a low bow. She could see small decaying teeth as he said, "Madame, I'm Pierre Garteau, booking agent for the Globe Theater. May I presume that you are Heather Cromwell, sent to meet me by my friend, Mrs. Goodlinger?"

It took Heather a moment before she was able to speak. "Yes, I'm Heather Cromwell. And I've come to see about a position in the theater."

Pierre was gazing at Heather in a way which made her uncomfortable. He gave her a peculiar smile and said, "I'm sorry that I was unable to meet you at the appointed time, but business detained me. However, after I spoke to Mrs. Goodlinger last night I arranged an audition for you."

Relief flooded over Heather and she smiled broadly. "Just come back here tonight at seven."

"I will be here, Mr. Garteau. How can I thank you?" Heather said.

"No need to worry, it has all been arranged. Now I must leave you. Remember to be on time. There are hundreds of young ladies begging for the opportunity that you have been offered." With that he bowed and was gone.

As Heather made her way back through the crowded streets to the inn, her steps were lighter and her face a little brighter. She did not stop to think that her business with Pierre Garteau was conducted in a very unorthodox manner. All she knew was that there was the possibility of work.

When Heather reached the inn, her face shone. Ma knew that her revenge was about to be accomplished.

Heather went directly to the old woman and took both of her wrinkled, crooked hands into her own. The smile on her lovely face seemed to bring the rays of the sun into the dark and dusty old inn. As she spoke, the old woman could not help smiling also. "Oh, Ma, how on earth can I ever repay the kindness that you have shown me? I have an audition for a part in a play. And I owe it all to you."

The old woman slowly pulled her hands free of Heather's and said, "Nay, lass, ye are a decent girl and needed a fair chance at something. With your looks the position that is waiting for ye will be just right." At that thought, she smiled and showed a few rotten teeth. "Yes, I think the position that is awaiting ye will suit ye to perfection. Now ye run along and get yer beauty rest."

Heather impulsively bent over and gave the old woman a quick kiss on the cheek before she lightly skipped up the stairs to her room.

Ma smiled to herself and rubbed a rough hand against the place where Heather had kissed her. "I've never in me born days seen a happier lass." With that she snickered. Yes, she had very special plans for Heather Cromwell.

When Heather entered her room it seemed as if the sun had come out after a long rainstorm. Everything looked different to her. She got into bed and was instantly asleep. She awoke with a start when she heard someone knock. It was dusky and Heather lit a candle before she opened the door.

Ma was standing there, her arm upraised to knock again. "Hurry, me girl, or ye will be late. It's nearly six and ye have a ways to go." Heather wiped the sleep from her eyes and hurriedly dressed. Ma watched her with interest. "Yes, me girl, wear the blue frock, it makes yer eyes show up," she said.

When she finished dressing, she turned to Ma and asked, "How do I look?"

Ma grinned. "Ye look lovely, me girl. Ye will do nicely but ye had better run along or ye will be late." Heather smiled at the old woman and then ran down the stairs.

She walked out into the streets, still crowded, but with a different kind of clientele. There was, it seemed to her, a more unsavory element about now that darkness approached. She looked around apprehensively. However, she did not let this deter her. She quickened her pace and did her best to avoid the rough-looking characters that cast glances in her direction. On several occasions, she heard someone call out and she quickened her pace. As she passed the dark alleys she heard several screams. London streets after dark were no place to be—least of all for an unescorted female.

It seemed to Heather that it had taken her forever to reach the street on which the Globe was located, but she made good time. Once again the theater looked deserted. As she'd done earlier in the day she headed

129

down the alley to the rear entrance. This time it took all the courage that she possessed, for it was pitch-black with barely a glimmering of light coming from the street.

By feeling her way along the walls Heather finally reached the door. To her amazement it was still locked. She knew that by now it must be seven and wondered why no one was about. *Maybe it's stuck,* Heather thought and pushed at the door with all of her strength. It would not budge. She had been so absorbed with the locked door that she had failed to hear the footsteps that approached until she felt a hand grip her by the shoulders and spin her around.

Heather screamed and a clammy hand was clamped down over her mouth. "Tie her hands and feet and then slip the bag over her head," she heard someone say and recognized the cool, smooth voice of Pierre Garteau.

She could not see with whom he spoke but she could hear a grunt. There seemed to be more than just two men because she could hear heavy, raspy breathing coming from behind her as her hands and feet were tied and the rough sacking was slipped over her head. She could not scream, for they had also put an evil-smelling gag across her mouth.

Heather thought that she would faint as she was roughly lifted up and thrown over someone's shoulder. The breath had been knocked from her and she found it hard to regain it in the tight sacking. "Easy there, mates, don't bruise the merchandise, 'cause it will bring a pretty tidy sum. Old Bess don't get this fine a piece often and ye know she don't like damaged goods. If there's any damaging to do, she'll do it herself. She's good at that." Heather knew that it was Pierre who had spoken, but he had lost his very proper accent and fallen back into the language of the streets.

An indeterminate time later, Heather was once again set down roughly. She knew that she must be inside, for she could see a little light seeping through the sack-

130

ing and she could hear a distant murmuring of voices as the door was opened and then shut.

Trying with all her strength, Heather worked to undo her bindings. After a few minutes the skin around her wrists was so raw from the ropes that she had to give up. Tears of frustration slipped from her eyes and ran heedlessly down her cheeks.

It seemed as if hours had passed. The silence made her even more fearful. Wild thoughts rushed through her mind and it took all of her will power to keep from losing complete control. She kept asking herself, *Why am I here and what do they want of me.* Presently, she heard the door open.

Once more she was roughly handled as the sacking was removed. Heather blinked her eyes, adjusting to the light. She could see that she was in a storage room. Huge boxes and barrels stood at the center of the room and lined its walls. It was damp and musty and an odor of wine pervaded the air. Someone was in the shadows near the door and she instantly recognized the figure of Pierre Garteau.

He waited for a few moments and observed Heather's reactions. He could see the fright in her, eyes glistening with tears. Her hair had come unpinned and now cascaded down over her lovely white shoulders. Pierre slowly walked to Heather, his eyes raking her body. As Heather grew more frightened his desire for her rose. He wanted to take her and feel her tremble naked in his arms and smell the sweetness of her fear. *If only old Bess would accept damaged goods,* he thought, *I would take her now. But the price is too high for me to throw away.*

Slowly he reached out to undo the gag. The movement made her shrink from his touch. "Ah now, me love, I'm just going to undo the gag. So sit still."

Heather did as she was told. Now able to communicate, she screamed in the hope that someone would hear and come to her rescue. "Now, me beauty, there's no one to hear yer screams except me and I don't like the noise. So if ye scream once more I'm going to have to slap that pretty face of yers."

Not heeding his warning, Heather screamed once more. The slap that resulted stunned her senses for a moment. "Now, me girl, let's not do it again because I hate to mess up a pretty face such as yers."

The pain that seared her face made Heather's eyes brim once more with tears. She did not attempt to scream again, but glared at Pierre contemptuously. "Why did you bring me here?"

"Ah, me beauty, ye will soon find that out," Pierre said as he sat down on a barrel.

Heather continued to glare at him but did not respond. What was the use of talk with such a man. He held her captive and she didn't know what else awaited her. She wanted to escape, to flee the terror that gripped her. Each time he looked at her a shiver ran up her back and it seemed to make the hair at the nape of her neck stand on end. Though she had seen a similar look in Captain Guyon's eyes, it had not made her feel dirty as Pierre's did.

Pierre moistened his thin lips. He was once more studying Heather and his breathing was coming faster. *God, I wish they would come. Watching her is enough to drive a man wild. I should take her but that would spoil everything and Ma would have my head on a pike. Maybe just one kiss. What could that hurt?*

Heather had been watching him from the corner of her eye and as she saw him move toward her, she caught her breath. What could she do? How could she stop him?

Pierre had heard the sharp intake of breath and knew that fear had once more gained control of her. Fear always excited him. Since he had been a small child he had loved to see fear on the faces of his victims. He had tortured other small creatures as a child, and now he tortured his wife. He loved to watch her frightened face when he beat her. It was like a cat-and-mouse game. He loved the torture before the kill.

132

Bending over Heather, he took her face between his hands and watched her lips tremble. A smile crossed his face as he kissed her roughly. She struggled as much as she was able but that only forced her against the wall, where she was trapped.

Pierre's intention had only been to kiss her but her fright had driven every rational thought from his mind. His hands roamed freely over her body, tearing at her frock. Finally he ripped apart the bodice of her dress and squeezed her breasts until they throbbed with pain.

Heather tried to cry out but his mouth was pressed tightly on hers. She could feel the skin break and taste the sweetness of her own blood. As his hands ripped the skirt of the dress, Heather tried to squirm out of his reach; it was a futile effort.

Pierre's breath became hard and raspy as he released her mouth long enough to look at her and see the blood on her lips. He now had to have her; with both hands he tore the last of her garments from her. She lay naked and trembling.

He slowly removed his clothing and folded it. As he divested himself of each item of clothing he would strut a little to show off his manhood. He knew that it terrified Heather.

Caressing himself as he walked toward Heather, he heard her whimper and knew the time had come. Untying her feet, he roughly spread her legs apart and ran his hands slowly up her thighs until it reached the mass of golden hair. He could feel her shudder and as his finger explored the depths of her private area, he fondled himself more vigorously.

He did not hear the door open and see Ma walk in. When she saw what was about to take place her first reaction was to sit down and savor her revenge. However, her greed took hold and she walked over to Pierre and gave him a hard kick in the rear. He lost his balance and fell to the floor.

Heather looked up and saw who her rescuer was and relief flooded her face, however short-lived it would be.

"Get up and put yer rags back on, ye dog," Ma growled at Pierre. Cursing under his breath, Pierre hurriedly put on his clothes.

Ma watched him dress and then turned back to Heather, who was struggling to sit up. "Ma," Heather said with tears of relief streaming down her cheeks, "I prayed for someone to save me but I never dreamed it would be you. God bless you."

Disgust showed on Ma's wrinkled face as she once more turned to Pierre. "Didn't I tell ye not to be messing with this un? She won't bring as much damaged. I'm glad I got here in time or I would have lost a good sum. Get some of them rags and cover her up before ye go wild again. Ye are like a dog in heat, but I guess ye are like any other man, wild over a pretty face!"

Heather gazed in bewilderment at Ma. The conversation puzzled her. Ma acted as if she were a friend to that fiend. Apprehension made Heather's skin prickle.

Turning back to Heather, Ma said, "How do ye like yer new accommodations?"

Heather glanced around more confused than ever. "What do you mean?" she asked.

Ma gave her a gaping grin. "Well, they won't be for long, only an hour or so more, and then ye will really have some fine living quarters."

"Ma, why am I here?" Heather asked faintly. The old woman touched her hair as if to straighten it but only disarranged it more. Then she explained the situation.

This really knocked the breath from Heather. "My mother? What's that to do with me? I never knew her," she said. Looking down at Heather and letting her hatred show for the first time, Ma spat out the words venomously. "Well, ye shall pay for what she done to me."

This was hatred such as Heather had never seen before, and she was afraid that she was in more danger

134

now than at any other time of her life. Once again she asked faintly, "What did she do to you?"

Remembrance made Ma's breath come in short little gasps. "She killed me only son." Seeing the doubt in Heather's eyes, she continued, "No, not with a knife, but just as deadly. Ye are like her with yer pretty face and graceful airs. Making all the men look at ye, and you're dumb like her too. Aye, making them want ye like a bitch in heat."

This had nothing to do with Heather. It was a sick old woman's revenge and Heather could not comprehend it. She just stared at Ma in a vague way, trying to take it all in and make sense of it.

The old woman continued as she bent over Heather. "But ye shall pay for her making my son fall in love with her. When she got knocked off, he drowned himself in that bloody river, the Thames."

Ma was so close to Heather's face as she spat out her vindictive words that Heather could smell the rank odor of garlic and wine on her breath. It made Heather want to retch but she swallowed it back, trying with all her might not to let Ma know how frightened she was.

"Aye, I'll have me revenge. Where she made him love her so will ye make men love ye. But ye won't ever have the kind of love that others have because ye will sell yer love to the highest bidder. They'll express their lust on yer body but never love ye for anything else. And maybe if ye are lucky ye will get the pox and it will end yer miserable life." At this thought Ma smiled and slapped Heather across the face. "That's all the abuse ye will receive from me, but me revenge will be in knowing what is happening to ye every day and night." Ma laughed loudly at this and then turned to Pierre. "Get the sack ready. It's time to take her to Bess."

Heather did not move; all this had the effect of a drug used to stun the senses. All she could do was to sit there in a daze, with the horror of Ma's words tumbling through her mind.

Pierre once again tied Heather's feet. He could not resist running his hand down the soft white thigh. A little mournful sigh escaped his lips at the thought of what could have been.

Heather did not resist as he slipped the bag once more over her head and picked her up. She knew it would do no good and if she resisted, they might beat her or do something worse. It was best to accept what was to happen and pray that she might find some means of escape.

She could hear the mumbled voices of Ma and Pierre but could not make out what was being said. Once it seemed as if Pierre had bumped into something because he had nearly dropped her. "Be careful, ye bloody fool, or ye will hurt her. All we need is to hand her over with a broke leg," Ma said. To this Pierre merely grunted.

After a while Heather heard a knock and then a door open, then a new voice that sounded husky and feminine. "Take her upstairs and I will be there shortly."

Heather was jolted by the climb but she could hear no footsteps and supposed the stairs were carpeted. Finally she was set down on a soft seat.

No one spoke and no one moved to undo the sacking until Heather heard the door open and the swish of satin.

The same husky voice said, "Take that bloody sacking off her so I can see if we can come to an agreement. Ma, if this one isn't better than the last few you have brought me I'm going to stop doing business with you."

Heather heard a chair squeak and knew that Ma was shifting in it uncomfortably. "This un here is the best that I have ever brought ye, mistress. She be as graceful as a swan and just as beautiful too. She also be a virgin," Ma said.

Bess looked quizzically at Ma and said, "How do you know that?"

Ma smiled shrewdly and said, "She done told me and she's just fresh from the country."

"Well, there are men in the country and she could have lied, but we'll see."

Shaking her finger at Pierre, Ma said, "Get that sacking off so Mistress Bess can see the goods."

Pierre did as Ma said and untied the sack, and when a glint of golden hair showed above the sacking a smile of triumph crossed his face.

The first person Heather saw was Ma with a smile of satisfaction on her face. She looked about and saw another woman. She was short and plump and dressed in a gaudy purple satin evening gown. It had layers of frills and bows which made the woman look like an overdressed doll.

Heather guessed her to be about fifty. There had been an attempt to mask the wrinkles with cosmetics, but it was unsuccessful. Nevertheless she moved with grace and spoke in the modulated tone of a lady. "You have done well this time, Ma, and you will be justly rewarded. I've found it difficult to acquire young ladies as beautiful as this one. I expect she will do quite nicely for my finer gentlemen. Let's go to the day room and we'll finish our business."

As they turned to leave Heather finally found her voice, practically inaudible though it was. "You can't keep me here!"

The woman Ma had called Bess turned back toward Heather. "Well now, she speaks as though she were a lady. You know, my girl—for you are my girl—just as soon as I pay Ma ten pounds you will do exactly as I say. You may even want to stay, when you learn the alternative."

As she spoke, Heather could see the hard, mean glitter in her eyes. Bess was ruthless, she had no doubt about that. Yet Heather's instinct to fight and to survive had returned while she sat listening to the women discuss her as though she were something less than human. She might regret speaking her mind but that

137

would be better than being half alive and used for the rest of her life.

"No matter what you do, I am not your girl and you have no right to keep me against my will. What can you gain if I will not cooperate with you? None of the—finger gentlemen—will want me when I tell them how I came to be here."

As Heather spoke a smile quivered on Bess's lips. "You think that, do you? Well, my customers never listen to the girls. They come only for a little pleasure. After they've had their fun, they can't even remember the girl's face, much less her tale of woe. As for not caring about what we do here, well, you may change your mind after a few minutes in our Spanish Room."

Cupping Heather's face in one hand, she twisted it between her short fat fingers. "I would hate to ruin that pretty face, but once you have tasted the pleasures of the Spanish Room I'll venture you'll not be quite so anxious to defy me."

"I'd rather be dead than a part of this house," Heather said.

Bess turned from Heather. "Well, Ma, let's finish our business. I've work to do on this lass."

Tears streamed down Heather's face as she worked at the ropes that bound her hands. Her wrists were already swollen, but she would not be deterred. Finally she realized it was useless. *I must bide my time,* she thought, *and when the moment is right I will find a way out. Now I must do all in my power to avoid the Spanish Room.* These thoughts cheered Heather a little; at least she was fighting back. A slight smile tugged at her mouth. She stared at the painted lovers on the ceiling for a while before she fell asleep.

When Heather awoke the candles were guttering. Obviously she had been there for quite some time. She wondered why they had left her alone. Soon the door opened slowly and a small, slim girl came into the room. The girl limped about the room, relighting and replacing some of the candles. After she finished she turned to Heather and said, "Miss, I'm supposed to take ye to Mistress Bess downstairs, so if ye will follow me." At this she turned and started to the door, until she heard Heather speak.

"How can I follow you with my feet and hands tied?"

The girl limped back to Heather's side. As Heather watched her, she thought she saw a look of pain on her face. Heather could not keep herself from asking, "Does it hurt when you walk?"

The young girl looked surprised at the question and it took her a moment to respond. "Yes, miss, it does hurt something awful when I have to climb the stairs."

There were droplets of perspiration on the girl's forehead as she bent to untie the ropes around Heather's ankles. "Would you untie my hands also? They are terribly swollen," Heather said.

"No, miss," the girl answered, shaking her head. "I daren't 'cause Mistress Bess didn't tell me to, and if I did she would have me back to the Spanish Room. Lor', I'd rather die than have that again."

To hear this young girl talk about the Spanish Room with such fear made Heather curious and she asked, "Why did a young girl like yourself have to go into the Spanish Room?"

The girl looked at Heather a little uncertainly and wondered if she had already said too much. However, she decided that Heather looked like a person she could trust. "Well, ye see, miss, some men like them young and real small, I was only twelve when it happened."

Heather listened closely as the girl spoke and it seemed to her that she heard the voice of an old woman. There was so much misery and pain in her. "What's your name?" Heather asked.

"My name, miss? Why, it's Missy, Missy Talbot, that's my name," the girl answered in a surprised voice.

"Well, how do you do, Missy Talbot. I'm Heather

Cromwell, and I need someone to help me leave this place."

As Heather said this a look of fright came to Missy's face and she slowly backed away from Heather. "No one leaves this place, miss, without Mistress Bess's approval." That brought the subject of Bess's Spanish Room back into the conversation. "If I were to help ye leave she would take me back to that room again and then I'd lose the use of me other leg." Missy's voice trembled at the thought.

Heather's eyes widened. "You mean that's how you lost the use of your leg? What could you have done that would have brought about such punishment?"

"I fought. I wouldn't summit meekly like Mistress Bess said I should do. I was scared of all those big men and what they tried to do to me." Missy shivered at the memory.

Bess loved to get hold of young pretty girls and torture them until they begged to sleep with her customers. Once in a while, she would go too far and would maim or disfigure one of the girls.

"So I daren't help ye, it would be worse on me next time. I don't believe I would live through it again," Missy said.

Heather realized that the girl was filled with so much fear that it would be useless to ask her again for help; instead she said, "I understand, Missy. Now take me to your mistress." Heather had decided to meet Bess with courage rather than cowardice. Somehow she'd find a way to handle the situation.

With hands tied and with a slight limp Heather followed Missy downstairs. When they paused at the door, Heather steeled herself. Missy knocked at the door and they entered.

Bess sat in a large comfortable chair in front of the fire. At first Heather felt as though she were in an elegant sitting room in a Spanish villa. Upon closer inspection she could see that it was not a place anyone would come to for pleasure.

140

Along one wall there was a large delicately curved cabinet. Its doors were open and she could see displayed an array of implements whose use she could only imagine. There were, among other things, thumbscrews, a whip and a chain—all hung decoratively on gold hooks. Heather noticed that the back of the room contained a small area draped with exquisite brocade. This too was filled with every conceivable means of torture. There was a whipping post, a rack and wheel, a ducking tub and a brazier for branding. Would anyone really be so cruel as to use these instruments? Perhaps they were indeed meant to entertain some sick mind. But then wasn't Missy proof that they had been used?

Heather realized that Bess had been observing her. The woman had a faint smile on her face. Bracing herself, Heather asked, "You wanted to see me?"

Bess was taken by surprise. She had anticipated some resistance from the girl, but assumed that once Heather had seen what the Spanish Room had to offer she would give in and agree to do anything she was asked to do. Ma had said she was docile. But there she stood, as regal as a queen. There wasn't so much as a tremor.

"Yes, I wanted to see you. I want to inspect you as I'd inspect any new possession," Bess said. "Come closer so I may see how well you will please my customers."

When Heather stepped closer the smile returned to Bess's lips. "Now, turn around slowly."

Heather did so and then said, "I don't think you will find me to your liking, nor will your customers."

Slowly Bess got to her feet and walked to within a few feet of Heather and slapped her across the face. Heather did not flinch, but stared at Bess coldly. "You will not presume to tell me what I may find to my liking. After a few minutes with black Josh you will satisfy any man that I tell you to and like it."

Waving her plump hand in Heather's direction, Bess

141

continued, "Take off your clothes so I may see more of your finer points." Heather did not move. Rage filled Bess and she shouted, "I said take off your clothes!" Still Heather made no move to obey. Turning, Bess pulled the servant's cord. After a few moments Heather heard the door open and then a deep masculine voice.

"Yes, madam, may I be of service?" Heather saw a huge man dressed completely in black, except for a flash of white lace at his throat.

"Yes, I need you to assist this young lady to undress, Josh."

Heather looked once more at Bess. She saw that the woman's face was full of triumph. Shaking her head and losing some of her self-control, Heather stammered, "No, I will not undress, with his assistance or without."

Smiling broadly, Bess said, "Josh, you know what to do." Before Heather could move, Josh took hold of her with one huge hand and ripped the gown from her.

"Now, madam," Josh said with a wicked, lustful grin, "may I have the pleasure of dealing with this one?"

To Josh's surprise Bess said no.

Heather glanced from Josh to Bess. She could see that a strange light had come into Bess's eyes, one which she did not understand. Bess continued to stare at Heather's naked body. She had never seen a more perfect body, with its firm round breasts and slender waist, softly curved hips that gave way to the pale golden hair that hid the secret place in which her clients would find their pleasure. Perhaps . . . but that was getting ahead of things.

Slowly Bess released Heather's body from her gaze and looked at Josh. She could see that he had been as affected by the sight of the beauty of this girl's body as she herself had been. She usually allowed Josh to take his pleasure with any of the girls, but this one was special, she was not to be abused. Bess knew she could

142

charge a huge sum to the first man who bedded her. Purity brought a high price in her establishment.

Josh did not understand what was happening. His usual privilege was being denied, and it disturbed him.

As though reading his mind, Bess repeated, "No, I've special plans for this one. Bring her closer, Josh."

As Josh pulled Heather to Bess, she was tempted to take her into her arms. For the moment she restrained herself, but *someday,* she thought to herself, *I will taste your sweet lips.*

As Heather stood before Bess she trembled with fear, for she sensed what Bess was thinking. Slowly Bess reached out and stroked Heather's breast. "Now, my girl, I can see that you are worth what I paid for you. When you learn all of the tricks of love you will be in much demand. My gentlemen will adore you, and I have a few noble ladies who will enjoy your companionship." Seeing the shock that this remark brought to Heather's face, she continued, "Yes, we have lady customers. And sometimes Josh participates too." With this she laughed and ran her hand down Heather's body. She had inspected her thoroughly and found her to her liking in every respect.

Heather shook her head to clear it. This must be some strange and ugly dream. But it wasn't. Bess was still there, and Josh.

"Now, Josh, take her back to her room so she can get some sleep. We've got to keep her beautiful. She is a valuable property."

Josh started to lead Heather from the room but her legs finally gave way and she collasped onto the floor. He picked her up as if she weighed no more than a feather and carried her from the room.

As Bess watched the scene she had a strong desire to tell Josh to bring her back, but her greed was more powerful than her lust. She turned her back to them and gazed with longing eyes into the fire.

Once in Heather's room, Josh gently placed her on the bed and then slowly ran his large hands down the body Bess had forbidden him to have. Heather lay there and stared at the huge man. She did not move as he touched her, for it seemed to take an effort to breathe and she knew that her strength had completely deserted her. Her only hope was that he would obey orders and not take her.

As if sensing Heather's thoughts about Bess, he slowly placed a soft blanket over her naked body and left the room. Heather gave an audible sigh of relief.

Sleep took possession of her body but her mind played back the horrors through which she had lived, and would live if Bess had her way. She awoke the next morning tired and restless.

The sun was not up yet as Heather looked out at the street below. It seemed as if it had been a lifetime since she had left the inn with high hopes for a career in the theater. And now not even twenty-four hours later she was trapped in a situation from which she could see no escape.

Still naked, she glanced at herself as the first rays of the sun came into the room. *Why has this happened to me?* Heather asked herself. *All I've ever wanted was to love and be loved.* She gazed up at the clear morning sky, as if to find an answer. Slowly she slid to the floor and leaned her head against the window pane.

She did not hear the door open or know anyone was in the room with her until someone touched her on the shoulder. Turning and with relief, she saw that it was Missy. "Miss, I've brought ye something to eat."

With a hint of a smile on her lips, Heather got to her feet and followed Missy to a small table where she had set the tray of tea and biscuits. "It's not much, but the mistress said that ye couldn't have any more than this until ye come to yer senses and cooperate with her demands. I'm sorry, miss, but this is the only thing that ye will get to eat today."

Heather's faint smile faded as she heard what Missy's orders were. "But a person can't live on tea and biscuits. Instead of beating me, she plans to starve

144

me into submission. But I will not do as she asks no matter what she does to me," Heather said.

"But miss, she will kill ye if ye don't. She don't want to beat ye because she don't want to scar yer skin, but she has other ways of punishment," Missy said and glanced down at her leg.

Heather looked at Missy and could see the fear in her face. *The poor girl has seen enough to make her afraid but I still can't do what Bess is asking.*

Missy limped toward the door. "I'll bring you some clothes after a while," she said, then left Heather alone with her thoughts.

As she nibbled on the biscuits, she realized how famished she was. It had been a day since she had last eaten. She did her best to prolong her meal, for she knew that Bess meant to make her suffer. For as long as possible, Heather was determined to defy Bess.

Angry, Heather abruptly pulled the sheet from the bed and wrapped it around her. She continued to be restless and walked around the room examining each object, then finally lay on the bed to await her fate.

With each sound that she heard, Heather tensed, ready for the worst, but no one came into the room all day. As dusk approached she heard someone unlocking the door. She sat up in the bed and awaited the visitor.

Heather did not get out of bed but sat staring as Bess walked into the room with a candle. She placed the candle on the night table. That way she would be better able to observe Heather's expressions. "Well, my girl, how do you feel after your fast?" Bess asked as she set a chair next to the bed.

"Just fine, thank you," Heather replied in a sarcastic tone. "Wouldn't anyone who has had only tea and biscuits for a day?"

A smile tugged at the corners of Bess's brightly painted lips. "But it would not have to be so if you would only do as you are told."

Heather smiled at Bess. "Yes, if I would only turn into a plaything for your customers. It would please you extremely, no doubt. But for your information, I had rather starve than become as low as you have."

Bess did not let Heather know how her words affected her. She knew they were both playing the same cat-and-mouse game. And each knew which was the captor and which the prey. "But you could save yourself a great deal of trouble in the long run, and much discomfort," Bess said as she patted a stray hair into place. "And it is not what you expect, you would only be entertaining the most affluent of my customers."

At this Heather laughed. "You must think that I am very stupid to believe what you tell me."

Bess straightened herself in the chair and said, "Now hear me out. I know that you don't believe me but I have a plan for you. Your beauty far outshines any of my other girls. If you will cooperate and not force me to use drastic measures things will go well for you. My other girls perform with whomever I designate but you will be given only to the richest. And you shall meet him first."

Heather laughed again. "But I will still be a whore no matter how prettily you phrase it."

"Yes, in the end you will take a man to your bed, but it will not be as the others; you will at least have been introduced. In the beginning you will serve as a hostess in the main salon. There will be numbers of men asking for you but you will not be sent to any of them. Then if my plans work well you will be the talk of all the rakes of London. 'The Unpossessable Beauty of Big Bess.' "

As Heather watched Bess, it seemed as though the woman was living out some kind of fantasy in which all of London's richest men would come begging Heather's favors. And Bess would stand in the background counting the money she would get from the lucky man finally chosen for Heather's bed.

While Bess formulated her plans, Heather was busy formulating some of her own. If Bess meant what she said, it would be a while before she would have to per-

146

form her duties, except that of hostess. This would give her time to plan some way of escape. Heather knew that time was what she needed. She began to feel more hopeful. If she played her part well, she would not be exposed to the horrors of the Spanish Room or to Josh. "I still don't believe you," Heather said, knowing that Bess would be suspicious if she succumbed to her persuasion too easily.

"Well, my girl," Bess said as she rose from the chair, "I will let you think on it awhile and see how you like the dark and your tea and biscuits. Perhaps after another day you will see my point more clearly."

As Bess started to leave the room with the candle, Heather pretended fright. "You're not going to leave me in the dark?"

Bess was delighted to think she was really punishing the girl and said, "Think of what I have said to you, and if you agree to do as I ask, it will be the last time you will be left in the dark."

Heather smiled to herself and then settled into a comfortable position. She marveled at how well she had managed to deceive Bess.

Sitting up in bed the next morning, she watched Missy limp in with her meager meal. "Good morning, miss, ye are looking much better today."

Heather once more settled herself at the small table to eat the tea and biscuits. "I guess I do feel better, even though I am starving," she said.

"Maybe, miss, ye won't have to starve much longer." At this Heather looked up expectantly. "I heard the mistress talking to black Josh last night as I prepared her room for the night."

Heather stopped eating and asked, "What did you hear, Missy?"

Missy stopped for a moment as if she had said too much. But as she watched the lovely girl sitting at the table gazing at her with hopeful blue eyes, she continued, "She says to Black Josh that he was not to touch

147

ye, for ye be special to her. Ye will not starve after to-day."

Heather stood up from the table and walked over to Missy. Taking both her small hands into hers, she smiled down at the small frightened creature. "I know that it took much courage for you to tell me this, Missy, and I shall always remember that you are my friend. If at all possible, I will help you someday."

Tears welled in Missy's eyes as she said, "Miss, ye are the first person that has ever acted kind to me and I do hate to see ye mistreated. But please don't mention that I told ye or she will beat me."

"You have nothing to fear on that count, Missy. I would not betray you. I do not want you to worry despite the fact that I may look as if I have succumbed to Bess's will."

Heather could see that the last remark had not been lost on Missy as she asked, "Miss, what are ye planning?"

Heather explained briefly what Bess had said to her and that she was planning to go along with her until a time when a chance of escape presented itself. "But miss, she will find out and then ye will have no mercy from her. She will kill ye just as sure as ye draw breath. She will beat ye and then turn ye over to black Josh. Oh, miss, I'm frightened for ye."

Heather gently squeezed Missy's hands and then said, "Don't worry, she is not going to find out if I have anything to do with it. And Missy, you must never breathe a word of what I have said to anyone. If I escape from this house of evil, I will, if at all possible, help you to leave it."

A gleam of hope flickered on the thin face of the girl. "I would rather die than betray ye to Bess, for I do hate her."

"Then, Missy, you must listen for any information concerning me. I will need your help with that."

Missy gave her a small curtsy, and smiled for the first time. She looked, Heather thought, like a pretty little imp. Now Heather realized why Bess wanted her for one of the girls. *Yes, I have made you a promise and I will keep it, if I myself survive.*

Restless, Heather once again examined every object in the room and then paced the floor until she thought that she would scream. She could not stand idleness. Not having chores was a new sensation, and Heather was uncomfortable with it.

If only Bess knew, Heather laughed to herself, she would lock me in a small room without even a window and I would die of boredom.

Finally, her nerves wearing thin, Heather lay down on the bed. *I must not do this. I have to keep up my strength and not waste it worrying about something over which I have no control. I have to be patient and wait for the right moment.*

As the evening sun cast the last of its rays over the roofs of the surrounding buildings and the gloom of dusk settled in her room, Heather once again heard the door being unlocked.

The lone candle that Bess carried softened the lines of her face and she looked younger. She was flashily dressed as usual. The frills and bows might have suited a much younger person, but on Bess they were vulgar.

"Well, how do you feel today?" she asked as she set the candle on the table. Seating herself in the same chair, she did not wait for Heather's reply. "Now do you agree to do as I tell you or are you willing to starve yourself to death?"

Heather pretended she was weak with hunger and slowly slid from the bed. To her own surprise she swayed slightly on her feet.

Touching her hand to her forehead as if to clear the dizziness, she then sank to her knees. Looking up at Bess she said, "How will I know you are telling the truth, that I will not be handed from one man to another instead of just one?"

Bess smiled at Heather and then, placing one hand

149

under her chin, she raised Heather's face to her. Before Heather knew what was happening Bess placed a light kiss on her lips. Heather was too shocked to move. But Bess did not seem to notice and she stroked Heather's breast. "Ah, my girl, I would not lie where money is concerned or where love is." As suddenly as she had touched Heather she let her go and leaned back in the chair, breathing heavily.

Heather was slow to react, but presently she gave her mouth a vicious rub. After a moment, she said, "If I agree to do as you ask, will you never touch me again?"

For a moment anger flashed in Bess's eyes. She had hoped that in time she would be able to persuade Heather to enjoy her own proclivities. Nevertheless, if that was the price that she herself had to pay, it would be worth it. But first she would make Heather worry because of the injury she had inflicted to Bess's pride. "Now, aren't you being a little presumptuous? I don't have to agree to anything that you ask. I can make you do what I want. And you well know it. If I were in your position, I would not ask too much."

Heather could see the fury in Bess's eyes and decided that she might have gone too far. Yet she somehow had to dissuade Bess from pursuing this course of action. "Please," she begged, "I will do as you ask, but I cannot endure something that is so against nature and God."

"Did I not tell you that you would beg to serve my customers?" Bess laughed as she stared down at Heather in triumph.

Heather realized she had made a mistake and now she would pay for it dearly. "Get up," Bess commanded and Heather did as she was told. "Now, since we are in agreement, you will have clothes and food. And tomorrow we will start on your training."

When Heather did not hear Bess turn the lock in the door she scrambled to her feet and tried it. To her dismay, she was still locked in. She stumbled back to bed, dejected. She had lost an important battle and she knew it. Bess knew her weakness and would use it to her own advantage. Now it would not be as easy as Heather had thought.

✑ Chapter Eight ✒

The morning sun shone brightly as Heather paced wearily back and forth in front of the window. Dark circles were visible under her eyes. She'd had little sleep after her encounter with Bess the previous night.

On the table set a tray that Bess had sent her after she had been to see her. It was still untouched. Heather had completely lost her appetite after the scene with Bess. Her stomach growled from lack of food but she paid it no heed. Her thoughts were on escape.

She knew that Bess would not live up to any agreement whether she obeyed or not. Bess would bide her time and after Heather had accomplished her duty, she would once again make advances.

Heather sat down at the small table. Picking up a piece of ham, she nibbled it slowly. Nausea gripped her but she forced herself to swallow. Her strength was already dwindling and she knew that she must eat to preserve it.

However, she couldn't bring herself to finish the

food. Soon Missy came into the room carrying a beautiful negligee.

"Good morning, miss. I would have been in sooner but Mistress Bess said for me to let ye sleep." As Missy looked at Heather's haggard appearance, she continued, "But miss, ye look as if ye did not sleep a wink."

Heather smiled feebly at Missy and said, "I didn't. Oh, Missy!" The distress that Heather felt could be heard in each word she uttered. She jumped to her feet and hugged Missy as though to gain consolation. "Missy," she cried, "she is so wicked. We must escape as soon as possible or I shall go mad."

Patting Heather gently on the head as if she were a child, Missy asked, "What has she done to ye?"

Breaking away from the girl, Heather explained as best she could exactly what had taken place. She did not look at Missy as she talked, for she did not want Missy to see the terror that she felt. After finishing her story, Heather glanced up to see that there was no surprise on Missy's face, only sympathy.

Missy gently put her arms around Heather, and then looking like a woman instead of a small crippled girl, she said, "Oh, miss, I should have warned ye. But now ye know, and will be able to deal with it."

"But how?" Heather questioned. "She knows how she can torture me now without even a whip."

"She will keep her promise if ye obey until at least ye have accomplished what she has planned for ye. Ye are safe until then. Her greed will not let her do anything else. Now we have to prepare ye for yer first lesson. I will bath ye and help ye to dress. But I'm afraid that is all I'll be able to do for ye," Missy said.

Heather looked at Missy questioningly and then asked, "What kind of lessons are these to be?"

Pity was visibly written on Missy's face as she said, "Miss, it will be yer first lesson in love." Heather shuddered and Missy continued, "Ye must be strong and

154

obey so she will not hurt ye, miss. Just remember that."

"I will do my best, Missy, but it's the worst thing I've ever had to do in my life."

"Ye can do it, miss! Now I must prepare yer bath." Missy went into the adjoining room and Heather slowly followed. It was a small room which contained a large tub already filled with steaming water. Beside the tub were countless bottles of oils and perfume. The water had the scent of lavender.

Heather gratefully sank down into the tub and relaxed. It was the first real bath she had had since leaving Dunhan Manor. The old Marquis was an unusual man, for he demanded that each one of his household take a bath at least once a week. Heather was even more of an oddity. She took a bath at least once a day if at all possible. Most lords thought it bad for the health to bathe too often and used perfume and cosmetics to cover the scent of unwashed bodies. And they certainly did not insist that their servants bathe.

Now as she slowly swirled the water around her body, she forgot everything except the enjoyment of it.

When Heather finished with her bath, Missy rubbed her body until it had a rosy glow. She then oiled Heather's skin until it looked like satin. After she finished, she helped Heather into the negligee.

In front of a mirror that showed her from head to toe, Heather gazed at her image. She was dressed in a black lace negligee which was cut into a low décolleté. The material of the gown was so thin that the nipples of her breasts could be seen clearly. Her hair had been piled on top of her head, and small curls framed her face. As she looked at herself, it seemed to Heather that she was staring at a different person. She no longer looked like the young housekeeper from Dunhan Manor but like some enticing young lady. "Oh, miss, ye are beautiful!" Missy said breathlessly.

Heather could not resist smiling at Missy. It was the first time that she had ever worn anything so lovely and Heather could not help enjoying the feel of it. She knew the purpose it was to serve but she still enjoyed the softness of the lace against her skin.

"Now, miss, I must take ye to Bess," Missy said as she opened the door for Heather. All the enjoyment that Heather had felt for the past few minutes left her as she stepped from the room.

Missy took her to a room down the hall. There her eyes focused on a large canopied bed. Everything in the room shimmered with gold. The drapes, wall coverings and bed were done in gold brocade. The rest of the room was white with gold trim. The chairs and tables were in white with delicate gold carvings of cupids. Large mirrors hung on the walls and reflected the gold of the room, which only added to its staggering brilliance.

"Welcome to your new lodgings. I think these should meet with your approval." Heather turned abruptly to see Bess standing behind her. As she stared, Bess continued speaking. "I thought the gold would go with your coloring. What do you think of it?" Bess's congenial tone surprised Heather. She had expected anything but this. For a moment she was unable to answer, but Bess waited patiently.

Heather spoke honestly and said, "It is beautiful."

"I thought you would like it. Now are you ready to begin your lessons?"

Heather paled at the thought but answered meekly, "Yes."

Pulling the servant's cord, Bess said, "Now you are acting reasonably, and you look beautiful in the negligee." As she finished speaking a soft knock sounded on the door.

When Heather saw Josh enter the room, she held her breath. Turning to Bess, she said, "I thought you would keep your word when I agreed to do as you asked."

Bess seemed puzzled by Heather's words and then a smile played on her lips as she spoke. "I am keeping my word. I promised not to touch you; yet if you remember, you did not ask that no one else be allowed to touch you."

Heather glanced from Bess to Josh. She wondered for a moment which was the lesser of the two evils. She knew that if she did not cooperate things would be worse. "What do I have to do?"

Surprised at Heather's reaction to the appearance of Josh and then at her seeming acceptance, Bess said, "Take off your gown." As Heather slowly slipped the negligee from her shoulders she could see the strange glow return to Bess's eyes. Yet she showed no other reaction but said, "Now go and lie on the bed."

When Heather lay down on the bed she closed her eyes. She could not watch what was to take place, but when she felt another's weight on the bed, she could not prevent herself from looking. As she opened her eyes she saw the dark eyes of Josh staring down at her. He saw her fright and chuckled. Heather had to think fast. These were not to be the lessons of Dunhan and Josh was already drawing closer to her, a playful gleam in his eyes. Breathlessly she spoke to Bess. "You said that the man would know that I was pure, yet if I am knowledgeable in carnal matters he will conclude you have lied."

Heather had made her point and Bess realized it.

"Well, I see that the girl has some sense. I'm sorry to have to admit it to you, but you are right. However, you will have some of the lessons nonetheless." Glancing past Heather, Bess said to Josh, "Get your clothes on; we don't need you any more for the time being." Heather did not look around but felt the bed give way as Josh's huge weight was removed from it. He soon left the room. "Now we have work to do. Walk across the room and let me see how you move." Heather slowly slid from the bed and walked to the other side of the room. "Well, I see that it will not take much training. You already have the grace of a lady. What talents do you possess other than a beautiful body?"

Relieved to find that further instructions did not entail the more disagreeable aspects of life in Bess's house of pleasure, Heather spoke freely. "I am told that I have a pleasant voice." Heather could see as she spoke that Bess was once again surprised.

"So? Well, let me hear you sing so that I may judge for myself."

Seating herself, Heather sang the only song that came into her mind, the one that she had sung for the Marquis so long ago. As she sang, her mind carried her back to those peaceful evenings when she had sat in front of the fire and dreamed of David.

As Bess listened to Heather's soft voice she noticed that tears glistened in her eyes. She almost felt sympathy for the girl, but then realized what a prize she possessed. Until now she knew that Heather was one of the loveliest girls she had ever owned. But now with all the fear and worry wiped from her face Heather was truly magnificent. She could rule the hearts of kings. Heather must indeed be treated with care. Her favors would bring large amounts of money.

She was now certain that every rake and those noblemen interested in satisfying their fleshly appetites would be clambering at the doors of her establishment.

"You sing very well, and it will help you in your duties tomorrow night in the salon." Heather looked at Bess and swallowed the lump in her throat. She had not expected to have to perform so soon. However, the sooner she was allowed to mingle with the guests the sooner she would be able to escape. "You will have Missy to help you prepare and I have already ordered gowns befitting your duties. I don't think you need the supervision that my other girls needed. You have been well trained by the Marquis."

Surprise showed on Heather's face when Bess mentioned the Marquis. Bess continued, "Yes, I know all about you. Ma told me the whole story. But now that's all in the past and I think it is time for you to set the gentlemen of London on their heels."

Bess rose from her chair without waiting for Heather to reply. "Now I will send Missy to you so you may start readying yourself for your debut."

When Missy entered the room, she saw Heather sitting in the same place Bess had left her. She was still naked.

Missy picked up the negligee and carried it to Heather. A smile trembled on Heather's lips as she quickly slipped into it. "Thank you, Missy," was all she could say.

"Miss, I've been told to help ye prepare yerself for tomorrow night. And I think the best thing for ye would be sleep."

"How can I rest thinking that tomorrow will be the beginning of it?" Heather asked as she lay down.

"Well now, I can help with that. I'll bring ye tea with a relaxing draught in it."

"Thank you, Missy. What would I do without you?" Heather said.

After Missy had gone for the tea, Heather looked about the room once more. It was the most beautiful place that she had ever seen and she knew that she could be happy here were it not for the horrors that lay before her. Her dreams had always been of splendor and fine clothes and of someone to love. Now she faced in these beautiful surroundings a life of degradation.

Heather was staring vacantly at the ceiling when Missy came back with the tea. For a moment Missy thought something had happened to Heather, but as she looked closer she could see that Heather was only in deep thought. As she placed the tray on the table beside the bed, Heather looked at her for the first time since she had entered the room. "Here, miss, drink this and ye will feel much better," Missy said, handing a delicate cup to Heather.

Heather swallowed the sweet tea and then lay back on the pillows and closed her eyes. It was a few

159

minutes before the draught began to take effect but then she slowly slipped into a relaxing sleep.

When she awoke, Heather felt better than she had in a long while. She had slept the night through without so much as one nightmare. She stretched slowly, enjoying the feeling of tranquillity. Then her lassitude was broken as her mind returned to her problems. This morning, though, she felt more able to cope with things.

Heather went over to a beautiful bureau and started to brush her golden hair. Before long Missy entered, carrying a tray with a delicious breakfast. For the first time since her arrival at Bess's, her natural healthy appetite returned and as soon as Missy set the tray in front of her she began to eat. She did not speak until she had finished every crumb on the plate. "Now let's begin so we will be free of this place all the sooner. Where do I start?"

Missy gave Heather a slight curtsy and said, "With yer bath, for ye have slept most of the day."

Astonished, Heather looked at Missy and said, "I thought it was morning."

"No, miss, it's nearly night."

When they entered the bath, Heather held her breath, for it was just as beautiful as the bedroom. Only the coloring was cool, light blue, trimmed in gold. She had seen baths with tubs before, such as the one of the previous night. But this one's tub was placed in the floor so you might walk into it. One did not have to sit up in it but could recline and relax as if lying on a bed.

Heather was eager for another hot bath, for when she was in the warm, scented water she forgot everything except the enjoyment of it.

Missy laid out a beautiful gown of white silk enhanced with tiny blue jewels which matched the color of Heather's eyes. A pair of tiny blue kid slippers also adorned with jewels completed the ensemble. She helped Heather into the white gown and then dressed

160

her golden hair, placing into it small blue gems which matched those of her gown.

As Missy finished she stepped back and admired Heather. "Oh, miss, there are no words to describe ye. Ye look as if ye were floating on a cloud with stars shimmering about ye."

They were both so absorbed in Heather's attire that they did not hear Bess enter the room. "Yes, I agree with you, Missy, she does look lovely."

Turning with a start, the two girls saw Bess standing in the doorway surveying Heather from head to toe. "Now you are ready for your debut to the salon?"

Heather paled but replied, "As ready as I shall ever be."

"Then let us proceed."

As Heather walked from the room she glanced back at Missy for reassurance, only to see the girl had also paled and tears brimmed in her eyes. Heather tried her best to give Missy a reassuring smile but the attempt failed. She then quickly turned and walked from the room and followed Bess to the salon.

Bess gave Heather an approving look and then opened the door for her to enter. For a moment Heather hesitated but then gathered her courage and walked boldly into the brightly lighted room.

The salon was elegant. She could not understand how a woman like Bess could have such fine taste in furnishings yet dress with such vulgarity.

Heather gazed about the room. There were many fashionably attired gentlemen and also a few lovely women. Her own presence created a stir and Heather glanced apprehensively at Bess.

"Ladies and gentlemen, I would like you to meet a new member of my establishment, Heather Cromwell," Bess said as she held out her hand toward Heather. Heather curtsied, then sat down where Bess had directed her. "From now on Heather will be the hostess when I am unavailable and she will also entertain us with her quite remarkable voice. Now, Heather, if you will consult with the orchestra we shall then have the pleasure of a song," Bess said, speaking both to Heather and her guests.

Heather spoke with the musicians and soon her clear lovely tones filled the air. She glanced at Bess's clientele as she sang. Most of them seemed to be high-ranking nobility. Among them were a few members of the King's Guard in their dress uniforms. Some reclined in graceful chairs or lounged on the striped silk sofas. Servants brought around champagne and caviar.

When she finished singing several songs, there was a round of applause and she was instantly surrounded by a group of admiring gentlemen of varying ages.

One gentlemen bowed over Heather's hand and said, "My dear, you sing divinely." Heather thanked him. She was embarrassed by his obvious stare.

He misunderstood the gesture as an attempt to flirt. "May I introduce myself? I am Count Perier de le Creusot, ambassador of France, at your service, mademoiselle."

As he spoke, Heather realized that his English was fluent with just the trace of an accent. He was a middle-aged man with cool blue eyes. Count Perier brought Heather's hand to his lips, and murmured, "I'm delighted to meet you Heather Cromwell, and I hope we will have a chance to further our relationship."

Heather did not miss his insinuation and lowered her eyes once more. Again he misinterpreted the action, but before he had time to say anything more, two young captains came over and introduced themselves.

Much to Heather's relief several others joined the group around her and no one was able to make more than a few complimentary remarks before he was interrupted. Soon Bess, too, was making her way toward Heather. And Heather was pleased. Perhaps she would be allowed to leave the salon.

The Count spoke to Bess as she approached. "Ah, my dear madam, where have you found this delightful creature? She has the beauty that would drive a man mad and the charm and voice of an angel."

At this Bess gave what she considered her charming smile and said, "So, my dear Count, you have enjoyed my little entertainment."

Bowing over her hand as if she were a duchess he said, "Need you ask? I'm looking forward to seeing what other delights this beauty has in store for us."

As he said this he glanced back at Heather and she sensed an offer would be made tonight. She could not refrain the shiver that crept up her spine as she watched the knowing look come into Bess's eyes. "Well, my dear Count, we will have to discuss this further. Right now it is time for Heather to retire."

When they at last reached her room, Heather threw herself on the bed. Tears of nervousness and fatigue rolled down her cheeks as she looked up to see Bess standing beside the bed with a smile on her painted face. "You were perfect. When I go back there will be at least ten offers for you, but none will be accepted. By tomorrow your fame will already have begun to spread." Bess could barely restrain her joy. "Tomorrow night the place will be packed, and when they find they cannot have you they will take my other girls instead. I had not thought of that angle before; you will bring more money than I had originally thought."

Looking at Heather really for the first time since they had entered the room, she could see that this first experience had exhausted her. Bess turned to Missy and said, "See that she gets to sleep so she will not look tired tomorrow night." Then she left the girls alone.

Heather looked at Missy and sobbed, "Oh, Missy, it was horrible! So many men, and knowing what they were thinking. We must leave this place soon!"

Missy wiped Heather's tears and then cradled her in her arms. "We will, miss. But ye must be strong and not let them upset ye so or ye will not be able to keep going on with yer plans."

Swallowing back the sobs that threatened to once more break loose, Heather sat up and said as she wiped her eyes, "Yes, you are right, I have to stop acting like a baby and crying at the drop of a pin." And then looking beseechingly at Missy she continued, "Help me undress and then give me one of your soothing draughts."

As Missy helped Heather undress, she said, "Miss I don't like to give ye something to make ye sleep, but if it will help, I will."

Heather again begged Missy with her eyes and said, "It's the only thing that makes me forget. I need to forget, if only for a little while."

Missy did not say any more but continued to help Heather undress with a worried frown on her face. She knew that the potion she used to induce sleep was habit-forming, since it was made from the flower of the poppy. She had seen many become dependent on it and did not want to see this lovely girl do so. As she watched Heather get into bed, she decided that she would not give her as much as she had the night before, and tomorrow she would give her even less. Maybe by that time she would only need to think there was something in her tea and she would relax. At that thought, Missy smiled to herself and left the room to fix Heather's draught.

∽ Chapter Nine ∾

Nicholas Guyon had been appointed Ambassador to France. Directly after the palace ceremony he rode through the night to reach Dunhan. The estate had been awarded to him by King Charles. The King had also decorated Captain Guyon for bravery in the battle at Gravesend. He'd been more than the observer he was meant to be.

His golden medal gleamed brightly in the morning sun as Nicholas put the large key into the lock and opened the gate to Dunhan. He then stood for several minutes and observed the grandeur that was now his.

Dunhan Manor had always intrigued him and he had loved it since his first visit. He could never have guessed that one day he'd be master here.

Gazing up the tree-lined drive, Nicholas envisioned what it would have been like had he grown up with estates of his own instead of living on the generosity of his uncle.

His mother still lived with his uncle. And it was she who evoked the elder Guyon's benevolence. As a young child Nicholas had thought his good fortune had been brought about by his uncle's love of his older brother. Surely the amount of care lavished on the young boy and his mother stemmed from enormous family devotion. As Nicholas grew older he began to notice the affection between his mother and uncle. Still he assumed it to be the love of a brother for a sister until, one day, after he had been on a hunt, he had rushed into his mother's apartments to tell her of his good fortune. To his astonishment, he found his uncle and mother entwined in a lovers' embrace. The two were naturally embarrassed but an explanation did follow. Uncle Thomas said that he had loved Alice for years, even while her husband had been alive. He had wanted to marry her but the family had betrothed Alice to his older brother. They could not now marry because of the laws and, further, it would besmirch Nicholas himself.

Nicholas Guyon never again felt the same way about his uncle or his mother. Somehow she had betrayed his father. As soon as he was old enough he had asked to be allowed to join the army. Something had hardened within the young man. He would never be able to look upon any woman without thinking of betrayal.

Remounting his black stallion, Nicholas rode up the drive with an anticipation he could not explain. He wanted to see Dunhan but more than that he wanted to see Heather.

In his mind's eye, he could see her beautiful golden hair and pale blue eyes. He knew that her reaction to him would be cold but he did not care. For with a start he had realized that possessing Dunhan Manor also meant possessing the servants. Heather was his at last. He knew in time he would be able to erase the hate that she felt for him.

As he entered the hall of the manor he saw but one servant, Hopkins, who had remained to oversee the estate. The rest, Hopkins informed him, had gone home to their families. Nicholas asked about Heather and was disheartened to find her gone. Some of his high spirits at owning Dunhan had been dampened. After a tour of his new estate he decided to return to London. Without Heather Dunhan suddenly seemed empty.

Several weeks had passed and Heather continued to appear nightly in the salon to entertain the guests. She was becoming a little more accustomed to the way in which the gentlemen acted. Their compliments combined with insinuating remarks about being entertained privately had not ceased to be embarrassing, and her shy demeanor seemed only to inspire the men to greater efforts at winning her favor.

Since Heather's first night in the salon, her fame had spread and in many of the clubs she was called the Unpossessable Golden Girl. And as Bess had predicted, the clientele grew. As Heather glanced around the salon she could see many new faces.

Among the steady devotees of the salon was the Count Perier de le Creusot, whom Heather had met during her first evening in the salon. Each time he came back, his compliments were more effusive and his courting more demanding.

"My dear Heather, must you torture me so? Cannot this game you are playing desist?"

Smiling at the Count, Heather said, "My dear Count, I'm sure there are many lovely ladies that you desire."

There was a gleam in his eyes this night. He was making progress, he thought, for Heather usually did not respond to his remarks. "Yes, there are many lovely ladies, but none as beautiful or as talented as you. From the first night my heart was laid at your feet."

As Heather started to give a clever rejoinder, one of the captains came by. He effusively paid court to Heather, then turned to the ambassador. "Sir, did you hear the news?"

The ambassador, irritated at the interruption, spoke

167

with a brisk and impersonal tone. "What news, may I ask, could be so interesting that it warrants discussion at this time and in such lovely company?"

The young captain was in no way put off and did not seem to notice the Count's irritation. "Nicholas Guyon has been made ambassador to the court of King Louis by His Majesty, King Charles."

"Yes, I was informed this morning of the appointment. But I was rather shocked to hear of it. I know he made a great show at Gravesend with his bravery, but he has nothing else to offer. His title is of little import."

The captain looked a little ruffled by the Count's words and said, "I beg to differ with you, sir. Captain Guyon is rather a rich man now. He came into quite a sum gaming, and then the King awarded him the holding of Dunhan. He was the one who arrested the traitor."

Both men had forgotten Heather and she listened intently to their conversation. She longed for word of the Marquis and the state of his health. She knew that imprisonment would impair his already weakened health. As though in answer to her question she heard the Marquis' name mentioned. "Yes, and I heard today that he has gone to his just rewards."

The Count looked surprised at this bit of information. "I had not heard of that. When did he d—" He was unable to finish the sentence, for he heard a slight cry and looked to see Heather in a dead faint. Rushing over to her, he picked her up and saw Bess hurrying to their side.

"Take her up to her room," she said as she led the way with a grim expression on her face.

After the Count laid Heather on the bed and Missy was in attendance, he turned to find Bess staring at him. "My dear Count, could you enlighten me as to what caused this collapse?"

"Madam, I haven't the faintest idea."

"Something must have upset her. Had anyone made an unkind remark?" Bess inquired.

"None whatsoever. We were discussing the death of the Marquis de le Dunhan," the Count answered.

At this Bess knew the reason for Heather's collapse and smiled at the Count. "Well, I'm sorry to have detained you," she said as she opened the door for the Count to leave.

"Just a moment, madame, I would like a word with you concerning mademoiselle."

"Well then, sir, would you follow me to my office?" Bess said, leading the way from the room. With one last glance at Heather, the Count followed Bess to her office.

Once Bess was seated behind the big desk she said, "May I ask what you have to say regarding Heather?"

"Yes," the Count smiled, "I want to know why you are playing games. You already know that I want her. I offered for her the first night and you turned me down. Yet you keep bringing her back night after night, luring me on."

Bess smiled at him. "But you know what I want and until we come to an agreement you will not have her."

Shaking his head, the Count said, "Madam, you are in the wrong business. You would do well as the King's treasurer."

Standing, to show that his mission had once again failed, Bess said, "When, my dear Count, you have what I ask, you will then find that you can possess the lovely beauty upstairs."

Giving Bess a slight bow, the Count said, "Madam, I will do my best."

As he started to leave the room, Bess said, "Sir, you had best act soon. Tomorrow night she will no longer be available. Several others are willing to meet the price. I would not have said anything but I know how you feel about the girl."

The Count looked at Bess and his lips narrowed into a thin line. "Thank you. And I shall try to have the required amount by tomorrow noon." He then left Bess's office and her establishment.

As Bess returned to the salon, she had a triumphant smile on her face. No one else had been able to come up with the amount she had asked for Heather and she was beginning to tire of the game. She had helped things along by telling the Count the lie. Heather had been spared long enough and she was ready to collect on her investment.

When the Count left Bess's, he went to the Silver Cock, one of the favorite gaming clubs of most of the high-ranking gentlemen in London. As he entered, there were numerous welcomes and invitations to join the games; however, he only wanted a strong drink and a place to think.

Finding a deserted table, he seated himself and ordered a brandy. As he glanced around the room, he saw someone approaching his table. At first he did not recognize Nicholas Guyon. "My dear Nicholas, may I congratulate you on your appointment?"

"Thank you, Jacques, and may I ask why you are sitting here alone? What deep thoughts keep you in isolation?"

Indicating a chair opposite his, the Count said, "Please be my guest."

As they sat down, Nicholas said, "Jacques, I've known you for many years and I have yet to know you to walk into a club and not gamble. Something must be bothering you and I'm willing to wager it is a woman."

The Count gave Nicholas a weak smile. He had known Nicholas since the beginning of his service as ambassador to England. They had never been close friends, but now he needed someone to confide in.

"You are a very shrewd person, Nicholas, and I think you will make a good ambassador after all," the Count said as he picked up his brandy and drank it down.

"So it is a woman. Can I do anything to help?"

Summoning the waiter, the Count ordered another

drink before he answered. "I'm afraid, Nicholas, there is nothing anyone can do. I long to possess the Golden Girl but it's impossible, for I have lost too much at gaming to afford such a luxury."

At the mention of the Golden Girl, Nicholas' thoughts went to his own Golden Girl. He knew how the Count felt. He too longed to possess someone who was out of reach. But he said, "Come now, surely it is not that impossible. Tell me about her."

After finishing his second drink, the Count related the story of Bess's Golden Girl. For a moment Nicholas just sat and stared at the Count and then said, "Does this beauty have a name?"

The Count smiled at Nicholas and said, "It is a fitting name. Heather, Heather Cromwell." As the Count spoke the glass in Nicholas' hand shattered.

Jumping to his feet and wiping the brandy from his coat, he said, "Jacques, I'm so sorry, but I have just remembered an important engagement, so I must be off." Giving the Count a slight bow, Nicholas turned and hurriedly left the club without waiting for the Count to reply.

The Count watched Nicholas' receding figure and was puzzled by his abrupt departure and obvious rudeness.

As Nicholas drove through the streets of London toward Bess's house of pleasure, his only thought was of Heather and the hope that he would not be too late.

When he arrived at the house, he disregarded the usual formalities but asked to be taken immediately to Bess's office. There he would await her. After seating himself in the same chair that the Count had occupied earlier, he looked about the room and another thought occurred to him. In his haste to rescue Heather he had failed to think that she herself might be involved in Bess's ploy. Perhaps she was to get a cut out of the fee charged. *Ridiculous,* he scowled at himself, *she is not that kind.* He knew how houses such as this came by their girls, who did not come willingly. But how would he deal with Bess and take Heather away with him?

Nicholas stood as Bess entered the room. "Bess, you are just as lovely as ever."

"Captain Guyon, I'm so glad to see you. I have heard of your good fortune. And which of my girls are you here to celebrate with tonight? The black-haired vixen is still free."

Nicholas casually seated himself once again and accepted the glass of brandy Bess offered. "I want none but the Golden Girl. That is what I'm here about. I heard of her in one of my clubs and thought that I would come and see her for myself."

"I'm sorry, Captain Guyon, but she has already retired. But you may see her tomorrow night."

Nicholas smiled charmingly at Bess, while on the inside he wanted to strangle her. "They say you are asking an outrageous fee for her. Is that true?"

Watching Nicholas with her calculating little eyes, she said, "When you meet her you may not think it too high."

"How much would you charge me, sight unseen?" he asked.

Bess laughed at his question and said, "You would do it too, just to say you had won that which all the others could not. But my answer is still the same. You would have to pay the price I have set."

Nicholas' eyes glittered dangerously as he looked at Bess. "Well, Bess, what would you say if I were to pay you twice what you ask, if you would sell her to me?"

Bess stared at Nicholas with open amazement. "Why should I sell her to you when after the appeal of her purity has worn off I can still make money from her?"

Nicholas' smile faded slightly as he said, "My dear Bess, have you forgotten to whom you are speaking? If I don't get what I want neither will you. Remember, there are others that would like to know your whereabouts and your real name, my dear."

Bess's face turned ashen. She knew she had much to

fear from this man. He had been the person who saved her from the gallows in Liverpool when she had been condemned for witchcraft. This was the first time he had ever mentioned the affair, though he had been to her house many times over the years. She knew that he meant what he said and she had to accede to his wishes. "I now see your point, and for a few extra shillings I shall throw in the girl that has been caring for her."

Nicholas leaned back in his chair and savored his triumph, relieved that one of his questions had also been answered—Heather was still pure and was not party to Bess's plan. "I will come back tomorrow night for her and I will pay for both the girl and her servant." And as if he could read Bess's thoughts, he said, "And she had better not be harmed or you will pay dearly. Also I do not want her to know of our discussion or for that matter that anyone has bought her. Have her dressed as usual and then I will do the rest." As he finished speaking, he rose from his chair. "And be warned, Bess, I mean what I say." With that Nicholas left.

Heather opened her eyes slowly to see Missy's worried face staring down at her. "Oh, miss, ye did frighten us," Missy said as she placed a damp cloth on Heather's forehead.

For a moment Heather only stared at Missy, and then she remembered the conversation between the Count and the captain.

"Miss, what has upset ye so?" Missy asked.

Looking at Missy, Heather said, "He's dead, Missy," and sobbed into her hands.

Patting her gently on the head, Missy asked, "Who's dead, miss? Someone ye know?"

Between sobs Heather gasped, "The Marquis." Through her tears, Heather could see Missy's puzzled expression and continued, "He was like a father to me, especially after David was killed. I was only his housekeeper, but he was kind to me and befriended me. Missy, they did this to him, Captain Guyon and all those like him. I hate them all and someday I will make them pay." Heather fell back on the soft pillows and covered her face.

She did not hear Missy leave the room but when she looked up sometime later it was to see Missy coming into the room carrying a tray of tea. Missy had changed her mind about not giving Heather any more of the sleeping draught, for she knew that Heather must rest so that her wounds would heal. She had seen Heather cry before but this was different. It was as though her heart were breaking. "Here, miss, drink this and ye will feel better," Missy said as she helped Heather to sit up and then drink her tea.

After a while Heather became drowsy, but before sleep overtook her, she said, "Yes, if ever I escape from this place I will make them pay, and Captain Guyon will be at the top of my list."

Missy watched Heather for a little while and then went back to her small room in the attic of the house. She did not sleep well and several times during the night she crept downstairs to check on Heather. The girl worried her. Not only did she have to bend her will to Bess's demands, but she was further hampered now by a desire for revenge. Such a feeling, Missy felt, made people do things that they normally would not do.

After a restless night, Missy went down to the kitchen, where she fixed Heather's breakfast. Tray in hand, she opened the door to see Heather awake and sitting up in bed. "Good morning, miss, I hope ye feel better this morning."

Heather slowly slid from the bed and walked to the window and stared down at the street. She did not speak to Missy, for her thoughts were on Dunhan and all that had once been there.

As Missy observed Heather, she sensed a change in the girl. She saw in Heather's eyes a cool, almost hard glint. As she spoke her voice also seemed to have an edge. It appeared as if she had become a woman overnight, and the soft gentle girl had vanished.

"Yes, Missy, I'm feeling better this morning. What do you have for breakfast? I'm starving."

"Yer usual, miss. So eat it all and ye will feel much better."

When she had finished she said, "Missy, I would like a bath, and then we will have to prepare for tonight, because we are going to have to speed up our plans."

As Missy prepared Heather's bath a frown wrinkled her forehead but she did not ask the questions that were in her mind. "Tonight, Missy, I'm going to tell the Count what Bess has planned and beg him to help me escape. I think he will if I promise to become his mistress," Heather said. Relaxing back into the water, she continued, "So tonight I must look special and I must do my best to be alluring."

Missy did not comment on what Heather had said. She knew that this was not the same girl she had helped dress the previous night.

A slight frown puckered Heather's smooth brow as she watched Missy go about her duties. She had expected Missy to give her opinion of her plan but she had said nothing. As Missy helped Heather to dry, Heather said, "What's wrong, Missy? Are you having pain from your leg?"

Missy looked up at Heather with a worried expression on her face and answered, "No, miss, it is not me leg that is bothering me."

"What is it then, if it is not your leg?" Heather said as she slipped into the robe that Missy held.

"It is ye, miss; ye don't seem like the same person this morning."

"What do you mean, Missy? I'm the same person," Heather said as she smiled down into Missy's worried face.

"No you're not, there is something different this

morning. Yer eyes have a cold gleam to them that was not there yesterday."

Seating herself in front of the bureau and picking up the hairbrush, Heather began to pull it through her hair. Watching Missy in the mirror, she said, "What do you mean, Missy?"

"Miss, I think that yer sadness last night has something to do with it."

Nodding her head in agreement, Heather said a little sadly, "I think it did, Missy. Now I have learned a hard lesson. I should have learned it sooner from being here in this house but until last night I had been living in a dream. I thought that everything would be all right. But now I know that it will not be unless I do something." Heather smiled at Missy and continued, "So, Missy, you see why I have to get the Count to help us. If I don't we will be here until we are of no use to anyone. And I have to get away so I may do something that I promised myself last night."

The frown deepened on Missy's face and she said, "Miss, I hope for yer sake that it is not a plan that will hurt ye worse in the long run."

Heather smiled at Missy once again and said, "Don't worry, Missy, we'll be all right."

At dusk Heather and Missy began to make their final preparations. Tonight Heather planned to wear a dark blue velvet trimmed in silver braid. The neckline plunged into a deep v-line in the front to show off her breasts. A tiny band of silvery-encrusted jewels accented her small waistline. And the velvet skirt gave way in front to layers of silver lace accented also with tiny jewels. The sleeves of the gown were long and also cut the same as the skirt with the same silver lace.

As Heather slipped into the gown she could not keep herself from stroking the soft velvet. It was the gown in which she was supposed to meet the gentleman that Bess had chosen for her. She knew that Bess would be in a fury when she saw Heather in it. No

176

matter, she needed all the ammunition she could muster if her plan were to succeed.

Swirling around, she smiled at Missy and gave her a slight curtsy. "My dear Count, would you not like to rescue me so that you alone may bed down with me?" Heather laughed, and then added, "Missy, don't look so shocked, for I am only jesting. I would do nothing like that and you know it."

Missy gave Heather a weak smile and said, "I know, miss, but ye do worry me."

Seating herself so Missy might arrange her hair, Heather said, "Please, Missy, don't worry over me. As I told you this afternoon, everything will be all right. Just arrange my hair and forget about it. I know what I am doing, and remember, it's for your sake too."

Missy blushed at this and said, "Yes, miss."

Heather realized that her voice had sounded angry and that she had hurt Missy. Patting the maid's hand, she said in a reassuring voice, "I'm sorry, Missy, if I hurt you. I'm not angry with you but please believe me, I will not get hurt if I can help it."

As Missy was putting the last touches to Heather's hair the door opened and Bess walked in. "Good evening, I see you are ready," Bess said as she eyed the blue gown.

"Yes, I'm just about to go down," Heather said.

She expected Bess to comment on the gown but to her surprise Bess only said, "Missy, you may be excused."

Bess waited for the door to close before she said, "Heather, I want you to wait here for another hour and then you can make your appearance. The Count has not yet arrived."

Heather's only answer was, "If it pleases you." She did not want to question Bess's reasons, though she was nervous about what the evening would bring. What if the Count refused her offer? But she couldn't think of that.

Bess had her own thoughts about what she'd like to

do to Heather. But she dared not touch her, for she knew that Nicholas would keep his promise to expose her and she would surely go to the gallows.

Bess walked from the room and locked the door behind her.

Heather did not understand why she was once more locked in. Since her appearances in the salon the door had not been bolted.

Going to the window, she stared out into the darkness. *What has Bess planned? Or has someone come up with her price?*

As Heather stared out the window, she did not hear the door open or the sound of the footsteps as they crossed the carpet. "Ah, my fair damsel, what thoughts could be so deep?"

Turning with a slight cry, Heather looked up into the dark eyes of Nicholas. "What are you doing here?" Heather asked.

"I've come to rescue you, my dear," Nicholas said as he smiled down at Heather.

"I would rather stay here than be rescued by someone like you," she said venomously.

Nicholas laughed at her anger, though his own anger began to grow. How could she prefer this degradation to what he offered? "Well, fair maiden, if that is how you feel, you may remain and be one of Bess's whores."

"I shall not be that either, Captain Guyon, because I have my own plans for escape!" Heather spat and turned her back to him.

Nicholas stared at her for a few moments before he walked from the room. He had thought that she would be glad to see him but she had spat in his face. He had paid Bess the price that she had asked and he meant to have Heather. Speaking from the doorway, he said, "I bid you adieu, fair maiden, but we shall meet again on my own terms." Slamming the door, he left Heather already regretting her words.

Why had she spoken with so much anger? Why was

178

she so hasty in refusing his offer of escape. True, he was the enemy. He had come to arrest the Marquis and his behavior toward her had been reprehensible.

Heather sat down on the floor in front of the fire. As she watched the flames her misery grew but her eyes remained dry with a hard glassy look. As she heard the key being turned in the lock she glanced up to see black Josh walk into the room with one of Bess's flunkies, carrying a large sack and some ropes.

Heather knew she had made a bad mistake and that Bess was now going to punish her dearly. She jumped to her feet as the men approached and backed away from them. Black Josh reached Heather first and took hold of both her hands. He did not hurt her as she had expected. He only tied her hands with the rope and just before he put the gag across her mouth, he kissed her. Heather had to suffer it since he held her face firmly with his hand. "That was goodbye, my beauty," he said and then tied the gag across Heather's mouth. Taking the sack from the flunky, Josh pulled it over her head.

The last words that black Josh had said to Heather made her shiver with fear. Were they going to kill her, or had she been sold into bondage? In either case she had lost control of her destiny.

~§ *Chapter Ten* §~

The day was clear and the water was a deep blue. A gentle breeze ruffled her hair as she peered out the porthole. The cabin was comfortable and had the voyage been of her own choosing she would have enjoyed it.

There was a soft knock on the door and a young boy came in with Heather's breakfast. He walked across the cabin and unlatched a cupboard which now became a small table. After setting the tray on the table, he slid the one small chair forward and motioned for Heather to sit down. He did not speak but lifted the cover of the tray to reveal tasty-looking sweet rolls and tea. "Thank you," Heather said. As she ate, she watched the young boy go about his duties of straightening the cabin. When he had finished and was about to leave, Heather asked, "May I ask your name?"

The lad turned and said, "Aye, miss, I'm Jon McHan, cabin boy." Hoping that this had broken the silence between them, she continued, "Would you tell me who's ship this is?"

Jon turned to the door once more and said as he left the cabin, "No, miss, I have me orders."

Disappointed at not finding any answers from Jon, Heather finished her breakfast. During the rest of the day no one came to disturb her. She had watched the sea until she was tired and then paced the cabin. Hundreds of jumbled thoughts poured through her mind but none made any sense to her. She could not fathom what might happen to her. She knew that whoever was behind her abduction had gone to a great deal of trouble.

Later that night two burly sailors walked into the cabin, "We're here to take ye on deck," one of them announced. And as he said this the second man handed Heather a velvet cape. As Heather stood and slipped the cape around her shoulders, the one that had spoken before said, "I have to blindfold ye, miss."

Heather looked a little startled but did not resist. She knew that it would be useless to argue with them. As he tied the blindfold across her eyes, she said, "Where are you taking me?" They did not answer, but guided her through the door and up the small flight of steps.

When they reached the deck Heather could feel the cool evening breeze fan her cheeks and hear the orders that were given to the sailors in a robust voice. That would be the captain, she thought.

The man who had blindfolded Heather never left her side and after a while he spoke again. "Miss, we're to take ye ashore now, so watch yer step." He guided Heather across the deck. "Don't be frightened, miss, I've got to carry ye down the ladder to the small boat," he said as he picked Heather up. He did not put her over his shoulder as Josh had done but carried her carefully down the ladder. Once inside the skiff, he set her gently down and rowed them to shore.

When they reached the bank of the river, he helped Heather from the boat and they walked a short distance to an awaiting carriage. Still blindfolded, Heather knew they were in a city, for she could hear the horses' hooves as they clipped the cobbled streets.

Heather was frightened and her breath became labored as she said, "Can't you undo the blindfold now?"

After a moment the sailor spoke. "No, miss, I've orders not to."

Heather tried once again to get some nformation as she asked, "Can't you even tell me where you are taking me?"

"No, miss, but I can tell ye we are nearly there. Then ye may be allowed to know more."

As the streetlights cast their dim glow into the carriage the sailor could see the paleness of Heather's face and hear the quick intakes of her breath. *She's a brave one, all right,* he thought, *determined not to show the fear that she feels.* As he watched Heather his thoughts continued. *The master has really picked a beauty this time, but why has he gone to all this trouble—made a hostage of her. He's got more than enough women chasing after him. Well, it's no concern of mine,* he thought as the carriage slowed to a stop.

Stepping down first, he then helped Heather from the carriage and up a flight of steps to the townhouse. At the slight sound of his knock the door was opened by an immaculately dressed butler. He did not speak as the sailor and Heather stepped into the hall, or as he proceeded to show the way upstairs to the room Heather was soon to know as her prison.

The blindfold was removed and it took Heather a few moments to adjust her eyes to the light in the room.

It was an elegant room. Dark rich paneling covered the walls. The drapes that hid the French windows were of deep red and gold, as was the bed with its counterpane and dust covers. The furnishings, like the rest of the room, were made of dark mahogany, polished to a deep rich luster. Most were massive and heavily carved.

Where the room at Bess's had been completely feminine with its light colors of gold and white and the delicate furnishings, this room was completely masculine. That was it! The room was entirely a place in which a man would be comfortable.

Instead of easing Heather's fears, this realization only heightened them. Wide-eyed, Heather turned to the sailor and said, "Why have you brought me here?"

Pity was in his eyes as he started to the door, and he said, "A maid will be here to help ye prepare for the night and she will bring ye something to eat."

After the sailor had gone, the first thing Heather did was to run to the windows and see if she might recognize her surroundings. The only thing that she could see in the darkness were the streetlights and the outline of the buildings against the dark sky.

Heather once more glanced at the room. Over the large fireplace hung a shield with a family crest carved across the face of it. She tried to read what the engraving said but it was in Latin. She had studied languages but had never advanced to Latin, and this crest was as much a mystery to her as was everything else that had happened since last night.

For a second as she heard the door being unlocked, it seemed as if her heart stopped, until the little maid came into the room carrying a tray of food for her dinner.

The maid curtsied slightly and then placed the tray on the table in front of the fire. "If Madam please," she said, "I will serve her dinner."

Seating herself in the chair that the maid offered, Heather said, "Will you tell me where I am?"

The maid lowered her eyes and said, "Paris, madam."

Startled, Heather said, "Paris! In whose house?"

The maid did not look at Heather as she answered, "Madam, I am not allowed to say. If that will be all I shall prepare your bath and help you get ready for bed."

184

Heather slid from the bed and padded barefoot to the window. In the early dawn she could see that the street was not in a district such as Bess's had been. She could see many beautiful houses from her window; however, the view of the street was blocked by a wall that surrounded the garden. It was a beautiful garden with a small fountain surrounded by delicate rosebushes.

As Heather gazed upon the garden a longing grew within her to see the gardens of Dunhan and the meadow in which she and David had played in their childhood. She sat down in front of the fire. In the glowing embers her eyes glistened with unshed tears.

The little maid came in and saw Heather staring into the dying fire. "Is Madam all right?" Glancing up at the maid, Heather nodded. "You gave me a fright, you stare so intently into the embers, as if you watch something which hurt you," the maid said in a light French accent.

"I was only remembering," Heather said as she rose from the floor.

"What is your name?" Heather asked.

"Marie," the maid said as she straightened the room.

"Marie, would you not tell me for whom it is you work?" Heather asked imploringly.

Stopping, she looked at Heather and replied, "Madam, I am told that you may not know from me."

"But why?" Heather asked.

"This I do not know, madam," Marie answered truthfully as she finished the bed. "Does Madam require anything?"

Heather looked at her and realized there would be no use in telling her what she really needed were the answers to her questions, and then said, "No thank you, Marie, that will be all."

When she was ready to be dressed, Heather found that Marie had laid a beautiful gown out for her. It was of the palest blue silk that Heather had ever seen.

As she slipped into it, she could see that it had a deep décolletage coming to a halt between her breasts. The cut of the gown was very simple with the silk clinging to her every curve. When she finished dressing and slipped her feet into a pair of soft kid slippers, Heather went to a small dressing table and seated herself.

When Marie finished dressing Heather's hair, she reached into a box on the table and brought out a pair of small diamond earrings with a matching necklace. These Marie fastened to Heather's ears and clasped around her slim neck. Stepping back, she said, "Madam is beautiful."

"Thank you," Heather said, as she gazed at herself in the mirror.

The butler had brought a small serving cart and Heather noticed that there were two place settings. She knew well what that meant.

After the butler withdrew, she poured herself a glass of wine. The meal looked appetizing but she had no appetite.

Bess has succeeded, she thought. Heather finished her first glass of wine, poured a second, and then a third. By the time her captor entered the room Heather was toasting the empty wine bottle. She was sprawled on the divan, her golden hair hung loose around her shoulders and she seemed totally oblivious to her surroundings.

The tall man in elegantly cut evening clothes roared with laughter. Heather did not have to turn around. She knew who he was. Jumping to her feet and turning quickly, she threw the bottle in the direction of the laughter.

The bottle shattered against the wall and he laughed once more. "Captain Guyon, what do you mean by bringing me here?" Heather demanded with all the dignity that she could summon.

"But fair maiden, I've come to rescue you from your ivory tower."

The wine that Heather had consumed had begun to

186

make her drowsy and she swayed against Nicholas. Reaching down, he picked her up and carried her to the bed. She looked at him pleading for a moment and drifted off to sleep.

Nicholas looked at the sleeping girl and smoothed back the curls that had fallen across her forehead. *Now you are mine, Heather,* he thought. *And no one will ever take you from me.*

Slowly he undressed Heather and gazed at her naked body. He had the desire to take her as she lay sleeping but pulled the soft sheet over her and sat down in front of the fire.

The butler arrived with another bottle of wine, and Nicholas poured himself a glass. He leaned back in the chair and sipped it thoughtfully, savoring his good fortune. Heather's voice brought him from his reverie. Getting up from the chair, he walked over to the bed. Heather tossed in her sleep mumbling something he could not hear.

Bending over her, he smoothed her hair once again and to his surprise, her arms came around his neck and she pulled him down so that their lips met in a kiss. As he released her mouth from his, she said, "David, I love you."

Abruptly he walked away and poured himself another glass of wine. Swallowing it in one gulp, he looked broodingly into the fire. *Damn!* he thought. *Will she never forget?* Glancing back at Heather, he said, "You may never love me but you are mine and will stay that way until I decide otherwise!"

After undressing, Nicholas slid into bed beside Heather. Gazing at the long lashes resting on her pale cheeks and at her pink, soft lips, he could not resist kissing her. This time she did not respond. Nicholas blew out the candle and went to sleep.

As Heather awoke the next morning the sun was shining brightly into the room. At first dazed and disoriented, she did not realize that her head rested on the chest of a man, his leg over hers. Fully conscious now, she eased herself out from under him and sat up.

A blinding pain shot through her head and she raised her hand to it as if to keep it from flying off. Then she remembered all the wine that she had drunk. Very slowly she slipped from the bed and as she stood up, her head began to spin so much that she had to sit back down on the side of the bed. As she did so, she heard a slight chuckle and turned to see Nicholas' dark eyes looking at her in amusement. As his eyes traveled over her body, Heather realized she was naked and grabbed the sheet and held it in front of her.

Heather's first thoughts were to flee and she made a move in that direction but before she could take a step from the bed, Nicholas' large muscular arms came out and pulled her back to bed. She struggled against him with all her power but he managed to pin her beneath him.

With blue eyes blazing, Heather said, "Let me go!" A smile appeared on Nicholas' full sensuous lips. "Why should I? Don't you remember, I told you one day you would be mine? Now that day has come."

Between her teeth Heather said, "I hate you!"

Nicholas threw back his head and laughed. "Is that anything new?" he asked as a strange gleam came into his dark eyes. He raised himself up on his elbows and gazed down at Heather. During their struggle, the sheet which Heather had wrapped around herself had slipped from her and she lay naked underneath him.

Heather's breasts pressed against his chest and he could feel her heart beat. Her eyes blazed at him and she tried to move but he lay on top of her and she could not move. A tear slid down her cheek and onto the pillow. She tried to contain her tears but it seemed as if they had a will of their own and they continued to stream down her cheeks. "Do you enjoy raping women? Because I will never give myself to you willingly," Heather said.

Nicholas smiled at Heather, showing his even white

188

teeth, and said, "No, I don't enjoy raping women and have never had to, but if you give me no choice in the matter I will."

Rolling her head from side to side, she said, "Never will I give myself to the man who has taken everything from me. I hate you! I hate you."

A puzzled look came over Nicholas' face as he said, "I have taken nothing from you yet, my love, but I will if you force me."

Freeing her hands and pushing him away from her, Heather sprang from the bed and ran to the door. It would not give. Turning, she saw that he had risen from the bed and was watching her futile efforts. He laughed and said, "Come now, Heather, you can never escape me." He walked to her and as he reached out to take her in his arms she shrank from him.

"Don't touch me, you murderer." Nicholas stopped.

"What do you mean? I have harmed no one," Nicholas said in a puzzled voice.

"Yes, you are a murderer, and you have taken everything from me," Heather screamed as she tried to claw at him. Nicholas realized that she had become hysterical and he slapped her.

Stunned, Heather looked at Nicholas and then crumbled to the floor. Picking her up he carried her to the bed and put her down. All the fight had gone out of her as she lay sobbing.

Nicholas looked at Heather and tried with all his power to understand what had possessed her. He had murdered no one, unless it was the Dutch that she was talking about. As he watched her he was bemused. Then he thought it just an excuse to delay the inevitable. Bending over Heather, he said, "Heather, do not take on so. I promise you, I have murdered no one."

Heather rolled on her back and said, "Yes you did, maybe not with your own hand but just as surely as if you had taken your sword to him."

Looking into her tear-filled eyes, Nicholas said,

189

"May I ask who it is that I am supposed to have murdered?"

Heather looked at him venomously and said, "The Marquis."

Surprise showed on Nicholas' face as he said, "I did not murder the Marquis. He is still alive and well in the Tower of London."

"No, he is not. I heard the Count and a young captain talking of it at Bess's. He is dead." Heather spat out the words at Nicholas.

At this Nicholas threw back his head and laughed. "My dear Heather, that is exactly what the King wants people to think. Don't you see, if the Marquis is believed dead maybe the others involved with him will come out of hiding."

Heather looked at Nicholas in disbelief. "You lie. You are only telling me this."

Nicholas' smile faded from his face. His patience was coming to an end. "Heather, I will not abide being called a liar. I have no reason to lie. I could have you without telling a lie."

Heather looked at him doubtfully and said, "You still don't have me."

"Yes, my little blue-eyed vixen, I do have you. Even though you persist in saying I do not. I think you had better accept your fate. As I told you some time ago, you will be mine, and you are unless you prefer the establishment in which I found you."

With that Nicholas slipped into his dressing gown and then walked to the door. He unlocked it with a key he'd taken from his pocket. "I think you will see the advantages of our situation," he added before leaving the room.

Heather sat still for a few moments, and then a rage grew in her until she could contain herself no longer. She ripped the covering from her body and then tore the sheet from the bed. She ran around the room smashing everything that would break. Finally she stopped and surveyed her handiwork. One thing still remained intact—the beautiful gown that she had worn the previous night. She pulled it from the chair and ripped it into tiny pieces. Exhausted, she sat down amid the ruins.

As Nicholas had left the room, he had summoned Marie to attend Heather. When she entered the room she could not believe her eyes. "Oh, madam! Are you all right?"

Heather glanced at Marie and gave her a blank look. "No, Marie, I'm not all right and never will be!" Jumping to her feet, Heather lunged at the door and tried to open it. Banging her fist against the dark wood, she cried, "Let me out! Someone please help me." Turning to a startled Marie, Heather said, "Marie, please let me out. Unlock the door for me."

Marie stared at Heather wide-eyed. "No, madam, I am not allowed to do so. Please, madam, be calm. It is not good to get so upset."

Heather could feel hysteria building once more, but she fought it with all her strength. Taking long deep breaths, she slowly regained some of her composure.

Marie left the room and was gone a short while, to return with a tray of steaming hot chocolate and sweet pastries.

Thoughts whirled through Heather's mind as she ate her breakfast. If she could only get Nicholas to care for her, she would be able to persuade him to help the Marquis. Yes, that was it. She would stay here and try to help the Marquis through Captain Guyon. If the price was her purity so be it.

⊷ Chapter Eleven ⊷

Nicholas was perplexed by Heather's calm, cool demeanor. What was she up to, he wondered. This sudden change in her unsettled him, but he'd wait it out, see what kind of game she was playing. She looked lovely in the flowing white silk gown. Its décolletage exposed her soft white skin. And the blue gems sparkling at her waist lent a delicate touch. She was indeed a vision.

He handed Heather the glass of wine, took one for himself and then sat down beside her on the divan. "To your beauty," he said. Heather acknowledged the toast and slowly sipped her wine.

When would she drop the facade, he thought. She seemed unperturbed, completely at ease, as though this happened every day of her life.

"Have you thought over our conversation of this morning?"

Heather tried her most beguiling smile while she swallowed the lump in her throat. "I have thought it over," she replied.

"Well, my dear, what is your decision?"

For a moment Heather could not answer as she watched his expression. It was expectant, attentive and far too eager, she thought. "I have one stipulation," she ventured.

"And what may I ask is that?"

"I would like to have the maid who served me at Bess's." She was not about to tell him what she really wanted, not yet, not until she was more certain of him. First she would ask this small favor, and later, if her plans worked well she would ask that he help her free the Marquis.

"My dear Heather, that is easily fulfilled. She is down in the servants' quarters now." Heather looked at Nicholas in surprise and said, "You mean Missy is already here?"

"Yes, I purchased her when I dealt with Bess for you."

A genuine smile formed on Heather's lips and on impulse she leaned over and gave Nicholas a slight kiss on the cheek. "Thank you."

As she started to pull away from him, his arms came around her and pulled her against his chest. "I want more than a kiss on the cheek." And as he said this, he lowered his lips to Heather's and kissed her long and hard.

Heather pulled away, her hands automatically coming up against his chest. "Are you already backing out of your agreement?"

A flush rose to Heather's cheeks as she said, "No, but you startled me."

Nicholas smiled at Heather and said, "If one little kiss startles you, what will the rest do?"

Her cheeks turned a deeper red. "I will keep our agreement," Heather said, shivering slightly. It was enough to signal Nicholas that her nonchalance was indeed a pretense.

He released her and rose from the divan. "Now if

you will allow me, I will escort you to dinner." Heather took his arm gracefully and walked to the small table.

Nicholas held the chair for Heather as she sat down and then seated himself across from her. He observed every little expression that played on her face during the meal. No further word of their agreement was mentioned during dinner or as they sipped their wine afterward.

Heather did her best to carry on a normal conversation. She was surprised to find that she had actually laughed at Nicholas' stories about court life and his army service. She tried to prolong their dinner as long as possible.

Finally she rose from the chair. A smile appeared at the corners of Nicholas' mouth. "My fair demoiselle, you are one of the loveliest creatures I have ever encountered. Now I will go to my study and have a brandy while you are preparing for bed. I'll send Marie to help you." Nicholas lightly kissed the tips of Heather's long slender fingers and then left her.

It was only a moment before Marie entered carrying a beautiful negligee. Where the one at Bess's had been black, this one was made of fine white lace. As Heather slipped it on and looked at herself in the mirror, she could see how transparent it was. Every curve was accented by the clinging nightdress and her breasts were clearly visible. Her first reaction was to cover herself, yet she resisted and let Marie assist her to bed. "I will let your hair down, madam," Marie said as she began to brush Heather's hair.

"Thank you, Marie. That will be all," she said, impatient to be left alone. She needed these few minutes to collect herself. She was deeply troubled and anxious. Yet she had to submit to Nicholas' will. The only thing that made what was about to happen bearable was the hope that she could help the Marquis.

Nicholas was wearing a velvet dressing gown of deep burgundy as he entered the room. All the candles had been extinguished except the one near the bed and it cast a warm glow over Heather's ivory skin. Her golden hair fell in a mass above her shoulders. Nicholas drew in his breath. He had long dreamed of this moment.

As he walked closer he could see that Heather's eyes were wide with fright, though she tried to conceal it. He could see the pink nipples of her breasts pressed against the lace and he wanted to taste their sweetness, to feel them taut beneath his fingers.

When he neared the bed, he said, "My fair demoiselle, you are Venus come down from Olympus." And he bent and kissed her. He slowly removed his robe and slid into bed beside her.

Taking Heather into his arms, he could feel her stiffen and said, "My love, don't be afraid, I will bring you pleasure." Heather did not answer, for she would not trust her voice. She thought if she made any sound at all it would be a scream.

Nicholas kissed Heather gently and he could feel her relax. Slowly he placed his hand on her breasts and caressed them until he felt the nipples grow taut. At this he could feel her stiffen once more. Raising up on one elbow he looked into her wide eyes. "I will not hurt you, my fair one. Your body was made for love. Can you not tell that by its natural reaction to my touch?"

Heather did not say anything but shook her head. "See, I will show you." Slowly he slid his hand down Heather's body and caressed her thighs. She did not move but only stared into his face. As his hand slid upward and his fingers entwined in her golden hair Heather's breathing began to change. Her body was beginning to betray her as he gently slipped his hand between her thighs and caressed the softness there.

Heather tried to move away but he said, "Lie still, my love, and let your body rule your mind." Then he bent and kissed her. This time was different. His tongue moved into her mouth and caressed and teased

196

her tongue and lips. It sent shivers over Heather and when he released her lips, she was breathless. He smiled at her and said, "See, my darling, you were made for love. And for me." His voice had grown husky and his breathing had become rapid. His lips brushed the softness of her neck and shoulders.

His hands sent tremors through Heather. There was a path of fire along her body as his lips traveled down to her breasts. His tongue teased the nipples and he could hear her quick intake of breath. Slowly he began to nibble their sweetness and savor the smell of her flesh and he quickly stripped her naked.

His hands continued to caress her and he could feel the sweet moistness of her as his fingers gently found their way into the dark passage of love. Heather moaned as he slipped his fingers into her and slowly withdrew them. Slowly his lips traveled between her breasts and he glanced up at Heather's face.

He could see her eyes were closed and she had caught her lower lip between her white teeth as she tried not to respond to his touch. Heather's head rolled slowly from side to side as his gentle lovemaking began to awaken her passion.

He kissed her soft flat stomach and moved slowly to the mass of golden hair.

Involuntarily she opened her thighs as his lips traveled through the golden fleece seeking the sweetness that was beneath it. As his tongue caressed the soft wetness of her, she let out an audible moan and thrust her hips to meet his seeking tongue. She trembled with desire, fought a losing battle with the forces deeply inside her. Spasms of pleasure ran through her as Nicholas kissed her body. Her own desire dismayed her. How could she be so weak, so unable to control her fleshly desires. Her body seemed to have a will of its own. She began to return Nicholas' caresses, wanting him close, closer still.

When it seemed as if she would scream with pleasure, Nicholas slowly came on top of her. Heather

197

could feel the hardness of him as he pressed against her thigh and then between her legs. Her arms encircled him and pulled him closer. Before their lips met, he murmured, "Now, my love, you are ready."

Heather could only nod her head as her lips sought his and kissed him deeply in return as he slowly entered the tight passage of pleasure.

Heather stiffened with pain for a moment. She moaned again and he slowly withdrew from her and looked into her passionate blue eyes. "Now, my love, there will be no more pain, only pleasure." He entered her once more and she responded, kissing him deeply.

With each thrust, her pleasure heightened and with each motion her body began to meet his. Suddenly it seemed as if the world was full of shooting stars as wave after wave of pleasure swept through her body. At the same moment she could feel Nicholas explode within her and then collapse against her hot and sweaty body.

Nicholas did not move for a few moments and lay on her, savoring the hot feel of her around him. He kissed her smooth shoulder and then slowly withdrew from her. Lying beside her, he turned to see tears rolling down her cheeks.

Nicholas gently swept the tears from Heather's face. "There is no need for tears, my love. You were made for love, so don't be ashamed of it."

Heather could not look at him and she rolled on her side and sobbed into her pillow. She felt betrayed by her body and could not forgive herself for it.

Nicholas did not say anything more. He knew that many girls had this reaction during their first encounter with lovemaking. He also knew that she hated herself for responding to him. He wanted to take her in his arms and comfort her, but was sure she would not allow it.

Slowly the sobs abated and Heather drifted off to sleep. Nicholas waited a few moments and then drew her gently into his arms. Her lashes were still wet from the tears and they glistened against her ivory cheeks. Several times her lips trembled and she drew ragged breaths.

As he looked at Heather, Nicholas was aware of an emotion that he had never felt before. She above all others had excited and challenged him. Her resistance had at first provoked a desire within him to ravish her, yet he held back, controlled his own passion until their bodies blended in mutual joy.

He gently kissed her lips and smoothed the damp hair from her face. *Heather,* he thought, *you are mine and I'll never let you go. You will come to love me, that I promise you. Your body already understands and soon you will also. No one else will ever have you.* A chill ran down his back as he thought of how close he had come to losing her.

❧ Chapter Twelve ❧

As Heather awoke she could hear the rain splashing against the windows. How appropriate she thought, for the gloom of the day matched her mood exactly. She could not move. Nicholas' arms encircled her. But as she looked at his sleeping face, she felt an emotion stir in her that she could not understand.

His black hair fell across his forehead and his long dark lashes lay on his cheeks. He looked almost boyish as he lay asleep beside her. There was a softness about him that was not present during his waking hours. His sensuous mouth, which had both smiled and sneered at her, was now in sleep relaxed and partly open. A stubble of black beard shadowed his square jaw and cleft chin. He had a straight nose with slightly flaring nostrils which suited the rugged face and added character.

The arms that encircled her were well muscled and the hands were large with long tapering fingers. Contemplating those hands, she remembered the passion they'd aroused. One of his long muscular legs was thrown over hers.

Heather could see why a woman such as the Countess Beaufort would love him. He certainly was one of the most handsome men Heather had ever seen and he had wit and charm, which she had found out at dinner last night. Still that did not change the fact that she was being held captive by him. Perhaps she could forgive him this. What she could not forgive was his arrest of the Marquis.

She knew that her body had responded to his caresses and would again, if he so chose. She had promised herself that she would die before becoming any man's whore, yet here she was lying naked in a man's arms. Heather could not resist reaching up and touching the scar on Nicholas' cheek, the scar inflicted by David's riding crop. Once again she was reminded that he was the Marquis' enemy—her enemy. But she would lie with him, must lie with him, to free the Marquis.

He opened his eyes and looked at her strangely. It was as though for a moment he did not know who she was. Finally he said good morning and asked if she had slept well.

"Yes, thank you. And now if you would please release me," Heather said, attempting to disentangle herself from him.

"Why, my love? I think it's rather pleasant to wake and find a lovely woman in my arms." Heather grimaced and he tightened his embrace. "Yes," he continued, "today you are a woman. And if I may say so, all woman!"

"Please, I must get up and dress before the maid comes," Heather pleaded, pushing at him.

"Oh, I think Marie will understand. Everyone in Paris loves lovers. This is known as the city of love, my dear."

"Please," Heather said again. "It will be embarrassing for Marie to find me in such a position." To

202

Heather's surprise Nicholas released her. But as she slid from the bed he whacked her bottom.

"How dare you!" she said with fury, only to have him laugh.

"Ah, that's the Heather I know, not the meek little lady who was with me at dinner last night. Now come here so I can give you your good morning kiss."

Heather backed away from the bed and said, "I will not and you had better keep your hands to yourself."

Climbing from the bed, Nicholas started toward Heather and she fled behind a chair. "Come here, my little vixen." Heather shook her head as he approached. "Have you forgotten our agreement?" Nicholas asked.

"Stay away from me," Heather said.

"No, I will not stay away from you, because you are mine. Didn't I prove that to you last night?"

Heather blushed and said, "I kept our agreement last night, and I hope to your satisfaction. But this morning is another matter."

A smile played on Nicholas' lips as he came toward Heather. "You are mine all the time, my blue-eyed demon, so draw in your claws."

Heather pushed the chair at Nicholas and he dodged it easily. She ran to the table and picked up a cup and threw it at him. He laughed as he ducked. "I said come here and stop acting like a child. You are a woman now."

"Yes, I'm a woman now, thanks to you, and I will not be ordered about like a child. I will have some say in what I will and will not do." She stood at the window now, her back to Nicholas. "I know I made an agreement with you last night and I think I have kept it. But now there is something else I would ask of you."

Nicholas was curious, and a bit cautious. There was a strained quality in her voice. Heather turned and looked at him. "I will stay here without further trouble and do anything you ask of me if you will help the Marquis."

He stared at Heather in amazement. "How can I do that? He is a traitor to the crown and you know he is guilty."

"Yes, I know that," Heather said calmly. "But I also know that he was your friend and he is an old man. He cannot be allowed to die in prison."

"I cannot do anything. It is beyond my power to help him. Can't you see that? Yes, he was my friend, but I'm a loyal subject of the crown."

As he said this he walked to Heather's side and took her face into his hands. "Heather, I did not like what I had to do but I was under orders from the King."

"I know that, but I also know that you have gained from his arrest. You now own Dunhan."

Dropping his hands to his sides, he said, "The estate was a gift. Don't question me any further, Heather. I will not tolerate it."

"You will not help?" Heather asked.

"No," Nicholas said as his anger began to build.

"Then I will not do as you ask," Heather said as she walked away from him.

Slipping into her robe, she went over to the fire. She dared not look at him because she knew he was furious.

Nicholas grabbed her by the shoulders and turned her to face him. "You forget you are no lady," he roared. "You are a servant, you will do as I bid you."

The pressure of his fingers cut into her skin and as she looked into his face she could see that he was livid. But she held her ground, firmly declaring, "I will *not* do as you say."

"Yes you will, my beauty," Nicholas said as he released her shoulders. I have bought and paid for you and I intend to use what I have purchased!" He ripped the robe from her and picked her up and carried her to the bed. Heather kicked and clawed at him but to no avail.

204

Throwing Heather down on the bed, he then fell on her and took her with all the rage that he felt. After he finished, he smiled at her and said, "Now, Heather, say you don't belong to me. You are mine, and you *will* keep our agreement."

Heather stared at Nicholas, her eyes blazing with hatred. "Yes, my love, and you will act like a lady and do whatever I ask of you. You will be my hostess when I have guests and you will escort me wherever I decide. And in public, you will display your devotion."

Nicholas could see the thoughts that ran through her mind and said, "No, you will not escape when you leave this room. At all times you will be watched and if the reports are not favorable you will be punished. Think it over, demoiselle, and make up your mind. I will not tolerate much more from you. Now I will send Marie to you. And the room had better not be destroyed as it was yesterday."

She sat up in bed and looked toward the door which Nicholas had just walked through. She ached from head to toe from his abuse and her thoughts whirled in her mind.

Stumbling from the bed, she picked up the gown that she had worn the previous evening and slipped it on just before she heard Marie open the door. "Good morning, madam. Did Madam sleep well?" Marie asked as she set down the tray, which held steaming tea.

Heather only mumbled a slight yes as she rubbed her bruised shoulders. As Marie straightened the bed a knowing smile played on her lips. "All is well now and you will be happy, yes?" Marie said as she looked at Heather. "Love conquers all, yes."

Heather only nodded to Marie and then said, "Marie, will you prepare my bath?"

"If Madam pleases," Marie said as she went into the adjoining room. When she returned she said, "It is ready." And as she started to follow Heather into the bathroom, Heather turned to her and said, "That will be all for now, Marie." Heather wanted to be alone and relax her hurt body with the hot water and try to assemble her thoughts.

She felt her efforts had been in vain. *He will not help the Marquis, and now I am in much worse trouble than before. He knows my weakness and will play on it. Oh God, what am I to do?* She longed to cry, to release some of the misery that she felt, but her eyes remained dry as she stared unseeing into the room.

Heather stayed in the bath until the water became cool and as she dried herself she saw the finger marks on her shoulders. *The brand of a whore,* she thought and rubbed herself viciously.

She lay down on the bed, still undecided on what to do. Someway and somehow she must formulate a plan of action. Slowly fatigue overcame her and she drifted into an uneasy sleep.

Nicholas paced his study like a man possessed. Last night everything seemed to be going smoothly. Now he had a battle on his hands. He was not surprised that Heather's sudden timid behavior meant something. But he was totally at a loss to explain the graveness of her request. She was a lot more tied to the Marquis than he had suspected. And he was uncomfortable about Heather generally. She wasn't like any other woman he had ever known. Never before had he allowed himself to succumb to such anger in the presence of a woman. He wasn't proud of what he had done to her. But no woman was going to dominate him. Heather was his alone and she would obey him. Yet some part of Nicholas felt great tenderness toward her. As thoughts of her filled his mind he could almost smell her sweetness and taste the lusciousness of her body. He poured himself a glass of brandy and downed it.

When Heather awoke it was raining and darkness

had fallen over the city. Marie came and helped her dress, and afterward, to her surprise, she dined alone. Marie told her that Nicholas had gone out for the evening.

ઓફ *Chapter Thirteen* ৯৯

While adding the finishing touches to her attire,
Heather trembled with apprehension. But she braced
herself as she walked from the room. Following Marie
through the corridors, she could see that the rest of the
house was just as elegant as her room had been. The
rich paneling continued into the hall and thick carpets
hushed their footsteps.

Heather's determination flagged and her heart raced
as they approached large carved oak doors. As Marie
knocked on the doors, Heather did her best to compose
herself. Why had Nicholas asked to see her in the
study she wondered.

The room was as masculine as the rest of the house
and for a moment Heather took in its richness and
beauty.

Nicholas was standing behind a large mahogany
desk cluttered with papers. He was dressed in a dark
blue jacket and his shirt was immaculately white, with
lace at the cuffs. His pale blue vest was made of rich
brocade and was studded with small diamond buttons.

The britches were also dark blue and he wore shiny black boots.

"Come in, Heather," Nicholas said. He offered her a chair and asked if she wanted any refreshment. She refused and he sat down across from her.

"Well then, let's get down to business. We are having guests the day after tomorrow, and I shall expect you to act as my hostess."

Heather studied Nicholas for a moment before she answered. She would not fulfill his every whim. "I'm sorry, sir, but I cannot," she said firmly.

Anger flashed in Nicholas' eyes as he said, "I thought we discussed this yesterday and had come to an understanding."

"You discussed it, sir," she said with a touch of anger. "I do not remember consenting to any agreement." She had to think of something, some ploy to put him off. And while it seemed silly, she blurted out, "I have nothing to wear."

Nicholas smiled, relieved. The little vixen did have feminine concerns after all. "You needn't worry about that. There are gowns already being prepared for you. All that is needed are a few fittings and you will have whatever gowns you require."

Heather looked at Nicholas with dismay. Her delaying tactic, flimsy though it was, had failed. She'd have to do better, but she could think of nothing substantial. "There is one more matter that we must discuss," she said finally. Nicholas lifted an eyebrow.

"It concerns Missy, the girl you brought from Bess's. I would like her to attend me."

"Does Marie not please you? She is a very competent lady's maid."

"Yes, she is very efficient. However I like Missy," Heather said.

Nicholas watched Heather a few moments before he gave his answer. He was trying to discern whether she had some scheme in mind. Momentarily satisfied there was nothing behind her request, he said, "I will see

210

that she is sent to you, but I insist that Marie escort you to the dressmakers because she knows Paris. You may need other items and she can help you. That will be all for now, and I will discuss further arrangements with you at dinner tonight." As he watched Heather walk to the door he said, "Heather, do not try anything. You will not escape."

Heather did not answer but only gave him a chilling look and slammed the door behind her. She ran up the stairs to her room.

Having Missy was a small concession but it was something. Between the two of them they would find a way to escape. And then she would see about the Marquis, even if it meant going to the King himself.

Missy gave Heather a slight curtsy and said, "Oh, miss, I'm so glad to see ye again." She then ran to Heather and threw her arms around her.

"And I'm just as glad to see you, Missy. Have they treated you well?"

Missy looked up at Heather and said, "Yes, miss, they be ever so kind, and look, miss, I've new clothes." A bright smile played on Missy's face as she turned round for Heather's inspection.

"Yes, I see, and you look wonderful."

Missy gave her another curtsy and said, "Thank ye, miss. The master says that I'm to be yer personal maid and I'm so glad. It's a nice household, miss. Have ye ever seen anything so beautiful?"

Heather could not keep from smiling at Missy's exuberant happiness even though she felt none of it. "No, Missy, I have not; however, we will be leaving it as soon as I can formulate a plan to get us back to London."

Missy paled as she listened to Heather. She could only remember the pain and horror that she had found in London and did not want to return to them. "Oh, miss, no! It is nice here and they treat us well. If we go back, Bess will get us again," Missy whispered anxiously as one small thin hand slid to her throat.

"No, Missy. That will not happen again, and I must return to London; I have to help the Marquis."

Missy looked at Heather for a moment with a puzzled expression on her face and said, "But miss, he is dead. You found that out at Bess's."

"No, Missy, he is not dead; that was a ruse to get the other people involved to come out of hiding," Heather said as she walked to the windows. "Missy, I can't stay here and be Captain Guyon's mistress. I must help the Marquis if at all possible. Don't you understand, Missy? He was like a father to me."

Missy nodded her head and said, "I do, miss, and I will help, but I'm still afraid."

Heather smiled at Missy and said, "I knew you would because you are my friend. Now help me change. Marie will be here to take me to the seamstress' in a few moments."

The streets of Paris were thrilling. There were stalls in which merchants sold their wares. There were old ladies with baskets full of flowers. Many elegant men and women strolled by, stopping here and there to examine an item that had caught their eye.

There were ragamuffins and cutpurses and beggars but they did not seem as aggressive as the ones that she had seen in London. When she mentioned this to Marie, the maid explained that this was where the rich traded and it was closely watched by the gendarmerie. Paris was much more brutal to the poor than London, she said. And if one decided to venture into the gutters where the real criminals did their work, instead of just losing your purse, you would most likely lose your life.

Heather nevertheless enjoyed watching the business on the streets. She savored every moment of the ride because it was the first time in several weeks that she had been allowed to go outside. The fresh air seemed for the moment to wipe away all her troubles.

As the carriage slowed to a stop in front of a

seamstress' establishment, Heather did not notice a tall slim man. And as she stepped down from the carriage she did not see that he had dismounted from his horse and crossed the street to observe their movements.

The visit to the seamstress did not take long. Heather and Marie returned to their carriage directly and the man who had been standing in a doorway across the street continued to follow.

As they approached the house Heather looked at Marie and asked, "Do you think Captain Guyon would mind if we walked in the garden?"

Marie shook her head and said, "No, madam, he will not mind. He has already suggested that you might like to use the garden."

"Then shall we stroll there before we go back into the house? The roses look lovely from my window," Heather said as she stepped down from the carriage.

"If Madam wishes," Marie said as she followed Heather.

The tall man relaxed under a tree as he watched Heather and Marie enter the garden. He could not see beyond the high wall that surrounded the garden but kept a close watch on the house. He was happier today than he had been in a long while because now he had some information to give Bagaudae. *Finally,* he thought, *we have found a crack in Monsieur Guyon's armor. The beautiful madam.* He smiled to himself as he stood watch.

Heather strolled among the roses, loving every intoxicating moment. She dreaded the thought of once more entering what to her had become a prison.

As she walked through the garden, she stopped to smell one of the beautiful roses. She did not know that at the same moment she was being observed from the windows above.

Nicholas watched her with pleasure and a troubled mind. He wished that she were not so reluctant to come to him. Still that very elusiveness enhanced her desirability in his eyes. The other women he had known had been all too ready to fall into his arms. That had made it too easy: Heather presented a challenge which both pleased and disturbed him. Why it disturbed him was a question he could not answer.

As she strolled among the flowers with the sun reflecting on her golden curls, Heather looked a true lady. A dull ache began to grow in his loins and he turned from the window. He would like to walk into the garden and take her on the soft grass with the scent of roses in the air. Yet he was determined not to touch her until she lost some of the hate that he could see in her eyes.

Heather stayed in the garden until the sun began to cast golden rays across the sky and the air became cool. Finally she told Marie that it was time to go inside. As she walked through the door she cast one last glance at the garden and longed to be in the meadow of Dunhan.

Missy was waiting for her when she returned to her room to dress for dinner. "Miss, yer bath is ready and I have laid out yer gown. It is late so ye must hurry."

"Yes, I know, but I was so enjoying the garden; it reminded me of home," Heather said as she stepped into the hot water.

"Yes, miss, but try not to think of it. It only makes ye sad."

"I do try, Missy, but it is hard not to think of the gardens and the meadow in which I used to play when I was a child. I miss them so." She did not add that she missed David all the more when she strolled among the roses. Dunhan's rose garden was a favorite place of David's.

Heather followed Marie down the stairs to a large dining room. It was a lovely room with a long table in the center which could seat a great many guests. Dominating the room was a huge crystal chandelier. Dazzled by its beauty, Heather just stood and stared at it.

214

"It is magnificent, isn't it?" Nicholas said. Heather glanced in the direction of the voice.

Nicholas was standing near a handsome black Italian marble fireplace which reflected the light from the chandelier. He was dressed in elegant evening clothes. He wore a deep red velvet jacket with ribbons about the collar and cuffs, from which fell rich lace. His shirt was white silk and his cravat was tied into many ruffles. His britches were also red and clung to his muscular thighs. The stockings were of the purest white silk and his evening slippers were black with diamond buckles and sported the red heels made fashionable by Louis XIV.

As Nicholas casually came forward to meet Heather, she was once again astounded by his good looks. "Yes, it's the most beautiful chandelier that I have ever seen. Its size is rather breathtaking."

"The chandelier was made for Lucrezia Borgia, and has been brought here from Italy. They say that each crystal was cut with such precision that it magnifies the light in such a way that it seems there are several chandeliers instead of only one."

"Your house is very beautiful."

Nicholas smiled and said, "It is comfortable. Now, shall we dine?"

Their conversation was on the whole impersonal until Nicholas said over dessert, "Did you enjoy your visit to the seamstress?"

Heather replied that it had been pleasant, a little annoyed at his possessiveness. But when he added that he expected her to be a lady when she entertained for him, she nearly exploded. "Just how can I be a lady when you have made it clear that I am no more than a servant?"

Nicholas stood and offered Heather his arm, and they walked across the hall to the drawing room. As she took the seat offered, he said, "Heather, you know as well as I do that you have all the graces of a lady,

215

thanks to your training at Dunhan. I am merely asking that you not spoil the illusion."

His attitude was bad enough but the mention of Dunhan brought a rush of emotion. Heather did not look at him as she said, "I will do my best. Now, if you don't mind, I think I will retire to my room." Standing, she started to walk from the room.

"Heather, I have not given you permission to leave," Nicholas said.

Heather looked directly at him, fiery rebellion in her eyes. "I'm sorry, I thought you had finished with your instructions for tomorrow night."

Chilled by the look, he said, "I have. Now good night." With this he turned toward the fire. Heather raced from the room, too upset to say anything else.

When the light from Heather's candle was extinguished, it was observed by the tall thin man now perched atop the wall. Across the street was another man. He was as tall as the first man, but he had a strong build, his hair was dark and a patch covered one of his dark eyes. "Monsieur Bagaudae, that is Madam's room," the slim man said as Bagaudae climbed up to sit beside him.

"Tomorrow, Piggot, Monsieur Guyon is to have guests for dinner, but afterward, I want you to climb up to that window and kidnap the woman. Then we will see how it affects Monsieur to have someone he cares about taken from him."

❧ Chapter Fourteen ☙

Heather did not sit down in the chair that Nicholas offered. He had called her into the study to give her instructions for that evening.

"I will be ready to receive your guests," she said calmly, "but I would like to know how you intend to explain my presence in your house."

Nicholas laughed. "My dear, I need not explain your presence. Mistresses are not unusual among my contemporaries."

Heather blanched at his reference to her as his mistress. While that was exactly what she was, she could not accept it. She did hope that somehow her presence in his home would be an embarrassment. While she realized that even the King in England had mistresses, she somehow supposed her own situation to be different, more clandestine.

"Shortly after luncheon Marie will go with you to the seamstress' for your final fittings. And," Nicholas said, taking a black velvet case from the desk, "I thought this would be suitable with the gown you are to wear tonight." He gave her a beautiful sapphire necklace with matching earrings.

Heather smiled broadly. She had never dreamed anything quite so lovely would be hers.

"I thought you would like them," Nicholas said as he watched Heather's eyes sparkle. "I think they will suit the blue brocade which the seamstress has for you. I wouldn't want my friends to think that I am not generous with my mistress."

Whatever joy she had felt was shattered at the mention of her position. Heather looked at Nicholas with the now familiar expression of loathing. "If that will be all, I will go to luncheon." She said the words but did not take the initiative to leave the room.

Nicholas noted this and commented, "You learn quickly, Heather. Yes, you have my permission to leave."

Marie and Missy helped her bathe and dress in the gown which Nicholas had chosen for her to wear. It was the pale blue brocade he had spoken of earlier. The gown glistened with hints of gold threaded throughout. The sapphires enhanced her white shoulders and when her hair was piled high on her head the earrings dangled enticingly from her small ears.

Heather turned for the maids' inspection and both smiled with approval.

Nicholas was waiting for her at the foot of the stairs. "My dear, you look lovely. I will be the envy of every man here tonight. Now, shall we greet our guests?"

Placing her hand on his velvet-sleeved arm, Heather let Nicholas escort her into the drawing room. Glancing about as they entered, she could see several gentlemen sipping wine and talking together. As their guests noted their entrance, every eye turned to Heather. "My dear friends, I would like to present my hostess, Mademoiselle Heather Cromwell."

The first gentleman to bow over Heather's hand was an elderly man with white hair and mustache.

"Mademoiselle, you are lovely. May I introduce myself, since this young rascal seems to be negligent of his duties as a host. I'm Count le Marignier de la Averyron." Then, gazing at Nicholas with envy, he continued, "Monsieur, she will set all Paris on its ears. I wish that I had half the luck that you have with the ladies. Not only are you one of the most popular men at court, but now I find that you have this beauty hidden away. I think it unfair for one man to possess such good fortune."

Nicholas laughed. "My dear Count, I do not plan to keep Heather secluded away. She is far too lovely to hide, and I expect to bring her out into society."

"That is admirable of you, sir, but if I were you I'd keep her here safe from all other men. Otherwise you will be fighting duels over her."

As the Count finished speaking two other gentlemen introduced themselves to Heather, paying her compliments on her beauty and commenting to Nicholas. She did not mind the compliments but when they turned to Nicholas and discussed her as though she were a prize he'd won at a game of whist, she was deeply insulted.

Heather glanced about the room looking for other women. But there were none. She wanted to question Nicholas about this but the opportunity never came and they went in to dinner.

Nicholas sat at the head of the table, with Heather to his right and Count le Marignier to his left. The dinner was sumptuous, an affair with many French dishes that Heather had never tried before. There was sauman à la Brantôme, which was salmon with shrimp and mushrooms, lobster à l'américaine served with wild rice and salade verte. Next there was caneton à l'orange, boeuf à la mode and blanquette of lamb. The vegetables were asparagus with hollandaise, artichoke hearts with lemon butter, stuffed mushrooms, peas parisiens and honeyed carrots. The desserts were tarte aux fraises, lemon soufflé with lemon sauce, and fruit and cheese. Each course was served with the appropriate wine which enhanced their flavor.

Though the food was delicious, Heather was unable to eat much because of her tenseness.

After dinner she was escorted back to the drawing room by the Count and as the men sipped their brandy, Nicholas asked Heather to sing. After her performance she asked to be excused. Nicholas noticing how pale and tired she looked, agreed.

Heather said her goodnights and accepted their regretful compliments and then left the room. When the door closed she leaned against it for a moment to gain enough strength to go upstairs.

After the door had closed Nicholas returned to his guests and asked them if they would mind joining him in the study. "Not at all, Captain Guyon," the Count said. "We know that you did not invite us here just to admire the beauty of your latest mistress."

"You are right, Count le Marignier, I did not invite you here just for pleasure. My country is in a difficult position now, and I hope you can persuade King Louis to help England defeat the Dutch. During the battle at Gravesend our fleet was nearly destroyed and it is urgent that we have France's cooperation."

As Nicholas spoke, Count le Marignier had his own thoughts on the situation. He knew he would support Captain Guyon's plea to King Louis, for he knew this was the opportunity that the King had been waiting for. It would give him more territory and another blow at the Spanish forces that he was determined to conquer. The King sought French supremacy. Even his marriage to the Spanish princess Marie Thérèse had served as a pretext for war. "Sir, you do realize that it will take time but I will give my full support to your cause. I don't know about the rest of you gentlemen but I'm sure that our King would help his relative across the channel." The Count looked around the room for corroboration among the others. He was convinced that they all seemed in agreement.

"Gentlemen, I appreciate your support," Nicholas said.

Missy could see the paleness of Heather's complexion as she entered the room and rushed over to her. "Here, miss, sit down and let me get you something."

Heather accepted the small brandy that Missy offered without complaint. "Missy, I can't go through with another one of his affairs. We've got to leave, and soon," Heather said as Missy helped her from her gown and into bed.

"Miss, you will feel better in the morning," Missy said as she blew out the candle.

Missy did not want to leave Captain Guyon's comfortable household. She wished that Heather would begin to like it, for she knew the master enjoyed having Heather there. She had observed them together and knew he cared for her mistress more than he wanted to admit. But it was no concern of hers. If Heather wanted to leave, she would go with her to the ends of the earth.

The moonlight streamed through the window, the air was soft and clear and after a while Heather began to grow drowsy. It was on such a night, she thought that David had told her he loved her. Gathering the pillow into her arms, Heather hugged it to her as if it were David and slowly closed her eyes to sleep.

A noise awakened Heather, and she sat up in the bed and glanced around the room. Her heart beat rapidly as she peered into the darkness. "Is anyone there?" she called, but there was no answer. She could not see anything in the darkness but she could hear heavy breathing.

Heather trembled and a hand clamped over her mouth to stifle her scream. *Nicholas!* she cried out to herself. *Help me!* But no sound came from her lips. She did not realize that she had called Captain Guyon by his Christian name, nor did she care; all she wanted was to see his strong figure come through the door to rescue her.

She had the sense of déjà vu as she was tied and gagged and thrown over someone's shoulder. The man then climbed down from the window and escaped through the garden unnoticed by anyone.

When they reached the street, Heather was roughly thrown into a carriage and the man climbed in beside her. She looked about with wide eyes but could not see the man's features because they were obscured by shadows. The carriage raced down the cobbled streets at top speed and Heather was jostled from side to side as it turned corners and hit deep ruts in the street. After a fifteen-minute ride, the carriage slowed to a stop.

Heather was then pulled from the carriage and carried down a flight of stairs. The stale, damp air had the stench of the gutter and once as she was brushed against the wall, she could feel the wet slimy surface within her every pore.

Heather thought that she was once more in the hands of Bess's men and she was terrified.

A torch smoked at the end of the passage and Heather could see a large wooden door. As they approached, it was flung open by what seemed like an overgrown boy with a stooped back. As he looked at Heather, a lopsided grin spread across his face to reveal only a few rotten teeth. He shuffled from side to side and swung his large arms at his side. "Tell Bagaudae we're here, Gluck." At this the boy slouched off into the adjoining room.

A large fireplace stood at the end of the room and Heather was unceremoniously dumped onto a stool in front of it. She could see the man who had kidnapped her in the light of the fire. He was tall and slim with mousy brown hair and watery eyes. He was dirty and dressed in a suit that looked as if it would have fit a much larger man.

He did not speak to Heather but held his hands out to the fire to warm them. Heather did not hear the approach of another man and as he spoke she turned to see a tall dark man with a patch over one of his dark eyes. A deep crimson scar ran down his cheek from the patch to his strong chin. "Is this the woman?" he said as he approached.

He could not see her features very well, for the light shone in his eyes, but it seemed as though he recognized her. As he came closer he stopped and stared into the frightened blue eyes. "Heather, is it really you?"

Heather stared in amazement at this tall man who spoke as if he knew her. "Speak to me, tell me it is really you," he said as he hunkered on his heels beside her and gazed up into the wide eyes.

"Yes, I'm Heather, but may I ask who you are and why you have brought me here?"

Something familiar tugged at Heather's memory but she could not define it. "Don't you recognize me?" he asked but could see that she did not. "It's the patch, that's the reason." The look of puzzlement remained on her face and he said, "It's me, David." For a moment the look remained on her face and slowly all color left her cheeks and she fainted.

When Heather awoke, she was lying on a straw pallet next to the fire. Its flames warmed her and for a moment she stared at them. Then, sensing someone near, she turned her head to see the dark man who said he was David. "Heather, my love, you frightened me to death. Are you all right now?" he asked.

Sitting up abruptly, she said, "How dare you. You have no right to be so cruel. David is dead. Why did you try to make me believe that you are he and why have you brought me here? To torture me? Are you one of Bess's henchmen?" As she spoke tears slid down her cheeks and suddenly her ramblings were stopped by his lips. Startled for a moment, she sat frozen, then surprisingly, she was kissing him back. Heather savored the kiss and let his lips renew their acquaintance with hers. It was David.

When he was finally able to pull himself from her, he gazed into her face and said, "You know me now and I have not forgotten the softness of your lips."

Tears of joy cascaded down Heather's cheeks as she spoke. "David, you are alive. Oh, my love!" And she threw herself into his arms again.

"Yes, I'm alive, but now I'm called Bagaudae," he said as he stroked her golden hair. He had dreamed of holding her and feeling the warmth of her body against his during all those agonizing months that he had spent enslaved.

David glanced up to see Piggot staring at them and he then remembered the reason for her being in his house. Pulling himself from Heather's clinging arms, he looked down into her beautiful face. It was even more lovely than when he had last seen her. She had matured into a beautiful woman. As he looked at Heather, he could see that she was dressed in an expensive negligee; it was thin and clung to her curves. No housekeeper would wear such a garment and this made his assumption a fact. She was Nicholas Guyon's mistress, there was no other explanation.

He stood up abruptly and briskly crossed the room to Piggot. "Are you certain this is the woman?"

Piggot glanced at David and then back to Heather and nodded his head. "It is she, monsieur. She is the one who rode in the carriage and strolled in the garden with her maid." David looked at Heather, still sitting on the pallet in front of the fire. He could see the reason for Nicholas wanting her as his mistress. However, it was hard to believe that Heather would want the same thing. But many things had changed since the day he had left the manor for his grand tour.

The manor was now in Nicholas' possession and his father was dead, and now here was Heather, his beautiful Heather, the mistress to his most hated enemy. He could not believe all the changes that had taken place in so short a time. But then he, too, had changed. He was no longer the young man of wealth but a criminal with but one thought in mind: revenge.

Revenge was the only thing that sustained him and made each day bearable. There had been the long months of slavery and then a torturous journey back to England and all the ugliness he had experienced thereafter.

David had joined London's underworld and soon became one of its leaders. It had been a hard battle to survive but he had done so for only one reason and that was to find his onetime friend and kill him.

. Now he looked at Heather, his hate reached new heights. There was one more reason to kill Nicholas Guyon.

Heather watched David and the other man as they talked. She could not hear what was being said but it obviously concerned her. She did not care what they said. David was alive, nothing else mattered.

She scrambled to her feet as David returned to her side and said, "Heather, I have to know something."

Heather looked up into his dark face. "Ask me anything, my love."

As he gazed at her, David could still see the innocent girl that she had been. "Are you Nicholas' mistress?" he said gently. Heather blushed and could not answer. She had no need to. David now knew the truth.

Heather could not stand the look of accusation that crossed his face and said, "No, David, it's not what you think! I'm not his mistress by choice. I could either live with him or be sold as any man's prostitute. Aside from that, I thought I could help your father."

David looked at her in disbelief. "How could you help my father when he is dead? There is no need for lies, Heather. I know you are his willing mistress; otherwise you would not have the use of his carriage, or your own maid." He glanced at her from head to toe, then waved his hand in Heather's direction and said, "Or expensive clothes."

Heather backed away from David and brought her hand to her throat in a helpless gesture. Slowly shaking her head, she whispered, "No, David, it's not true, and your father is not dead."

The scar on David's cheek turned a deeper crimson and his mouth was set in a hard line as he looked at her. He wanted to slap the lies from her lips and brought his hand up to do so. "No, David! He is alive. I'm not lying. It's the truth."

His hand fell to his side as he asked, "How do you know this?"

"Nicholas told me. It was only a plan of the King's to bring the others out of hiding. Your father is alive in the Tower."

David sank down onto the stool and put his head into his hands. He could not doubt her word, for in her eyes he could see that she was telling the truth. Heather crossed to him and placed her arms around his shoulders. Laying her cheek against his dark hair she said, "He is alive and we must help him."

David glanced up into Heather's face and said, "Is it true what is said about him? That he plotted against the King?"

Heather nodded her head. "Yes, it is, but he is an old man and when he thought you were dead it seemed to do something to him. I begged Nicholas to help, but he refused because of his loyalty to the crown."

"His loyalty to the crown! It is more his loyalty to the riches that once were my father's. I will kill him for it!"

Heather could see the hate that David felt for Nicholas and she shivered. "Don't kill him," she said, not knowing why she said it. Surely he had mistreated her. He'd kidnapped her, made her his whore. Why then did she want to defend him? She could not explain it, but the feeling was palpable.

"I will make him pay," David said harshly as he stood up. "And it will be through you, my love."

226

Heather looked at the expression on David's face, but could not read it.

"How do you mean, through me? He cares nothing for me."

David laughed at Heather's remark and bent down to brush Heather's lips with his. "Oh no, my love? He cares or you would not be in his house meeting all his fine friends." He took her face between his hands. "Heather, will you help me?" Heather looked into his face and knew that she would do anything that he asked her to do.

David released her and turned to Piggot. "Go and get the carriage." He took Heather into his arms and kissed her deeply. "It will not be easy for you, but you must play up to Nicholas and make him believe that you care. You must listen for any information that will help us in planning my father's escape."

Heather listened to every word David was saying but she felt uneasy. He didn't seem like the David she had known. She did not question him, for she was certain he knew what was best for her and the Marquis. She had to believe in his wisdom.

Stepping back from Heather, he escorted her up the slippery wet steps and out into the street. It was an ominous place, but with David at her side, she had no fear.

As he handed her into the carriage, he kissed her once more and said, "Do as I ask, my love, and then we will go back to England together."

As she walked across the garden, a chill ran down Heather's back. Piggot had taken her from her room without a wrapper. She did not see Nicholas standing in the French doors that led from the study into the garden and as she approached, he said, "Isn't it rather chilly to be taking a walk in the garden by moonlight?"

Heather straightened her shoulders. "I needed some air and it is such a beautiful night. The stars look close enough to touch."

Nicholas gazed at Heather as the moonlight shimmered about her and he took a quick breath and said, "Yes, it is lovely, but you are shivering from the night air. Come in and I will get you something to warm you."

Nicholas sat down in a chair across from her, handing her a glass of sherry. "It will take the chill away in a few moments." He then smiled and continued, "You were marvelous tonight, and every man in Paris will be longing for a glimpse of you after the Count has spread word of you."

Heather smiled at Nicholas. "I am glad that I was able to please you," she said sweetly.

Nicholas looked at her, a little puzzled by her congenial mood. Was it a combination of the sherry and the lovely evening? No matter, he would not question it. It was pleasant sitting quietly with her.

Heather became uncomfortable with his gaze. She realized that she was still in her negligee. It had completely slipped her mind in her excitement at finding David.

A smile crept to her lips as she remembered his touch and his lips upon hers.

"May I ask what makes you smile so secretively?"

Disturbed, Heather said, "It was only a memory of the past. It would not interest you. Now, if you will excuse me, I will go to my room. My walk in the garden has made me sleepy."

Nicholas escorted her to the door of the study and then said, "Good night, madam, I hope you will sleep well."

Heather glanced at him worriedly and wondered if he might know that she had not been walking in the garden. But she put the idea quickly aside, for she knew if he had known, he would surely have said something about it.

Nicholas sat down once more in front of the fire and sipped his brandy. The evening had been a success and he was happy as he stretched his long lean legs out to the warmth of the flames. He thought of Heather as

228

she had looked walking in the garden. She had seemed happy for the first time since she had left Dunhan. It was strange, because he could see no reason for the change in her.

Setting his glass on the table, he stood and walked from his study and up the stairs. At the top, he stopped and looked down the long hall toward Heather's door. He was tempted to go to her but instead he turned and walked to his room at the end of the hall. He would wait until she was willing, he thought.

The next morning Heather awoke and stretched leisurely as she looked at the bright sunlight that came through the windows. It was a beautiful day and her spirits were high.

She rose from the bed and rang for her breakfast. As the door opened, she said, "Come in, Missy. Isn't it a beautiful day!"

Missy looked at Heather in surprise, for it was the first time that she had seen a truly happy expression on Heather's face. "Yes, miss, it's a beautiful day, and I'm glad to see ye feeling better."

Heather danced happily around the room and said, "Yes, I'm happy, Missy, for the first time in months."

"I can see that, miss, with ye dancing all about the room. Come and have yer breakfast before it is cold," Missy scolded.

Heather came to Missy and hugged her. "Oh, Missy, I'm too happy to eat. All I want to do is to dress and go into the garden where I can enjoy this beautiful day."

"Miss, has something happened to make ye so happy? Ye seem as if ye will burst," Missy laughed.

"Yes, something has happened, but for now I cannot tell you. You will learn it soon enough and we will both be happy, Missy," Heather said as she dressed in a light print morning gown.

"Well, I'm happy, miss, as long as I can see the smile on yer face and watch yer light steps."

As they were finishing with Heather's toilette, there was a slight tap on the door and then Marie entered the room. "Is Madam ready?" she asked.

"Yes, Marie, I was just going into the garden."

"Monsieur would like to see you in his study."

The look of happiness left Heather's face but then it returned with a bright smile. "Tell him I will be down in a few moments, Marie."

Marie did not move and said, "Monsieur Guyon said he would like to see you now, madam."

Sometimes this little maid with her willingness to please Nicholas irritated Heather. She knew that Marie would not move from the door until she was with her. As she left the room, she turned to Missy and said, "I shall meet you in the garden."

Missy gave Heather a slight curtsy and said, "Yes, miss."

Heather walked into Nicholas' study to see him busy with his papers at his desk. He did not realize for a moment that she had entered. She watched him while he worked intensely, his dark hair falling over his forehead and his full sensuous mouth set in a firm line.

Heather walked to his desk and said, "Marie said you would like to see me." Nicholas looked up and motioned for Heather to be seated, then went back to work on the papers that were scattered across his desk.

After a few moments, he looked up and said, "I'm sorry if I have been rude, but I had to finish these papers this morning." He leaned back in his chair and observed Heather. "Now that they are done we can discuss what I asked you down for so early in the morning. I have just received a dispatch that we are to have an important visitor from King Charles's court. The Duke of Monmouth has arrived in Paris on official business and will dine with us tonight. I shall expect you to be my hostess."

Heather looked at Nicholas in surprise. She had met royalty before, but never the King's son. "Are you sure that you do not want someone other than a mere serving girl to act as your hostess?"

Nicholas threw back his head and laughed. "My dear Heather, that is of no concern because we are all in the same boat. You are a serving girl and the Duke is a bastard and I am nothing more than a lord with an empty title. If it had not been for the goodness of the King, I would be only a Captain in his army. Do not concern yourself with the propriety of it. You will be lovely enough that no one would ever think of your background."

Heather thought of what David had asked her to do and smiled. "It would be a pleasure to see the Duke."

"You will only be required to be my hostess through dinner, because afterward we have business to discuss. I hope it will not be as trying on you as last night," Nicholas said as he rose from the chair and walked to the window. He could see Missy in the garden and said, "Now you may go for your walk in the garden."

"Sir, do you have any preference as to what I should wear tonight?"

Nicholas glanced back at Heather and said, "The pink velvet, I think. It would look lovely with your coloring."

As Heather left the room Nicholas looked back at the garden to see her after a few moments join the maid. They began chattering as soon as Heather approached and he could see the happiness that was obvious on their smiling faces. There was something that kept nagging at the back of his mind as he watched the two stroll among the flowers. Nothing that he could place, but something that just did not fit the pattern that Heather had set before her walk in the garden last night.

He watched them for a while longer and then went back to his desk to finish his work. He hoped that the Duke would have some information on the Marquis and his associates.

That evening Heather dressed with all the gaiety of a

231

young noblewoman going to her first ball. She looked lovely in the pink velvet with its gold trim. The small diamonds that Nicholas had given her sparkled around her graceful neck and lent just the right touch to her costume.

Missy smiled at Heather's appearance and commented, "My, miss, ye do look radiant tonight. Yer happiness seems to make ye glow all over."

"Thank you, Missy, and I am happy, for soon we will leave this place."

Missy looked up at Heather and the happiness that she felt vanished at Heather's words. "Miss, is this the reason that ye were happy all day?"

"Yes, Missy, but all I can tell you is that we will be leaving soon and no one will be able to stop us. Now it is time for me to greet Captain Guyon's guest."

Heather walked from the room and Missy watched her with worried eyes. She could feel it in her bones, and she knew that Heather was headed for more trouble than she had known.

Heather knocked on the drawing room door and entered. She stopped for a moment when she saw the Duke of Monmouth leaning casually against the mantel of the fireplace.

He was an extraordinarily handsome young man, not many years older than herself, but he had the air of sophistication. He had dark hair and a thin face and the only flaw to his appearance was his mouth. It gave him a cynical, contemptuous expression.

As he looked at Heather, she remembered her manners and gave a deep curtsy. Nicholas came forward and escorted her into the room and said, "My lord, may I present Heather Cromwell, my hostess."

The Duke of Monmouth took Heather's hand and smiled at her charmingly. "It is my pleasure. I must commend Captain Guyon on his taste."

Heather blushed at the compliment and said, "Thank you for your kindness, Your Grace. And may

I say that you are everything that I have heard of you."

The Duke laughed and turned to Nicholas as he placed Heather's hand on his arm. "Nicholas, she is charming as well as beautiful. Where did you find this gem?"

"My lord, that is the question that many seek the answer to, but I shall never divulge that information." Both men laughed and looked at Heather, who continued to blush. "My dear, can I offer you a sherry?" Nicholas asked.

"Yes, thank you," Heather said as she sat down in a chair across from the Duke.

The Duke sipped his wine and observed Heather. He envied Nicholas his good fortune in women. Even now the Countess Beaufort waited anxiously at Versailles, hoping that the ambassador from England would appear at court. Had she known that he had such a luscious morsel under his roof she might well have come and created a scene. The Countess had begged and pleaded with the King to be allowed to accompany Monmouth to France. The Duke knew enough about the Countess to realize that it was not he that she wanted to be near, though she tried to make it seem so. She had given her favors freely just so she might make her way to Captain Guyon's side. He always had all the luck—in gaming, women and earning the respect of other men. This disgusted the Duke, for he had always had to fight for whatever he wanted.

This man had even won the respect of his father, King Charles. The Duke of Monmouth was still a long way from achieving that. It angered him to think that even now he was still considered a bastard, and not the proper heir to the throne.

"Nicholas, I hope you are planning to bring this lovely creature to court. It would be a pity to deprive the Dauphin of his chance at seeing such a beauty."

"Yes, I have made plans to do so, but Heather is still adjusting to Paris. It will be a while before she is ready for court life." Nicholas handed a small crystal glass to Heather.

"You mean that you have just arrived in Paris?" the Duke asked.

"Yes, only a few weeks ago, but I have already fallen in love with this wonderful city."

Nicholas looked at her quizzically as she spoke. It surprised him to hear her say she actually enjoyed Paris. But then, she was just making polite conversation.

When Heather admitted to missing the rolling hills of England, the Duke smiled and said, "So you come from the country."

Heather enjoyed talking with someone other than Nicholas and she could see that it was annoying him. Perhaps he was afraid that she would mention the Marquis and her involvement with him.

"Did you never visit London?" the Duke questioned.

"Yes, but it was when I was very young. After my father died I was unable to have a coming out as other young ladies do."

The Duke smiled and said, "It is a shame, for you would have instantly had all the young men's hearts."

Nicholas shifted uneasily in his chair as the Duke and Heather carried on their conversation. Though she was not actually telling the truth, her talk was precariously close to it. And he was afraid that at any moment she would mention Dunhan. It was to his great relief that the butler entered to announce that dinner was served.

Both the Duke and Nicholas offered Heather their arms. Heather smiled at each, then chose the Duke to accompany her to dinner. Nicholas followed, frowning.

The conversation did not return to Heather's life, much to Nicholas' relief.

After dinner Heather excused herself and went upstairs to her room. Missy was waiting to help her undress, but Heather made an excuse to remain dressed and sent Missy away for the night.

234

Heather waited a few minutes, then went to the door and peered into the hallway. When she was sure no one was about she crept downstairs.

The Duke and Nicholas had gone into his study to discuss matters of state.

Heather tiptoed to the door and opened it, just enough to overhear their conversation.

"You know, Nicholas, this is vitally important to England. If Louis does not help, England will be virtually bankrupt. We must get this treaty signed." The Duke sipped his brandy while Nicholas pondered the matter. "You are ambassador to France and His Majesty thinks you can be of invaluable assistance."

Nicholas was standing by the mantel of the baroque fireplace with its gilded figures looking down into the room. "You know I will do everything in my power to help get the treaty signed." Heather continued to listen to the grave political discussion. The treaty would free the King from dependence on Parliament. The introduction of Roman Catholicism also played a part in the King's plans. Nicholas and the Duke also discussed the assassination attempt on Charles's life.

"Has any more developed on that situation?"

The Duke shook his head and said, "I'm afraid it hasn't. The old Marquis is still in the Tower and his friends are still being sought. We had hoped to uncover them by now, but it seems as though they have vanished from the face of the earth."

Since his conversation with Heather, Nicholas had been wanting news of the Marquis. It pleased him to hear that the old man was still alive. "What are the plans for the Marquis?"

"He has undergone extensive questioning and has admitted to his involvement, but he has not divulged who the others are. The only reason the death sentence has not been carried out is that his testimony will be needed should the others be found. However, the King is losing patience. The Marquis may well be beheaded shortly."

Heather clasped a hand over her mouth to silence a gasp. She leaned against the door for support and willed herself not to faint. She dared not risk exposure. Pulling herself together, she fled up the stairs to her room. Quickly she must get this information to David.

After the Duke's departure, she would go through the garden to the little door and find Piggot. He would take her to David.

The meeting between Nicholas and the Duke of Monmouth seemed as though it would never end, and Heather began to tire. Just as she had decided to give up and go to bed, she heard the carriage pull away.

As Heather was getting a wrap from her wardrobe the door opened and Nicholas came in. "Are you going for another moonlight walk in the garden?" he asked.

"Yes, it is such a lovely night," Heather lied convincingly.

"May I join you?" he asked and opened the door for Heather.

Her plans were doomed and she knew that she would be unable to meet with David tonight. As they strolled through the garden and talked she did her best to keep the agitation from her voice.

"Heather, I must compliment you again tonight. You were marvelous and the Duke was enchanted. I had feared you might accidently mention the Marquis but you handled it magnificently. I am proud of you," Nicholas said as he took her arm.

"I am glad that I was convincing as a lady, and I thought the Duke was very interesting," Heather replied.

Nicholas took Heather into his arms and kissed her. She resisted and he released her. Looking into Heather's eyes, he saw the old hatred and knew her pleasing behavior had been a pretense. "I thought you were beginning to enjoy being here."

"I am," Heather lied, "but you startled me."

"It seems, demoiselle, that I am always startling you," he said. Nicholas could see that she was trying with all her power to produce a charming smile. But she didn't fool him this time. He suggested she go back to her room.

Heather did not argue with him. She was shivering.

As he watched Heather walk into the house, Nicholas mused, *She is planning something in that devious little mind of hers. But she will not succeed.* With that thought in mind he walked swiftly into the house and up the stairs. He locked Heather's door.

Angrily Nicholas strode down the hall to his own chambers, but as he looked around at the empty room he realized that he would be unable to rest. He put on his long black cape and called for his coach.

As he went downstairs he decided he would go to Versailles. Perhaps the beauties in Louis's court would amuse him, and take his mind off the vixen upstairs.

The beauty of Versailles never ceased to amaze him. The artisans who had constructed this huge masterpiece had accomplished perfection. And as he waited in the famous Hall of Mirrors, he could not help but marvel at the gilded bronze sculptures and beautiful paintings reflected in the hundreds of mirrors.

As the page showed him into the main salon his heels clicked loudly on the black and white Italian marble floors. He gave King Louis a low bow.

"Rise, Captain Guyon. You are a welcome guest," the King said. "And I know the ladies of the court will agree with me," he laughed. Nicholas smiled stiffly.

Louis waved a lace handkerchief and the musicians resumed playing. "I have certain matters of state to discuss with you later. But now you must join my ladies. They would think it most inconsiderate of me to keep you from them. And there are also the ladies of your own court," Louis said, glancing in the direction of the Countess Beaufort.

Nicholas ignored the Countess and soon was enjoying the pleasures of Versailles. He drank champagne and danced with many of the beautiful women, each of whom tried to capture his attention. He smiled and flirted with them, yet he could not put out of his mind the vision of Heather.

The chandeliers of Versailles were ablaze with hundreds of candles. A swirling rainbow of silks and satins filled the salon as courtiers and their ladies gracefully moved about the floor, dancing to the beautiful music.

Nicholas' spirits rose with each succeeding glass of champagne. Soon all his wit and charm began to surface, and he centered his attention on a raven-haired beauty with huge dark eyes. She was well known in Louis's court for her haughty demeanor, but she seemed to respond graciously to Nicholas.

Several of his friends, including the Countess Beaufort, noticed what was happening. All but the Countess smiled, for they knew that Captain Guyon had once again broken the defenses of a beautiful woman.

King Louis had also noticed what had happened. It always amazed him that Nicholas was one of the few men who were irresistible to women and could also command the respect of men.

Jealousy blazing in her eyes, the Countess Beaufort went swiftly to Nicholas' side.

He smiled at the Countess, though there was no warmth in his eyes as he looked at her. "My dear Meg, how surprising to find you here at Louis's court when all the time I thought you safe in Charles's bed."

"What is so surprising about my being here? Didn't the Duke tell you that I came with him?"

"I'm afraid not. We had things of importance to discuss," Nicholas said. Just then the Duke joined them.

"Indeed we did, and I do not think that it would have been proper to mention you, my dear Meg, in front of Captain Guyon's beautiful hostess." It amused him to divulge that tiny bit of gossip to the Countess.

Nicholas bowed to the Duke cheerfully and said, "I appreciate your discretion, my lord."

By the time the two men turned their attention back to the Countess, she had reddened with anger and was nearly speechless. "How dare you," she exclaimed loudly and brought her hand up to strike Nicholas.

He caught her wrist easily and said, "My dear Margaret, I believe you could use some air." And he led her away from the Duke.

Tears of rage filled her eyes as she looked up at him. "Why didn't you ask me to come with you, Nicholas? I would gladly have come, and you know it. Who is this person that makes you forget I have always loved you?"

"My dear Meg, you do look beautiful with tears in your eyes, but I would dry them quickly if I were you. People might guess that you aren't as heartless as they all suppose."

"Nicholas, you have not answered my question. Who is she?" The Countess placed her hand on his arm and looked into his dark eyes.

"Don't worry, dear Meg, it's only the little housekeeper from Dunhan. She is serving as my hostess while I am in France. She does have the facade of a lady, you know. And she can be rather entertaining."

"Does she mean anything to you?" Meg asked.

"Nothing—nothing at all. She is no more than a possession, a part of the Dunhan estate."

Meg sighed with relief. She still had a chance with him and she was determined that she would not let this night pass without leaving him with something to think about. "Shall we walk in the gardens?" she said.

They strolled aimlessly about until they came to a small secluded alcove. Leading Nicholas, Meg entered the enclosure. She was determined this should be a night he'd long remember and she pressed her body to his. Nicholas seemed preoccupied. Had Meg realized he was thinking of Heather, she would not have persisted.

"My dear Nicholas," she said, molding herself against him and moving sensuously. Her lips caressed

239

him and she ran her fingers through his hair, moved them along the contours of his face. It was a beautiful night. The moonlight shone down on them, and the faint smell of blossoms filled the air.

Nicholas began to respond despite himself. Heather might reject him, but Meg was all too willing. Gradually his kisses became more passionate, and their bodies sank to the soft grass. He fondled her breasts, kissed her neck, her shoulders, explored every curve of her luscious body. Suddenly he drew up her gown and plunged into her brutally, releasing all of the pent-up emotion that had been building toward Heather.

Meg had never experienced such lust from him. She soared with the moment, savoring its pleasure in every pore of her body. All of it had been worthwhile, the waiting, the years of longing. He was hers at last.

As quickly as it had begun, it ended. Nicholas climaxed. "Heather darling," he said. Meg was shocked and angered. Her pride had been shattered and tears rolled down her cheeks. Flustered, Nicholas attempted to apologize. But for Meg it made little difference. She realized she had lost him.

❧ Chapter Fifteen ❧

Heather awoke with nausea tearing at her insides again. She had thought her illness was due to nerves, but now suspected it was a child.

She wiped the tears from her eyes and stared out at the garden. Would it ever be possible to escape, she wondered. She looked longingly at the garden, to the place in which the small opening was hidden. She was desperate to reach David, but Nicholas watched her more carefully than ever. Missy had even been taken from her and there was no hope of ever enlisting the aid of Marie.

It had been three weeks since the Duke's visit and she had been unable to find a way in which to leave the room. She was only allowed out an hour or so each day to walk in the garden. Even then she was watched closely by Marie. There had been no chance to go to the opening to see if Piggot was waiting.

She knew David would think that she had changed her mind and decided to stay with Nicholas. As this thought crossed her mind a frown creased Heather's brow. *No, he should know that I love him and would come if at all possible.*

Going to the dressing table, Heather studied herself in the mirror. She looked a fright. Her face was swollen from all the crying that she had done and her hair had not been cared for. Marie had tried each day to persuade Heather to let her dress her hair but she had refused. She hoped Nicholas would become disgusted with her if she neglected her appearance. Yet nothing seemed to affect him; each night he would come and talk to Heather as if she were still beautiful. The only mention of her appearance had come during the previous night when he had noticed the slight thickening of her waist. "You must get more exercise, my dear, you are beginning to gain weight," he had said.

Heather had glared at him and said, "How can I get exercise locked in my room?"

He had smiled at her and said, "My dear, it is your choice. If you would only behave yourself, you would not have to stay in your room. And you have yet to tell me of the plans your devious little mind was working on that night in the garden."

Heather had jumped to her feet and thrown the glass of wine that she held into his face. "Yes, I was planning to leave this house and I will continue to plan until I succeed."

Nicholas had stood up and casually wiped the wine from his face. "You will never leave here, my dear. I thought I had made that clear in the beginning but I see that you will have to learn it the hard way. You will stay in this room until you come to your senses."

As she sat looking at herself, Heather heard Marie enter the room with her breakfast. As Marie set the tray down on the table, Heather said weakly, "Take it away. I don't want anything to eat." Marie looked worriedly at Heather and said, "Madam, you must eat, for in your condition you must have your nourishment." Heather glared at the maid. "And what do you mean by my condition, Marie?"

242

The maid blushed and said, "I have noticed that you have been ill in the mornings, and you have gained weight. Is it not a baby that causes these things?"

"Yes, Marie, you are right, but I forbid you to mention it to Monsieur. Do you understand?" Heather said a little more gently.

"Yes, madam. You would like to be the one to tell Monsieur, am I not right?"

Heather nodded her head. "Yes, Marie, that is right."

She did not feel like arguing with Marie and thought the little lie would help keep her secret from Nicholas. As she tried to swallow a bit of the food, her stomach gave way and she rushed from the room.

When Heather came back weak and pale, Marie was waiting to help her back to bed. "Madam must rest for the sake of the baby."

Heather nodded her head. "Thank you, Marie, you are kind."

Shaking her head so the light brown curls bounced, Marie said, "No, madam, I only want to please Monsieur. He would not be happy if something happened to you or his child." Heather did not answer the maid but turned on her side to rest.

Marie went downstairs to the study. Nicholas had asked her to stop by after she had helped Heather with her morning toilette. There were a few answers that he needed to make his assumptions fact. "Is Madam resting, Marie?" he asked.

"Yes, monsieur, but she is ill again this morning," Marie said.

"Marie, do you think that Madam is ill for the usual reasons a woman is ill in the mornings?"

"Oui, monsieur," Marie said. She had promised Heather not to speak about it to Captain Guyon but she knew that he was concerned about Madam's health and she could not lie. He had been so unhappy and she knew that news of a baby would make him happy. And perhaps bring the lovers' quarrel to an end.

"Thank you, Marie. That was all I wanted to know." As Marie left the room, Nicholas leaned back in his chair and stared out the window into the garden. Fall would be here soon and the flowers were already beginning to fade. As he thought of autumn, he also thought of spring, when his child would be born.

Joy flooded his veins. He wanted to rush up the stairs and take Heather into his arms and tell her about his happiness. Yet he would wait until she told him about the baby. He leaned over his desk and placed his head in his hands. He knew that he shouldn't keep Heather locked in her room but he was convinced that she would leave him. He could not permit it—especially now that she carried his child.

Deciding to retire early, Heather climbed into bed and blew out the candle. Just as sleep had begun to overtake her tired body, the window opened and Piggot climbed into the room.

She sat up and started to light a candle but he cautioned her not to. "Monsieur is still awake and in his study." Heather nodded her head to show that she understood as he continued, "Please dress quickly and I will take you to Bagaudae. He is waiting."

Heather did not need any further persuasion and jumped from the bed and hurriedly dressed.

Piggot easily lifted Heather into his lean arms and carried her down from the window. She glanced back at the house as they were leaving the garden. Nicholas was pacing the study.

Heather drew a deep breath, savoring the freshness of the night air and her freedom. After Piggot helped her into the carriage he climbed in and they rode off. Heather smiled at him. He didn't exactly return her smile, but she could see that his jaw muscles crinkled in the attempt. He looked as though he had lived a hard life. Everything about him was rough, his scarred face, his disheveled clothes, the worn boots on his feet.

They did not speak during the ride through the Paris

streets. As the carriage rolled to a stop, Piggot opened the door and Heather could see David waiting in the shadows of the building.

She jumped from the carriage and ran happily into David's waiting arms. He held her for a few moments and then said, "Come, let's go inside." Once more they descended the damp steps to the cellar below.

When they were alone Heather turned to David and threw herself into his arms. "I thought I would never see you again." She clung to him as their lips met for a long deep kiss.

He stroked her golden hair and gazed down into her blue eyes. "Nothing could keep me from you when I found out you were being held against your will."

Heather's surprise showed on her face as she asked, "How do you know?"

David laughed and said, "I have ways, but this time, it was your crippled maid who told Piggot of your situation."

"Missy? But how did Piggot come to talk to Missy?"

David led Heather over to the stool in front of the fire and said, "Sit down, my love, and I will tell you. You are so pale. Are you all right?" he asked.

Heather nodded her head and then remembered how dreadful she looked. "Yes, I'm all right, only I haven't been sleeping well from lack of exercise. Now tell me how Piggot was able to talk to Missy."

David sat down on the floor beside Heather. He picked up a piece of straw and twirled it between his fingers. It was all quite simple. David began, "Piggot watched the house every day and then as we were about to give up hope, he noticed the crippled maid. He began talking to her, escorting her to the market, and soon she began to trust him. She talked about her mistress, and as he prodded her with questions, it finally came out that you were locked in your room."

David was anxious to hear Heather's news and she quickly told him what she had learned.

"How did you find this out?" David asked.

"I listened at the door while Nicholas and the Duke of Monmouth discussed it."

David threw his arms around Heather. "I knew you would help. Now we must make plans to return to London."

David called Piggot in and began giving him instructions. He was to go to Rafael's an set things in action. Piggot agreed and left, calling David Bagaudae again.

"David, why do they call you Bagaudae?" Heather asked as David walked back to her.

"It is a new name for a new life, and was given to me by my friends. It also helps keep my real identity secret." David's words were sharp, and there was a finality to them. She wanted to ask him more about his life, but dared not.

"When do we leave for England?" she asked instead.

David glanced uneasily away from Heather and said, "You will not be going, Heather."

Heather could not believe what she had heard. "What do you mean?"

David walked into the shadows away from the fire so Heather might not read his expression and said, "You must return to Nicholas. When things are settled I will come for you." For the moment he'd put aside his revenge. Nicholas would have to wait until his father was free.

Heather went over to David and said, "I will not go back. I want to help the Marquis."

Shaking his head, David said, "No, Heather, you will not, because you might hinder our plans."

Heather clutched David's hands. "I will not hinder you or your plans. I might be able to help. If you will only let me. I could go places you will be unable to go."

David contemplated what Heather had said for a moment and then pulled her into his arms. "Yes, you might be right. You might be able to help at that."

Heather's face brightened and she pulled his face

246

down to hers and kissed him deeply. "I could never go back to that house. Not now."

David looked at Heather quizzically and said, "Why not now?"

Heather paled visibly and said, "I can't tell you."

Grabbing Heather by the arms and shaking her, David said, "Tell me, Heather! There isn't anything you can't tell me."

"If I do, you will not let me go with you."

David shook his head. "Heather, I will not go back on my word. Just tell me so I may justify the wrong that I know has been done to you."

Tears ran freely down her cheeks. "You cannot undo this, David, and it would serve no purpose to be revenged."

David looked down into the tear-streaked face and said, "But you still have not told me the reason."

Heather took a deep breath as if to draw courage from it, then said quickly, "I'm to have Nicholas' child."

A strange look came into David's eyes and Heather automatically stepped back from him. To her dismay, he threw back his head and laughed until tears streamed down his face. After a few moments he wiped his eyes and said, "Does he know?"

Heather shook her head. "But he will as soon as I'm found missing."

"That will be the ultimate revenge, my dear Heather." He laughed. Heather smiled as if she understood his meaning, but she did not.

She did not understand the David that she was looking at, but when he smiled at her and held out his arms she went into them gratefully.

"Come, my love," was all he said as he pulled her to the straw pallet near the fire. She went with him eagerly and snuggled close as they lay down.

As he kissed her and caressed her body, she was unable to respond and it puzzled her. This had been her dream for so long. Why couldn't she feel anything?

Why wasn't fire flowing through her body as had happened with Nicholas? Heather pretended a passion she didn't feel and soon David released her. She was concerned about what she had experienced. Perhaps she was nervous, perhaps it was their surroundings. True, David was not as gentle as Nicholas had been, but she loved him, she reasoned, and that would make up for it. As she snuggled against him, she thought, *It will be better.*

Marie entered Heather's room at the usual time carrying her breakfast tray. She noticed that Heather was already up and went into the bath to see if she might be of service. To her surprise, Heather was not there. She then returned to the bedroom and looked about again. Walking over to the windows, she saw that they were not locked as they had been.

Marie ran from the room and down the stairs to Nicholas' study. She knocked on the door and without waiting for an answer rushed in.

Nicholas was sitting behind his desk working. "And what makes you burst into my study without waiting for permission, Marie?"

"I am sorry, monsieur, but it is Madam. She is gone!"

Nicholas stood up abruptly and said, "What do you mean, Marie, by gone?"

"She is not in her room, monsieur. And the window was open."

"Maybe she is in the garden. Did you check?"

Marie blushed and said, "No, monsieur, but the door to her room was locked and she could not leave by it."

"Check the garden to make sure she is not there and then send Missy to my study."

Marie gave a slight curtsy and then hurried from the room. When she did not find her mistress in the garden, she went to fetch Missy.

"Do you know where your mistress is?" Nicholas

asked Missy when she entered the study. She paled and shook her head. "Did you help her to leave this house, Missy?"

"No sir, I have not been permitted to see me mistress in over three weeks," Missy said as she shrank under his hard gaze.

"Well then, Missy, what do you know of her plans to leave this house?"

Missy shook her head again. "None, sir. She would not tell me. She only said that we would leave and be happy."

"Did she tell you where she planned to go?"

"Sir, I promised not to speak of it to anyone. The only reason that I have said what I have is that ye already know of her plan to leave," Missy said stubbornly.

"If you don't tell me, Missy, I will send you back to Bess with my blessings," Nicholas said as he towered over Missy.

She trembled visibly and said, "Please, sir, don't send me back!"

"Well, tell me then what I want to know. It's for her welfare that we must find her. She is going to have my child." Nicholas' voice broke as he said this and Missy looked up to see that he was more upset than she had realized.

She knew now that she had been right in thinking that he cared for her mistress. "To England to help the Marquis."

Nicholas shook his head and ran his hand through his thick dark hair. "Do you know how she planned to do this?"

"No sir. She would not tell me."

"Do you know if she has any friends in Paris?" Nicholas asked.

"None that I knew, sir. She never left the house."

"Missy, have you met anyone who was interested in your mistress while visiting the market?"

Missy trembled as she answered, "Piggot."

"Who is Piggot, Missy?" Nicholas said as he stopped his pacing.

"A man I met while on me way to market, sir. But he never asked about me mistress. I was the one that mentioned her, meself. He was only sympathetic about me unhappiness for me mistress."

"Missy, what did this Piggot look like?" Nicholas questioned. He had noticed a tall slim man several times across from the house as he was leaving but never paid him much attention.

"Piggot is tall and slim and was a perfect gentleman. He never tried anything with me and that's why I liked him. He did not know my mistress. I did not meet him until after she had been locked in her room." Missy watched the color heighten in Nicholas' face.

"Where can I find this Piggot, Missy?"

"I don't know, sir, he was always waiting for me when I left the house," Missy said.

"Missy, if you see this man again let me know. That will be all, Missy," Nicholas said.

Missy slipped from her chair and hurried out of the room, relieved that she had been dismissed but worried about her mistress.

Nicholas watched Missy limp from the room and then seated himself behind his desk. He did not know where to begin his search for Heather but he knew that he must find her or die trying.

The first thing he must do was to locate this man Missy called Piggot. He would write to his friend Monsieur Colbert, of the secret police. With his help Heather could be found. Colbert knew everything that went on in France and would be able to advise him. His men worked in the gutters as well as at court.

Nicholas finished his letter to Monsieur Colbert and sent it by his footman to the Colbert's house.

A thought crossed his mind as he had looked out of the study window. Heather had an unusual interest in the garden at night. Perhaps there was an entrance to it that he did not know about. He decided to explore that

250

possibility. Searching carefully, he came upon a small vine-covered area not normally in view from the house. And as he came closer, he could see that the grass and vines had been broken as if someone had walked across them recently. Then he found a small door in the wall. He now knew how Heather had escaped without anyone seeing her. Obviously she'd had help, he thought, she could not herself have climbed down from the window. If Piggot was not the answer, he did not know where to look. The man definitely had something to do with Heather's disappearance. It was too coincidental not to be so.

Heather was startled by her surroundings when she awoke. But gradually things came into focus and she wondered where David was. She rose from the pallet and went closer to the fire to warm herself. The cellar was damp and chilly. Heather threw the few remaining pieces of kindling on the fire to make it blaze and then looked about the room in hopes of finding something to eat.

. All she could find was a piece of stale bread, which she ate. But once it reached her stomach, nausea overtook her. She rushed to a dark corner and threw up. Weakly she went back to the pallet and lay down.

She didn't know whether it was day or night nor did she know how long she sat huddled on the pallet before she heard someone coming down the steps.

David was smiling as he came into the cellar. "Good morning, my love," he said. "How are feeling?"

Heather smiled up at him weakly. She said she was fine, not daring to tell David of her nausea. She was afraid he would send her away.

"Well, my love, our plans are already started. Rafael has a boat that will take us back to England tomorrow," David said as he pulled Heather to her feet.

Heather hugged David and said, "I'm so glad. We will be free of Nicholas forever and we will be home in

England again." She looked up to see that David was not smiling. "What is it, David?"

As he walked away from her, David said, "England. Yes, it's my home but I have nothing to return to. Dunhan belongs to Nicholas. The only reason I'm returning is to free my father." He then came back to Heather and took her small oval face into his hands and gazed down into her pale blue eyes. "And you will help me, Heather. We will have our revenge on Nicholas as well."

Heather pulled herself free of his hands. "I do want to help with your father's release, but there is no need for revenge on my part."

David gazed at Heather with his dark eyes as if trying to solve some enigma. "Why don't you want to be revenged? Is it that perhaps you have some feeling for Nicholas that you do not want to admit?" He pulled her to the light of the fire so he might better observe her expression.

"David, you're wrong. I have no feelings except those of contempt for Nicholas. But once your father is free I want us to be happy. Let there be no more anger."

David could not understand the expression in Heather's eyes but he accepted what she said. No matter what Heather said, though, he would be revenged on his onetime friend. He'd say no more of it to Heather. "If that is the way you feel, my love, I will agree." And he hugged her.

As the day wore on several roguish-looking characters came to see David. There was a great deal of camaraderie between David and these men. They joked and laughed as they made their plans.

Heather, not included in their conversation, observed closely how David, the son of a marquis, bantered with these common men. It was as though he'd known them all his life. How different he was from the David she had known. Then Nicholas' name came up in their talk and David's reaction was such that she felt him capable

252

of almost any cruelty. That was a more familiar David, for she had sensed his cruelty even when they were young. She could see him trying to control it, but it often surfaced. Even now she remembered how he had forced her to ride a horse knowing how much she feared them. Heather shuddered at the thought, but she pushed it from her mind. She loved David—nothing could change that.

As night approached the men left except for Piggot and the man called Rafael. She knew he was the one who was to take them back to England in his boat.

Gluck came staggering into the room carrying a basket of food. He set it on the table and then left. David turned to Heather and said, "My love, would you see to our evening meal?"

Heather opened the basket and took out a bottle of wine and some cheese, bread and sausage. She placed these on the table and said, "Is this all there is?"

David glared at her. "We are not in a fine house now, my love, and have to make do with whatever there is."

David turned to Rafael. "She still thinks of me as the future Marquis. It does not occur to her that I am a rogue of the gutter." At this both men laughed.

Heather was embarrassed. "I'm sorry," she said. "I forgot for the moment where we are."

She sliced the bread and cheese and the men ate eagerly. She nibbled at her portion, no longer hungry. As they finished, David said, "I'm forgetting my manners. Heather, this is my friend Rafael. He is the one who will take us back to England and help us free my father."

Heather smiled at the little man who sat across from them. He was short and fairly well built, with wide shoulders. He had shaggy brown hair and greedy eyes.

"Madam, it is my pleasure to be of service to someone as beautiful as you," he said.

Heather nodded to him. "Thank you. Will both you and Piggot be helping David?"

The men glanced at each other and David answered her question. "Piggot is not going to England with us. He is to remain behind and finish some business that I have already begun. Once that is done he will await our return."

"We are to return to Paris?"

"Yes. We could not remain in England. They would find us there and then we would all be in the Tower. Don't you see, this is the only place where we'll be safe."

"Safe from Charles's men," she said, "but not safe from Nicholas." Heather had moved to the fire and pulled her wrap closer about her shoulders.

David came to Heather and placed his arms around her. "My love, don't worry, we will be all right. Nicholas will not be a problem." Heather looked up into David's face. She trusted him. He would take care of her, she was sure.

The night was foggy as they set sail up the Seine and then across the channel to England. They would not reach London before the next night and Heather did her best to make herself comfortable in the small boat.

The journey to Paris had been on Nicholas' sumptuous yacht and Heather did not then have her present condition to contend with. She suffered nausea most of the time but did her best to control it so that David would not know how ill she was.

The fog grew denser as they sailed up the Thames to London, and they were able to enter the city unobserved.

As they stumbled up the London streets Heather had to rely on David's help several times. He did not seem to be hindered by the darkness or the fog and led them through the streets as if he had known and traveled them all his life.

After what seemed like an eternity, they came to a small dark inn. Heather sat down in a crude chair in front of the fire as David went to get them some ale.

She did not relish the thought of ale but needed something to calm her.

When he returned, he handed Heather a mug of ale and she drank it down without tasting its bitterness. She did not listen to the conversation between Rafael and David but sat quietly savoring the heat of the fire. Slowly she began to doze.

"My love, you are tired and I have found us a room," David said. "With a little sleep you will feel better tomorrow." Pulling her from the chair, he led her to a dirty room at the back of the inn.

Heather followed him willingly and did not notice the filthy cot that she fell onto gladly. She slept soundly through the night and most of the day. Dusk was settling across the city when she awoke.

As she looked about the grimy room, she could see that it was very small, not much larger than a closet. There were no windows, but a shuttered opening let in the fading light. Rats scurried about in the corners, and Heather had no desire to leave the cot. She watched the rosy clouds disappear from the sky. Her mind dwelled on David and meadows splashed in sunshine. Finally, the rough wooden door creaked and David appeared with a candle. "Get up, lazybones, you've slept through the day," he said happily.

Heather gladly climbed from the cot and stood up and stretched her aching limbs. "I'm sorry I slept so long, but I was so tired."

"Yes, you were dead to the world and I could not have wakened you if I had tried." He laughed as he hugged her.

She smiled at him and said, "Now I feel much better. And I'm hungry—it must be the London air."

"Yes, you must be famished, you haven't eaten in two days. So let's go down to the public room and get something into that beautiful body of yours before you die of starvation." They laughed and walked hand in hand down to the tavern below.

Heather ate every crumb on her plate and drank the

bitter ale. The meal seemed to her like a feast. It was the first time in several weeks that food had had any appeal.

Heather glanced around the tavern as she sipped the last of her ale. The room was dingy and nearly as filthy as the room in which she had slept. The customers eyed the new arrivals with open interest. Heather dropped her gaze, trembling. She had seen their kind before, from Bess's window. They were an unsavory lot, beggars and thieves, she was sure. When David had finished eating and suggested that they return to their room she was relieved.

Once the door was closed David turned to Heather and held out his arms. She went into them and he kissed her deeply. David released Heather and then went to the cot and motioned for her to come and sit beside him. Putting his arms around her, he told her that their plans were under way. "Rafael has already begun to gather information. He's been to the prison and has contacted a prisoner who will help us."

Heather looked up into his face and smiled. "Then we will be able to help your father sooner than we had thought."

David nodded his head and said, "Yes, however, I think you may be the one to find out the most vital piece of information—where my father is kept. Are you willing, Heather?" She nodded her head and he continued, "Police Inspector Hough is in charge of prisoners at the Tower. It is through him that you will gain entry into the prison and learn what we need to know. He rather thinks himself a rake, and with your charm and beauty you should have no trouble winning him over."

"But how will I go about meeting this Inspector Hough?"

"You will go to the prison to see your dear brother. You will be dressed like a lady fallen on poor times. You have lost your post and have no money with which to secure the release of your dear brother, who

256

was arrested for bad debts." David smiled before going on. "The inspector will probably suggest that you work your brother's way out of prison, and you understand what that means. However, before you have to pay that debt, you will already be in the possession of the information that we need. You will have visited your brother and he will have let you know my father's location and details about guards and how we might best enter the prison. Once this is done you shall not return to Inspector Hough." Relief showed on Heather's face as David said this. She had thought for a moment that David had meant for her to give herself to the inspector.

Heather laid her face against David's chest. She was frightened at the prospect of what she had to do; but she trusted David. He would protect her.

"Now let's forget everything," he said, drawing her down on the cot. Heather pretended to respond to his caresses and when he was satisfied he turned from her and slept. But sleep did not come as easily for Heather. She kept going over their conversation, thinking of all the possibilities for something to go wrong. After what seemed like hours she finally drifted into an uneasy sleep.

❧ Chapter Sixteen ❧

Nicholas was sitting behind his desk when the butler showed the man into the room. He gave Nicholas a rather stiff bow and said, "Monsieur Guyon, I am Jean Lurcerne. I was sent by your friend Monsieur Colbert."

Nicholas stood up and came forward. "Did Monsieur Colbert inform you as to why I need your services?"

"No, monsieur, he did not elaborate on the subject. He only said that I was to be of service to you and do it with the utmost discretion, since it was a personal matter."

"Won't you have a seat, monsieur, and I will give you the information that you need."

For a few moments neither of the men spoke and it gave Nicholas time to regard the man sitting opposite him. The man was of regular build and of average looks, the sort of person one would not pick out in a crowd or remember seeing. Nicholas suspected this made his job all the easier.

Nicholas leaned forward tensely. "Monsieur Lurcerne, I want you to find a young lady for me. It will not be easy, for I have no clues except I think a man named Piggot helped her leave my house. And, as Monsieur Colbert has said, it must be carried out with the utmost discretion. I do not want anyone to know about your investigation and you will report all your findings to me alone."

The man nodded in agreement and said, "Monsieur, if you will give me the description of the lady and tell me why you suspect this man, Piggot, of helping her, I will begin my investigation."

Nicholas described Heather for Lurcerne and told him all he knew of Piggot. As he finished the man stood up and said, "Now I will question the maid." He bowed and left Nicholas.

David woke Heather at the first light of dawn.

Heather rose from the bed and slipped on the only clothes that she had. They were dirty and she could hardly bear to put them on.

She longed for a bath, yet she knew there would be no chance of getting one in a place such as this. It appeared to her that no one in the inn knew what the word meant.

She glanced at David and realized that he was as dirty as herself. He had come a long way from the immaculate young heir of the Marquis de le Dunhan. Often during these last days Heather had wanted to question David about what had happened to him during his capture but the place and time never seemed right. She longed to know what had changed him.

Heather had not realized that she had been staring at David until he said, "What is it? I know we both look a fright but that will change today."

She smiled at him and said, "Yes, we do. I was thinking that we have come a long way from Dunhan and the two children who played together in the meadow."

He nodded his head and stroked the stubble on his

face. "Yes, we have come a long way from Dunham and it is best we do not remember those days."

Heather went to David and took his hand into hers and said, "David, what is the future going to be like?"

He kissed her hand lightly and said, "That I cannot answer, Heather. The only thing now that I know is that we must rescue my father. After that is accomplished we will go back to France or maybe to Italy and proceed from there. We will never be as rich as before. However, I have friends in many places who will help us. Don't worry your pretty head over it. Now hurry and finish dressing so we can get you the clothes you will need to meet Inspector Hough."

When she was ready they went down to the tavern and had a simple breakfast and then went out into the morning streets of London.

The fishwives were setting up their stands and the merchants were opening their shops. On this side of London the shops were not as clean as the ones Heather had observed when she had searched for a position.

Many of the beggars lay in the filthy streets sleeping off the effects of drink. Heather's stomach turned several times as they walked along, and she fought with all her strength to keep from throwing up her breakfast.

After they had gone several blocks, David led her down an alley and into a small dark dressmaker's shop. As the door closed a tiny old woman came scurrying into the room. She stopped when she saw who her customers were. "Bagaudae! Oh, Bagaudae!" she cried, embracing David in arms so short and thin she could barely get them around him.

David laughed and pulled free of her. "Lizzy, you have not changed since the last time I was in London. Do you ever?"

The old woman brushed a lock of stray white hair from her face and said in a sharp, high-pitched voice,

261

"You know I will never change and why should I want to?"

"We don't want you to, Lizzy," David said and pulled Heather forward. "Lizzy, this is Heather and she needs a new gown to make her into a fancy lady."

"I can see she does," Lizzy said, her cold, black eyes appraising Heather.

David laughed again. "She is beautiful when she isn't covered in dirt. And I know we can count on you to do your usual fantastic job on the gown."

Heather blushed at David's remark about her appearance. She knew that she looked like one of the tramps in the street but she had been unable to do anything about it. David knew it too. His comment had been thoughtless and she was embarrassed.

Stepping around David, the woman took hold of Heather's wrist and pulled her into the light. "What kind of lady would you like her to be? A duchess or countess?" She laughed.

David shook his head and said, "None of those; just a simple lady who has fallen on hard times, but the gown must be pretty even if it is simple."

Lizzy grinned at him and said, "So you're up to your old tricks, Bagaudae. When do you want it ready?"

Heather looked at David quizzically but he avoided her look.

"Today, Lizzy. Can you do it?"

She nodded her head and said, "You know it will be ready, but the price will be higher."

David laughed again and said, "See, you never change, Lizzy. Don't worry about the price; you will be paid."

Heather was puzzled, she wondered where the money would come from. She knew that David could not have much or they would not be living as they were. However, she was unable to ask him about it, for she had to spend the rest of the day being fitted for the gown.

262

After David paid for the gown and a wrap that Lizzy provided he took Heather to one of the public baths. For a little extra money she was given oils and perfume. Heather scrubbed herself vigorously to remove the filth and grime from her body. The water was not hot as she would have liked but she enjoyed the feeling of it against her skin.

When Heather finished with her bath she dressed in the lilac gown trimmed in simple black lace. The only extravagant thing about the gown was the neckline, which showed her white shoulders to perfection. Tiny black bows accented the front of the waist, making it seem smaller than it actually was; since the gown had been fitted to her new measurements her pregnancy was not as apparent.

Heather walked from the bath feeling like a new person. David had also taken a bath and dressed in new clothes. They laughed as they looked at each other, remembering how they had been.

"Now, my love, let me take you to dinner and then we will visit your dear brother in prison," David said.

Heather curtsied to him and said, "Sir, you do me an honor and I would love to see my poor wretch of a brother, for I love him dearly—though he loves his cards more than he does me." She laughed as she placed her hand on David's arm. Heather had thought they ought to visit the prison during the day, but David was anxious that they begin immediately to activate their plans.

After they dined, David hired a cab to take them to the prison. As they approached the Tower, Heather tried to calm her shaking nerves. The closer they had come to their destination, the more uncertain she became. If everything did not go as David hoped, all their lives would be in jeopardy. She would not even let herself think about that. David had said everything would work as planned, and she had to believe that, otherwise she would not be able to play her part.

The cab stopped at the gates of the prison and just

as Heather started to alight David took her hand and squeezed it. "Heather, remember, no matter how distasteful this is, you are doing this to save my father's life."

She took a hard seat across from a large paper-strewn desk. The guard informed her that the inspector would be back momentarily. Heather glanced around the large office, curious.

The room was large and austere. The only decoration was a pair of sabers hanging over the fireplace. Her attention was involuntarily focused on the large desk which she sat before. She wondered how many men had sat in the same chair and gone through grueling interrogations. Would she too be sent to the chamber of torture if she did not give the right answers? She had heard of the famous chamber and its horrors which caused even the innocent to plead guilty to charges directed against them.

Footsteps echoed down the stone corridor and then a short plump man in his middle fifties entered the room.

Inspector Hough gazed at Heather curiously as he walked toward his desk. He did not speak for a moment and then fumbled with some papers on his desk. Clearing his throat, he said, "Um, now, madam, what can I do for you?"

Heather was taken aback for a moment by his gruff manner and answered in a weak voice, "Sir, I've come to visit my brother Raoul Lyauty. I believe he is being held in your custody and I would like to know how I will be able to obtain his release."

The inspector studied Heather a moment before he answered. "Madam, I'm afraid that you cannot visit your brother, and as for obtaining his release, that will be impossible until his debts have been paid. If you are willing to pay them it will then be easily arranged."

Heather lowered her eyes as if she was embarrassed and said, "Sir, how much are these debts?"

The inspector watched Heather with an all-knowing eye. He could see that she would never be able to produce a sum large enough to cover the debts. She was a lady, he could see that despite her simple gown. The embarrassed expression told him everything that he needed to know. "The debt totals several thousand pounds."

Heather looked up at the inspector and brought her hand up to her throat as though aghast. "Sir, there is no way in which I can pay such an exorbitant sum."

The inspector chuckled beneath his breath as he raked Heather with his gaze. Leaning back into the chair and stretching his short legs beneath the desk, he said, "Then it is impossible to arrange his release." Seeing Heather's somber expression, he knew that he was on the right path and that it would be easy to manipulate a bargain with her. As Heather rose from the chair, he stood also and said, "Madam, there might be other ways of arranging for your brother's release. If you would care to take some wine with me, we can discuss things more fully."

Heather looked at Hough and her stomach churned. She could see the old familiar look of lust in his eyes as he walked around the desk. Cupping her elbow with his hand, he led her into another small room which was warmer and more cozily furnished than his office had been. This was obviously his residence, for it contained a huge four-poster bed and several cupboards. Chairs were scattered about the room and there was a small table which held a bottle of wine and several glasses.

He poured the wine and held the glass out to Heather. "Now, if you will join me we can discuss this further." She accepted the wine and sipped it as Hough pulled two of the chairs close to the table.

Heather seated herself and Hough took the remaining chair. She looked at him innocently and said, "Sir, what other means can there be to release my brother? I have no money, for he has gambled away whatever was left of our father's estate."

Hough smiled at Heather and said, "There are ways, my dear. I might be persuaded to assist in his release if I had the right incentive."

Heather gazed at him with her large blue eyes and said, "Sir, I love my brother dearly and I must help him obtain freedom, but I still do not understand."

Hough placed his arm across the back of Heather's chair and leaned forward so he might look into her eyes. "Madam, you are a beautiful woman and I should think you would understand my meaning when I say other means can be worked out if you cooperate."

Heather blushed under his direct gaze and looked down at her hands, which were tightly clasped in her lap. "I seem to understand now what you mean, sir. If you will let me visit my brother, I might be able to give you the answer that you require."

Hough let his hand drop familiarly onto Heather's bare shoulder as he smiled and said, "I think your answer will be yes, my dear. But I shall let you visit your brother, though it is against orders. Your brother is being held in the Beauchamp tower, where our more affluent prisoners are housed. It is against all rules for them to have visitors, but for you Madam Lyauty, I will break the rules. However, before you see him you must give me your word that you will give me your answer afterward so we may complete our business tonight."

As Hough's fingers caressed Heather's shoulder, she held back the revulsion that crept through her body. His touch revolted her. She forced a weak smile and her lips trembled as she answered, "You have my word, sir. And I will discuss your proposition with my brother. If he agrees, I will consent to whatever you may ask."

Hough removed his hand from Heather's shoulder and stood up. "Madam, I think that will not be necessary. If you want his freedom, I suggest that discussion remain between the two of us. Don't you agree?"

Heather could hardly keep the smile from her lips as she watched the agitation on Hough's fat face. She had wanted to make him uneasy and she had succeeded. He thought he had her exactly where he wanted her. Though Heather was frightened, some part of her enjoyed the game. He had won the moment he had come into the room but she did not want him to know it. Heather lowered her eyes to keep the mischief from showing and said, "If you insist, sir."

Now, Hough thought, *that's more like it.* For a moment she had scared him, saying that she would ask her brother. Maybe the brother would have given his permission. Most men would sell their souls to get out of the Tower. But he did not want anyone other than the young woman to know his proclivities. Blackmail was all too possible with a man like Raoul Lyauty.

He looked at Heather sitting demurely with downcast eyes and thought, *Damn me, she is a lady all right.* And he did not think he would have to worry about her repeating to anyone what went on between them.

She was beautiful and there was nothing that he appreciated more than beauty—nothing except having someone confess under torture. To Hough it was nearly the same thing as having a beautiful woman in his arms. Violence always excited him physically, heightened his sexual appetite.

"Now, if you will follow me, I will take you to see your brother," Hough said almost eagerly. The faster he got her in touch with her brother the faster he would reap his reward.

Heather followed the little man into the long dark corridors. Their footsteps echoed ominously. The few torches, placed far apart as they were, were of little help. They walked mostly in darkness.

The air was damp and chilly and Heather pulled her wrap closer about her shoulders. Several times Inspector Hough would take her by the arm to lead her in a

267

different direction and each time he would give her a familiar squeeze.

As they passed different cells, she could hear sobs and moans. Heather shivered, the sound was almost inhuman. "How could anyone escape from a place such as this?" she said in a whisper.

Heather had not realized she had spoken aloud until Hough said, "No one does, my dear. Prisoners are either released on orders or put to death." He laughed and pulled her along still another dark passage.

"Ah, my dear, you are in luck, for you will get to pass the cell of our most famous prisoner, the Marquis de le Dunhan. If you had been a day later you would have been too late."

Heather gazed at Hough in the dimness and she sensed delight in his voice which she did not understand. "What do you mean?" she asked.

Hough laughed. "Tomorrow he will be executed, if he is not dead by then. He has been ill for the past several weeks, so the King decided not to wait any longer before carrying out the sentence."

Heather did not answer. He started to lead her away from the cell when the door opened and a priest walked out. "Sir, I was just coming to inform you that the Marquis has died."

Heather could not hear the rest of the conversation that went on between the priest and Hough. The corridor began spinning and she slipped to the floor.

"No! No! No!" was the first thing Heather heard as she began to regain consciousness, and she slowly realized that it was her own voice she heard.

Tears were streaming down her face as she looked up to see Inspector Hough leaning over her with a smile on his fat face. "So, madam, you are awake. You gave us quite a scare when you fainted. You hit your head as you fell."

Her head was throbbing, and she felt a bandage over her right temple.

She looked about the room and said, "How long have I been here?" She could not tell in her dazed state whether it was the light of dawn or dusk which streamed through the lone window.

Hough sat down on the bed and said, "You have been here since last night. I'm sorry I was unable to call a physician but it was not possible since you were not supposed to be in the Tower. I hope you understand."

Heather nodded her head and started to get up from the bed, only to realize that she was naked. Pulling the sheet up around her, she said, "Who undressed me?"

Hough's smile became more prominent on his face as he leaned closer and said, "I did, madam, and it was I who bandaged your head."

Heather shrank back from him. "Thank you," she said, "and if you will get my clothes, I shall dress."

"Not so fast, my little blue-eyed impersonator."

Heather paled at his words. "I don't know what you are talking about and I insist that you allow me to get dressed."

He laughed at her and leaned closer. "You mean you don't know what I'm talking about? When you raved about the Marquis for most of the night?"

Heather felt the blood rush to her face and looked for a way of escape. Finding none, she looked back to the inspector and said curtly, "I don't know what you are talking about. I came here only to see my brother, as I told you last night."

Hough took Heather's face between his fingers and squeezed it. She recoiled in pain. This made him laugh again. "So you insist on saying you know nothing. Well, let me help you remember." He jerked the sheet from her and pulled her viciously from the bed, dragging her to the window. "Look down there and tell me you know nothing," he said.

As Heather's eyes adjusted to the light she could vaguely make out two bodies hanging from a gibbet,

269

and then she recognized what had once been Rafael. The other she assumed was Raoul.

Realizing that she was starting to faint again, he turned Heather from the window and slapped her across the face. "Oh, no you don't, my beauty, not this time. You're going to talk just as your so-called brother did."

With tears cascading down her face she tore herself from his grasp and ran to the door, to find it locked; then she turned to watch as Hough slowly came toward her. "You're going to talk and tell me everything you know about the Marquis and all his associates. I want full details of their plans. I don't like being made to play the fool." He grasped her by the wrist and threw her across the bed. She did her best to escape his probing hands but his strength was too much for her. He took her brutally, leaving her sore, bruised and feeling soiled.

Hough left her for the moment. He poured himself a glass of wine and sipped it happily. He was not finished with the young woman. He would force from her yet the names of the Marquis' accomplices. He would then have everything that his heart desired. A grateful King would be generous.

Going back to the bed, he stared down at her and watched the fear in her eyes as he slowly lowered himself onto the bed. "Please no," was all she could say before he took her once more.

After what seemed like hours, Hough finally left her alone. Heather lay on the bed naked and bruised from head to toe. She had never known that she could suffer so much pain. She wondered if she would lose her baby.

She had not thought of the baby until this moment and she looked down at her rounding stomach. Placing her hand on it, she said softly, "Please, God, let nothing happen to it." Lying back on the bed, she tried to organize her thoughts. If she only knew what Rafael and Raoul had told them before they died she would have been able to lie her way around Hough.

It was a futile thought. They were gone and she was on her own. Perhaps Hough would slip and reveal something. Perhaps she could escape. Shaking her head, she turned painfully on her side and tried to sleep.

Just as sleep was about to take her, the door opened and Hough returned. "Get up!" he shouted. Pulling Heather by the ankle, he jerked her onto the floor. "I said get up, you bitch!" Heather pulled herself to her feet with great effort and he surveyed his handiwork.

She swayed unsteadily on her feet as she stood before him. He did not let her sit down and she looked at him pleadingly. "Please, may I have something to drink?"

Standing with feet apart and his hands on his fat hips, he said, "Not now, not until you have told me all I want to know."

Heather shook her head and her golden hair fell into her face as she whispered, "I don't know anything."

"You know more than anyone else, my dear," he snarled, "and until you tell me you will receive nothing to eat or drink." Going to the door, he opened it and called, "Gaston, come here."

A tall man in uniform came into the room. "Gaston, take her to her cell, where she may contemplate on what she will tell me when we next meet."

The man he had called Gaston took Heather roughly by the arm and led her stumbling form the room. They had not given her anything to wear and as she stumbled down the dark corridors, she felt the chill of the stone beneath her feet.

When he opened the heavy door, she could see that it was a small cell with nothing but bare walls encrusted with dark green slime. The floor was cold and damp. They had not even given her a blanket to cover herself and as she walked into the cell, she trembled.

Gaston then closed and locked the heavy door and left Heather in darkness.

Heather slumped to the floor and crawled into a corner. She felt like a caged animal. The darkness was so intense that she could not see the hand she held before her. She wrapped her arms around her knees and lowered her head. She wept in terror and pain.

At the sound of the door being unlocked, Heather awoke chilled and feverish. Through her dazed state she could see Hough standing in the doorway, smiling down at her. "Now are you ready to tell me what I want to know?" She tried to speak but her throat was swollen and no sound escaped. Hough took it to mean that she refused and he pounced on his chance to inflict further punishment upon Heather.

He threw a blanket onto the bare floor, and dragged her to it. "I don't want to dirty myself." He laughed and then fell on top of her and took her again.

Hough then left. Heather wrapped the blanket around her battered body. Had he forgotten it? Would he return and rip it from her hands? No matter, at least for now she was grateful for its meager warmth. She crawled back to her corner hoping something, perhaps even insanity, would relieve the brutal reality of what she was experiencing.

She whimpered when the door opened again the next day. She was unable to move. She stared in horror as Hough entered the cell. This time he had brought a small loaf of stale bread and some water.

"Come, bitch, crawl for it," he said as he threw the food onto the floor. Seeing the bread lying at his feet, Heather did crawl over to it. But once she was within reach of the bread he kicked it aside. "Tell me or you will not eat."

Heather looked at him and it took a moment for his words to sink into her mind. She could stand no more. All of her strength and resolve left her. Through thick, swollen lips she whispered, "Phillip Hastings and Millard Fairbanks." And she went on to describe every aspect of the plot against the King.

A smile spread across Hough's face and he bent and looked into Heather's face. "I knew you would tell me. Even though your supposed brother would only tell me of Bagaudae. It confirms your prison sentence, my dear. Now you will be mine to keep and to use as I please." He laughed as he rolled onto her and took her once more. When he finished he threw her the bottle of water and then left her in darkness to search for the bread.

Heather bit off a large chunk of the bread, barely chewing before she swallowed it. The moment the bread found its way to her stomach, she retched. After a few minutes of nausea, she tried to eat once more. This time she found the water and ate more slowly, savoring every mouthful. When Heather finished, she crawled back to her blanket and wrapped it tightly around her and slept.

Days passed and grew into weeks and then months. Heather had no idea of time. With each day only came the horror of Hough's visits and then the bread and water and sometimes a piece of cheese or some rotten vegetables.

Her stomach had become prominent and she could feel the baby move. It was strong, this she knew from its kick. The baby she carried within her actually preserved her sanity. She was obsessed by it. She had to keep it alive. Each day after Hough had used her she groveled for the food he left behind.

It seemed to please him all the more that she was great with child when he took her. He would run his fat clammy hands over her swollen belly and smile and Heather would cringe at the thought that he might harm the child in some way if she displeased him.

There had been little conversation between them since she had uttered the names of the two men who had been the Marquis' accomplices. Then one day when he had brought her food, he said, "You have helped my career a great deal. I have captured the two men you named. They have confessed and been beheaded. Now all I need is to find this Bagaudae and I will have everything."

Heather did not comment but let him use her as before. She was not worried about the men who had been beheaded. She did not concern herself any longer about the Marquis' fate. She thought only of her bread and water, and of the child that grew within her.

As her time grew near, the baby grew stronger and Heather began to wonder how she would manage to have the baby alone. She was afraid to ask Hough because it might anger him and he might injure the child. Yet she made up her mind to try and find a way to question him when he brought her food that night. To her amazement he did not come, nor did he come the next day. Several times she thought she heard footsteps near the door but there was no one. She sat cowering in a corner of the cell. Then she began to scream. She continued to scream as the men came into the cell and picked her up and carried her into the sunlight.

⇜§ Chapter Seventeen §⇝

Heather awoke and blinked her eyes at the light. Glancing around with terror-filled eyes, she could see two men standing in the distance. She jumped from the bed and ran into a corner of the room and crouched there. There was fear in her face, yet she seemed ready to do battle.

The two men studied her, then looked at each other. As Heather gaged her enemies something tugged at her memory. But she did not move. She had to protect herself and her unborn child.

One of the men slowly came toward her and began to speak in a low gentle voice. "Have no fear, we will not hurt you. Come, lie down and rest. You must for the babe's sake." At the mention of the baby Heather began to whimper and to clutch her large belly. The man slowly came closer and then picked her up and carried her back to bed. Laying her down gently, he then covered her body with a soft sheet. She continued to watch him with fearful eyes.

Gazing down into the too thin face and the fearful

blank eyes, he sighed. "Only a cruel, vicious, inhuman creature could so brutally have done this to her." Shaking his head, he went back to his friend.

"Monsieur Lurcerne, have you found out anything about this Bagaudae?"

"No more than I have you told you, monsieur. It seems as if he vanished into thin air. But as the king of the rogues I'm sure he will turn up sooner or later in some part of London."

"I want it sooner and I want to make him pay for what he has done to her," Nicholas said as he turned back to Heather. She continued to stare at them fearfully.

"I understand and I will do my best to uncover this rogue." Lurcerne picked up his hat to leave and as he opened the door he paused and turned back to Nicholas. "Monsieur Guyon, you will not be returning to Paris?"

"No, Lurcerne, I will be here in London until all has been settled."

"Then, monsieur, I will notify you here at your townhouse as soon as I have any information."

Nicholas watched the man leave and then went over to the table and poured himself a glass of brandy. He then walked to the chair beside the bed and sat down. Heather stared at him until sleep possessed her. The drug that Missy had given her earlier had worked, to Nicholas' relief. He could not bear the look in Heather's eyes much longer and he yearned to find this Bagaudae and squeeze the life from him with his bare hands.

As he watched the sleeping girl toss restlessly on the bed his thoughts returned to the time when Lurcerne had informed him of her whereabouts.

When Lurcerne entered the study in his house in Paris, Nicholas was unable to believe what the detective told him. He had tracked down Piggot and made him confess that he had knowledge of the girl's whereabouts. After learning that she had made her way back to England, he had gone there and found that she had been in the company of a man called Bagaudae. There was talk of her involvement in a plot to free the Marquis. He had heard rumors from some of the unsavory populace of London that a beautiful girl had been seen to enter the Tower and disappear. After that he had been unable to find any information concerning the girl, and that was the reason for his return to Paris to consult with Nicholas.

Nicholas sat and stared at the detective for a few moments without speaking, and then, slamming his fist down onto the desk, said, "Damn, where in this bloody world could she have gone?"

The detective shook his head and said, "That I cannot answer, unless she is being held without knowledge in the Tower. And that is one place I am unable to enter without some influence."

Nicholas walked to the fireplace and kicked a log with the tip of his boot. Then turning to Lurcerne, he said, "I can arrange those matters. We will go to England as soon as I finish some of the business I have at the Embassy. That should not take over a day or so. Be prepared to leave by then."

Lurcerne bowed to Nicholas and said, "I will be ready to leave when you say. Now I believe I will have another talk with that rogue Piggot, and squeeze some information from him about this Bagaudae."

After Lurcerne left Nicholas, he dressed and called for his carriage. The business of state had to be finished before he would be able to go to London. He must go to Versailles and request an audience with the King.

On the journey through Paris, Nicholas wondered at the possibilities of Heather's escape. But soon the carriage was on the road to Versailles and he repressed his personal concerns and began to think of the urgent business ahead of him.

Nicholas was shown through the palace and waited as the page went to announce his presence to the King. It was not long before he returned to show Nicholas to the apartments of the King.

As he entered the magnificent chamber, Nicholas could see the King relaxing in one of the gilded white chairs that he was making stylish.

Nicholas bowed deeply and looked up to see King Louis smiling.

"You may rise, Captain Guyon. I know we must hold with tradition and etiquette, but as you can see we are among friends. Come and join us."

"Thank you, Your Majesty. I am most honored to be allowed to intrude upon your leisure. If it had not been imperative, I would not have disturbed you." Nicholas approached the small group that surrounded the King.

"But you do sound as if I must now end our little relaxation and be pressed back into the ritual of work." Louis waved his attendants away. The musicians and courtiers who had been entertaining the King scurried to the doors.

"I'm afraid, Your Majesty, that I am here to do just that, with your permission," Nicholas said with another slight bow.

Louis laughed and said, "That is what I have always liked about you Captain Guyon, your directness. Not like most of my courtiers, who take all day and half the next to ask or request even the slightest favor."

"Your Majesty is most kind."

"No, not kind, but also direct. So let us dispense with this flattery and get to the heart of the subject that brings you here." Louis indicated a chair for Nicholas.

The Englishman smiled and seated himself across from the King.

"Your Majesty, I have come to you on the behalf of my royal sovereign, King Charles. As you have been informed, the Dutch have been trying to usurp England's rule over the seas and have also had the effrontery to attack England itself. I have been informed that Your Majesty and my sovereign have come to an agreement of terms which shall be signed into a treaty."

Louis leaned back in the chair and pressed his hands together. Looking at Nicholas he said, "You have been informed correctly, but this was settled several weeks ago while the Duke of Monmouth was here."

Nicholas nodded in agreement with Louis's statement, then said, "Yes, Your Majesty, I am aware of that, yet now there have been some unforeseen happenings and if it could be agreed upon there must be another treaty signed which shall camouflage the previous one. This one shall make no mention of King Charles's religion."

A frown creased King Louis's brow as he said, "And what unforeseen happenings have arisen to cause such concern about the treaty?"

Nicholas explained all of the exigencies involved in England's domestic situation and then waited for Louis's reply.

Louis did not speak for a few moments and the frown deepened on his forehead as he thought. "Captain Guyon, I see the reason for Charles's concern and am willing to agree that it might be advisable to camouflage our treaty, yet I will have to consult my ministers and then make my decision. I will inform your King as soon as the decision is made."

Realizing the audience was over, Nicholas rose from his chair and said, "Thank you, Your Majesty. I shall inform King Charles as soon as I return to England." Bowing deeply once again, Nicholas backed from the King's apartments. He went directly to his townhouse to prepare for his journey back to England.

Two days later, as the first birds of spring began their morning song, Nicholas and Lurcerne boarded his yacht. It had been eight months since Nicholas had been to England and he was looking forward to seeing his homeland. Despite the unpleasantness of his errand,

Nicholas enjoyed the crossing. He had always loved the sea; it seemed to have a soothing effect on his nerves.

As a boy, he had spent many wonderful days sailing with his uncle—until the rift developed between them over his mother. Since then pleasure cruises had lost their appeal and he only used his yacht for special journeys.

The warm spring breeze fanned his face as he scanned the horizon for the English coast. The day was peaceful and his life would be at peace were Heather by his side. The tranquillity of the scene was shattered by the screech of a seagull as it dipped into the water intent upon its prey. Nicholas studied it for a while and then became aware of the blue water, so much like the color of Heather's eyes.

Nicholas did not completely understand the hold that Heather had on him but he knew that he must find her, especially now that she carried his child.

Lucerne joined him on deck as they approached the coastline. The sun cast a multitude of colors across the evening sky, but Nicholas' mind was not on the glories of nature. "If she's anywhere in London, we will find her."

Lurcerne looked at the young man and wondered at his determination to find this young woman. "Oui, we will find her," he said simply. They did not speak again until they reached London and then only briefly, for both had things to do before going the next day to the prison.

Nicholas went first to his townhouse and sent the footman with a message that he sought an audience with the King. The footman returned with word that the King would see him the next morning. Nicholas was relieved that he would be able to get such an early appointment with the King. That meant he would be able to search for Heather by tomorrow afternoon at the latest. He went to his bedchamber still agitated and anxious but hoping to get some much needed rest.

Nicholas tossed about for hours. Over the past

months Heather had been in his thoughts constantly and until now there had been no word of her whereabouts. Now they were close to finding Heather, Nicholas could sense it. He wanted so much to see her face, to put his arms around her and hold her close. With these thoughts he finally slept.

The next morning he awoke early and went to the palace to deliver the message from King Louis about the treaty and to receive permission from the King to search the Tower for Heather.

As soon as he was allowed to absent himself from Charles's presence, Nicholas rushed back to his house to send word to Lurcerne to meet him at the Tower.

The sun was shining brightly as they walked into the cold dark Tower and asked to see Inspector Hough.

Hough was seated behind his desk when they entered his office and he stood to greet them. After the formalities, Nicholas came to the point of their visit. When he asked the inspector about a young woman who had been seen entering the prison but not coming out again, Hough paled. He denied having knowledge of any such woman. He assured them that he would have known if such a person had come, as he was informed of all visitors.

Nicholas asked Hough if he would be so kind as to let them search the prison. Inspector Hough began to perspire and wiped his forehead with his hand. He could not grant such a request, he told Nicholas.

"Well, sir, I think you should read this," Nicholas said as he handed Hough the writ from the King. He watched the inspector as he read and could see that his agitation had increased. This only added to his certainty that they were close to finding Heather. The inspector grudgingly gave his consent to the search but refused to aid in any way.

The first day had been their worst, for they had not been prepared for the horrors they witnessed. As they passed down the long stone corridor they could hear the moans of the prisoners. Long skinny hands, covered in so much filth that it was hard to determine the color of the skin, reached out imploringly. Some begged for food and water, others pleaded for release and still others asked only for death. And as they unlocked each cell door to inspect it Nicholas and Lurcerne were appalled at the filth and vermin inside. In many of the cells they came upon men who had already lost all their sanity. On several occasions they found men who had been dead for days. They later discovered that guards had failed to note that there was no sound of life coming from the cell and continued to remove food trays which had been cleaned by the rats. Nicholas' stomach rebelled at what he was seeing and he quickly fled back into the corridor. Yet he returned to the search and continued until exhaustion forced him to stop.

The next day turned up one interesting fact. The inspector had disappeared. They returned to their search convinced that they would be successful. But after another day of searching through the quagmire of human excretion and mold and mildew with rats and cockroaches scurrying in the darkness, they still had not found Heather. Night had fallen as they walked from the Tower. They had only one small section left to explore. If she was not there they could think of nowhere else to look.

When they entered the prison the next morning the spring sun was bright and warm and it seemed to caress the earth, to bring forth the sleeping life which lay beneath. Nicholas' spirits had risen. They would find Heather. They did not waste time but went directly to the Beauchamp tower. Each went to different sections and searched each cell. As the afternoon began to pass their hopes began to diminish. And then they heard the screams.

Now as he sat and watched her sleep, he longed to find the man called Bagaudae and make him suffer for the torment that he could see in Heather's face. The man had to be somewhere in London and he was determined to find him. But before he ended his miserable life, he would find the answers to some of his questions.

The man called Bagaudae had to be connected in some way with the Marquis, but he could not understand how. The King had informed him that Fairbanks and Hastings had been captured and that both had been executed for their treachery. Neither had known anything of Bagaudae.

Slowly he reached out and took one of Heather's small, thin hands into his and gently brushed it with his lips. Even in sleep, she trembled from the touch. He released her hand and placed it where she might feel the child. This seemed to comfort her and she released a sigh. Nicholas slowly shook his head and then leaned it against the back of the chair. He was tired, but kept his vigil. He had been at her side since the day he carried her from the prison. And he would remain there, he promised himself, until she was well again.

Missy had been of valuable service to him and he was glad that he had sent for her as soon as he had found Heather. He did not know what he would have done if she had not known how to help Heather sleep. He had called his physician, who had been of no assistance at all. He could only recommend that she be bled, and Nicholas would have none of it. He knew she needed what little strength she possessed and bleeding would only serve to weaken her more.

When Nicholas awoke, it was to find a pair of pale blue eyes staring at him in puzzlement. He smiled at Heather and said, "How are you feeling?" He received no answer but had not expected one. Yet it seemed that some of the fright she had shown before had diminished. He smiled again and gently touched her hand, but she quickly withdrew it. "I will not harm you," he said gently, but said no more. He would not force her to regain her memory. Reality might only make her withdraw even further.

Nicholas slowly rose from his chair and rang for

Missy. She would perhaps be more comforting, for there had been a friendship between them that had not existed between Heather and himself.

When Missy entered the room Nicholas asked, "When do you think the child is due?"

Missy shook her head and said, "That I do not know, sir, but by the looks it should not be long from now. But I'm no midwife and don't know much about these things except what I learnt from me ma and all her bairns."

Nicholas moved back to the bed, a worried expression on his face. "See that she has everything she needs, and notify me if there are any changes in her condition. I will be in my study."

Missy went into the adjoining room to prepare a warm bath for Heather. When she returned Heather was not in her bed. As she glanced around, she saw the door was ajar. She quickly ran into the hall just in time to see Heather going down the stairs wrapped in a blanket. "Miss!" she called, but Heather did not slow her pace. Missy did not know what to do except scream for Nicholas who had already heard the commotion in the hall and had walked from his study. He caught Heather just as she reached the main door. Picking her up in his arms, he carried Heather screaming and kicking back upstairs to her room.

Once he had managed to calm her, he turned to Missy in a rage. "What in the bloody world do you mean in letting her leave this room?"

Missy paled as she looked at Nicholas. "Sir, I did not think she would leave her bed, and was preparing her bath. In her condition I didn't think she would be able to leave the room. But it won't happen again, I promise ye."

Scowling at Missy, Nicholas said, "It had better not or you will regret the day you ever made such a mistake. I grant you that. She must be watched so no harm comes to her. Do you understand?"

Missy nodded. "Yes sir."

With that Nicholas said, "Well then, see to your mistress." He then stalked from the room, slamming the door behind him.

Descending the stairs, Nicholas suddenly realized why he had lost his temper. When he had seen Heather running toward the door, he feared he would lose her. He couldn't stand that again, for he loved her.

☙ *Chapter Eighteen* ❧

The drapes fluttered in the warm spring breeze, and the full moon cast its luminous rays onto the bed in which Heather lay bathed in perspiration. The pains of birth had begun at sunset and now they had intensified until she whimpered and tossed about on the bed. The pains became stronger and Heather began to scream.

Missy wiped the perspiration from Heather's brow with a cool cloth and did her best to calm her. Nicholas sent for the midwife but she had not yet arrived.

As Missy watched Heather writhing in pain, her own fears increased. She had never helped deliver a baby before. Her mother had been pregnant every year, but Missy had been too small to assist in the actual births. All she knew about the birth of a child she had gotten secondhand—overheard discussions and whisperings. She had listened carefully and remembered much of what she had heard, but she was afraid to handle the birth of Heather's child by herself. Nicholas had stayed with her until Heather had screamed. Then he had paled and left the room abruptly. Missy was now alone and afraid.

Nicholas paced the floor of his study and waited. The brandy decanter stood on the table with half its contents gone. He had drunk it without realizing or feeling its effects. He had tried to occupy his time by reading but could not concentrate on the words before him. Finally he had given up and started his wearisome pacing, until he heard a scream more piercing and agonizing than the others.

Rushing from the study and up the stairs, Nicholas burst into the room to see a small, pink, squirming creature being held by its feet as Missy slapped its bottom.

As the babe let forth its first cry it was a heart-stirring experience for Nicholas. He walked quickly across the room and took the child into his arms. He turned to Missy with a smile that would have lit up the world. "My son, Nicholas Guyon II," he said with pride. Then looking to Heather he ordered Missy to see to her mistress. "I shall tend the babe until you have finished."

As he walked to the fire, the midwife burst into the room, flustered. Observing the scene, she slowed her pace and went to the bed to tend her patient.

Missy took the babe from Nicholas. "He is a fine bairn, sir. And has the look of his father about him. By the looks of his eyes they will be like his mother's.

Nicholas was filled with emotion. For a moment the words wouldn't come. At last he said, "Yes, he is a fine boy. How is his mother?"

Missy glanced back to Heather as the midwife made her comfortable. She was sleeping peacefully for the first time since she had been brought from the dungeon. "She is resting now and will do just fine, sir. Her labor was not as bad as we had thought it might be. We be lucky that it wasn't because that lazy woman did not arrive in time. But I did me best, sir."

Nicholas nodded his head and said, "Yes, you did, Missy, and you'll receive a new frock for it."

Nicholas glanced once more at the child and then went to Heather's side. Gazing down at the golden curls clingling damply to her forehead, he gently brushed them with his hand and then bent and kissed her lightly on the lips. She did not stir. How lovely and innocent she looked, now that the lines of pain had left her face. She was again the young woman he remembered and loved. And at that moment, he loved her move than he had ever thought possible.

The morning sun seemed brighter and the day more cheery for Missy as she watched the child nuzzle at its mother's breast. It fed hungrily and Heather watched contentedly. She had seemed herself this morning even though she had not yet spoken. Missy's one consolation was that Heather had smiled at her when she had given her the infant to feed.

As Missy watched a slight tap came at the door and Nicholas entered. Heather did not look up but kept her attention focused on the babe. When Nicholas saw Heather and the child bathed in the morning sun his face shone with pride. He walked slowly to the bed and stared down at the two for a few moments before he spoke. "Heather, he's a beautiful child."

At the sound of his voice Heather looked up, smiled and said, "Thank you." Then she once more looked to her babe.

Nicholas was pleased. "She has improved," he said to Missy. "The coming of the babe may be the very thing that is needed to bring her back to the person we knew."

Missy nodded her head at Nicholas and beamed. "Aye, sir, she even smiled at me this morn."

Heather's gaze rested one moment on the two people speaking across the room and the next on the child that fed at her breast. Totally relaxed for the first time in months, dim recollections began to shape themselves within her mind.

She felt that she had known the girl and had been friends with her. She could not remember when or where she had known her but she was certain that she had. As for the gentleman, he engendered in her a desire to flee. What he had done, she could not say, but there was a feeling of unease, of suffocation, something akin to being locked in a dark cold place.

As Missy and Nicholas glanced back at Heather, she quickly lowered her eyes and resumed her watch over the child. She caught shreds of their conversation and she tried desperately to piece together something that made sense. But nothing they said had any meaning except the name Bagaudae. The man asked the girl if she knew anything about someone called Bagaudae. The girl denied having any knowledge of such a person.

After a while the man returned to her bedside. But when Heather did not raise her eyes to him, he left the room.

The child slept peacefully in Heather's arms, but Missy came and took him from her so she could also rest. She gratefully released the babe into Missy's care and leaned back into the pillows. Her strength had not yet returned. Before long she slipped into a restful sleep, only to be awakened by a dream. She was with a man and someone repeatedly called him Bagaudae.

As the weeks passed Nicholas continued to visit Heather each day. She did not speak to him again after that first day but listened intently to the conversations between him and Missy. Heather hoped to hear more about the man called Bagaudae.

As Heather's strength increased, she was allowed to go downstairs to the dayroom so she might enjoy the sight of the garden. It was spring and everything was in bloom. Missy stayed close by should Heather decide once more to leave the house. However, she was fairly certain this would not happen. Heather would not go without the child.

One morning they were in the garden when they heard voices coming from the study. Listening closely, Heather recognized Nicholas' voice, but did not know who the other man was. Missy did not try to get her to go back into the house when she heard the two men speaking. She was as interested in their conversation as Heather. She also did not think Heather was paying any attention to what they were saying.

Nicholas did not see the two women in the garden and continued talking to Monsieur Lurcerne. "Have you learned anything of Bagaudae?" he asked as he motioned for the detective to have a seat.

Lurcerne nodded his head. "Only one small item that could be of interest, but it led nowhere after I checked into it. He is still in hiding but I have reason to believe he will surface soon. I saw the man Piggot in a tavern on the lower side of the city yesterday. Luckily he did not see me and I was able to follow him to a small dress shop. He remained there for some time and then went back to the tavern. I have a man watching him now."

Nicholas looked grim as he said, "Do not let him slip through your fingers. He will be the one to lead us to Bagaudae." Slamming down his fist on the desk, Nicholas continued, "This time we will capture him. Do you understand, monsieur?"

The detective nodded his head and said, "Yes, we are bound to find him this time."

In the garden Heather's mind was spinning. The name Bagaudae brought with it this time the memory of love. And mention of the dress shop rekindled a walk down a street with David. There was some errand they had to accomplish. A frown wrinkled Heather's brow as the name of David came into her mind. Gradually the feeling arose that the two names belonged together. Bagaudae and David were the same person and she loved him and had loved him most of her life. A wave of dizziness overwhelmed her. She placed a hand to her temple as though to stop the reeling, then looked at Missy to see if she had noticed anything. Fortunately Missy was intent on listening to the conversation of the two men.

Heather knew that she had to be alone for a while to sort out her thoughts. Slowly she rose and went into the house and up to her room. Missy watched her go, but was reluctant to follow. She was intrigued by what she was overhearing. Still, she knew her duty—and the consequences of its neglect. She glanced once more in the direction of the study before she followed Heather into the house.

Heather lay on the bed trying to sleep, but flashes of the past spun around in her head. As the pale gray light of dawn seeped into the room, Heather lay exhausted, but things had begun to sort themselves out.

Tears slid down her cheeks as she remembered the death of the Marquis and her cold dark months in the cell at the Tower. She realized that she was once more in the hands of Nicholas and that he had hired men to search for David. She also knew that she must take her child and seek out David herself and warn him of the danger that lay ahead.

Quietly Heather slipped from her bed and dressed herself. Missy was sleeping in the adjoining room and she knew that she must not make a sound.

She went to the wardrobe and took what few clothes she and the child possessed and wrapped them in a small bundle. Then she went to the heavily carved crib and took the babe and dressed it warmly and wrapped it in a soft warm blanket.

Heather stealthily made her way out of the house and walked swiftly in the direction of the city.

In the early morning, Heather was unhampered by street crowds and in a little over an hour she had reached the tavern. How she knew the way she could not have said, but her feet carried her in the right direction.

As she walked into the tavern the child squirmed in her arms, wanting its morning meal. Heather was also beginning to feel the need of rest. The exertion of the walk had taken its toll on her meager strength, and she felt shaky.

She approached a strong and burly-looking man who was dozing at the bar, and tried to regain her composure.

Her hand came forward to shake the man awake when she heard someone clear his throat as if about to speak to her. She turned with a start to look into a pair of dark eyes. "Heather, what are you doing here? I thought you were dead," David said as he reached for her and she came into his arms.

It took Heather a few moments before she was able to speak and the child squirmed between them and David had to release her. "I was looking for you." A dark brow rose questioningly as he looked down at her and then at the babe. She also glanced down at the child and said, "I mean we were looking for you," giving him a weak smile.

"Well, let's not stand here. I will take you to my room so we may talk," David said as he led her up the stairs. The room was located at the back of the tavern where no one would be likely to disturb them. It also had a door leading out to the alley behind the tavern, which David checked should he need to escape. Perhaps Heather had been followed.

When Heather had seated herself on the small cot and begun to let the babe nurse, she saw David watching with interest. She could not read his expression, but it was similar to the one he'd had when he learned she was with child. She did not speak and David noticed that he was being observed and smiled at her. "Now, my love, we can talk. I can hardly believe you are here. We thought you dead also when we heard of Rafael's abrupt departure. How did you escape and where have you been?"

Heather shook her head and smiled at David and

said, "It's a long story but the main thing I want to say is that I've come to warn you. What has happened to me does not matter, but I've come to tell you that you are in danger."

David stood and came to Heather, looking down into her worried eyes. "What are you talking about? Why am I in danger?"

Heather looked at the cold, deadly expression that had come into David's eyes as she answered, "Nicholas has hired someone to search for you."

David did not move and smiled at Heather, but there was no warmth in the smile. "How do you know this?"

"I heard them talking as I sat in the garden yesterday morn. I have been at Nicholas' for a while but I cannot tell exactly how long I have been there because I am still a little uncertain of some things. It was only last night that I was able to remember what had happened to me. I lost my memory while locked in the Tower."

David looked at Heather in surprise and said, "You mean you were locked in the Tower?"

Heather nodded her head and said, "Yes, since the night I went there to help your father. That was the night he died, and they found that I was involved with him. I don't know exactly how long I was locked in the cell, but Nicholas found me there and took me to his house. The child was born there."

David dropped down on one knee beside Heather and pulled her into his arms as he said, "My dear Heather, you have been through hell, but Nicholas must love you or he would not have sought you out after all that time. How does he feel about the babe?"

Heather glanced at the small pink bundle, sleeping peacefully on the cot, and said, "He has been to see the child each day but I don't know how he feels."

David looked down at the babe and then back to Heather, and smiled at her. "Oh, I think he cares a great deal about you both."

294

Heather shook her head as she looked into his smiling face. "No! I don't think we mean anything to him. We are possessions and he is not yet ready to release us. He is angry that I escaped the first time."

As David stood up and shook his head, Heather reached out and took his hand into hers. She rubbed it against her cheek and said, "His reasons don't matter now. The main concern is that you are in danger and must escape before his men find you."

David looked down at the lovely young woman before him and said, "Don't worry your pretty head on my behalf. There have been many who have sought me and failed." Pulling her to her feet, he continued, "But we will go now before anyone is about."

Gathering the baby and her few belongings into her arms, Heather followed David through the door into the alley. They walked through the litter-strewn alley for some time until they came to the back of the dress shop that he and Heather had visited months before. This time he did not knock on the door but opened it and walked in. He motioned for Heather to follow.

David moved through the shop with ease, unhampered by the bundles of cloth that were stacked everywhere. As they approached the back of the shop, David opened a door that led down into what Heather presumed to be the cellar.

She shivered as she followed David down the stairs. It reminded her of the prison. When they reached the bottom of the steps, David opened another door which led into several different rooms. The first room had a fireplace from which emanated a warm glow. There were several chairs placed around the fire looking as though they had recently been occupied.

Heather stopped for a moment in front of the fire to rid herself of the morning chill. David motioned for her to follow him into the adjoining room. Here there were only a bed and a straw pallet.

Turning to Heather, David said, "Lay the babe on the pallet. He will be comfortable enough there."

Heather looked at the pallet and then down at her child and said, "He will take a chill lying on the pallet. Can he not sleep with me on the bed?"

David came over to Heather and took the babe from her arms. "He will later, my love, but now I will be the one to share your bed." He bent his head and kissed her and then placed the baby on the pallet. Coming back to Heather, he took her into his arms and kissed her deeply. He then led her to the bed.

As David made love to her, Heather could not keep from thinking of the babe lying on the cold pallet and of the warm crib that she had taken it from to come in search of David.

When David was satisfied he rolled from her and was instantly asleep. As Heather lay beside him she glanced at her baby. It was awake once more and wanted to be fed. She slipped from the bed and went quickly to the pallet. Bending down, she picked up the child and held him to her breast and crooned to him softly one of the old lullabies that she had learned many years before.

As she started to take the child back to her bed, she stopped as she saw David watching her. He was looking at her strangely and then said, "I forbid you to ever sing that song again. Everything about my past must be forgotten. I am not the same person I was. There will be no future Marquis. I only have one thing left to do to bring my past to a close and that will soon be done."

Heather nodded her head as she realized David's pain. She must not remind him of the past. As she sat down on the bed with her child, he continued, "I hate everything and everyone that has anything to do with the past, especially Nicholas Guyon. But that will soon be taken care of also."

Heather looked at David and realized for the first time that the strange expression that sometimes played on his face was hate. And she knew that it was directed at her as much as anyone. She shuddered and clutched her child closer to her breast.

David glanced down at the child that Heather held in her arms. "And I will not have Guyon's bastard in my bed, so take the child back to his pallet."

Heather gazed at David in disbelief. "You cannot mean what you say! My baby will become ill if he is left to sleep on that cold damp pallet. If he sleeps there so will I!"

David threw back his head and laughed. "Oh no you will not, for you are here for one reason and that is to warm my bed. If you care for the child you will not question my decisions in the future. If you don't do as I say I will slit the child's throat, as I plan to slit his father's."

Heather abruptly jumped up from the bed and ran to the door to find that David had locked it. He was reclining on the bed casually, watching her. "David, I don't understand. This is not like you; you have always been a kind person."

David looked at the young woman standing against the door, clutching her babe to her breast. He laughed once more. "You're a fool, my dear Heather. I was never the person you conjured up in your mind. And being a slave of the Saracens certainly does not improve one's character. Were my father alive, perhaps I'd feel different. But you and Nicholas Guyon helped destroy my father and with him my hopes for the future." He laughed cruelly and continued, "Yes, you and Nicholas finished it for me. He had my father arrested and you betrayed him even in death. I know you were the one who revealed the plot against the King, so don't deny it. And, on a more personal level," he added venomously, "I loved you, but you chose to bed down with Nicholas and bear his child."

Heather shook her head in denial. "You must listen to me. I am not responsible for what has happened." She wanted desperately for him to understand and to forgive.

But David would not hear her out. "Can you deny the bastard you hold to your breast? Did you think I wouldn't know where you were when you did not return from the prison the night my father died?"

Heather turned ashen as he spoke. It was futile to explain what had happened to her. He really didn't want to hear. He had known all along where she had been and had made not the slightest effort to rescue her. His display of affection had been a farce. She meant nothing to him. What a fool she had been. How misplaced her love had been all these years. He had never returned her feeling, even when they were children. He was the Marquis' son and loved only the legacy now denied him.

David laughed at her expression and then lurched at her, wrenching the infant from her arms. "I will bash the child against the wall if you deny it any further." Heather had no choice. Her child's life was in jeopardy. She would have to agree to whatever he wanted. She accepted all blame.

But David was not finished with her. "You are mine now," he said. "And anything I ask of you you will do."

"Anything," Heather sobbed, "only don't hurt my baby."

Kicking her away from him, David looked once more at the babe before handing it back to its weeping mother. Heather held the child so close to her breast that it began to whimper. She trembled and tears flowed freely down her cheeks as she tried to comfort the child.

"Yes, my dear Heather, you will do my bidding."

For the first time in her life, Heather was aware of true hatred. She found it hard to contain the feeling, to be in the same room with the man she so loathed. And as she watched David she began to realize what folly it had been to hold on to childish dreams. Why hadn't she seen how the Marquis and David had used and abused her? The Marquis had said he felt as if she were his daughter. Perhaps that was true to a certain extent, but he had also used her to ward off the loneliness that he felt after the loss of his beloved son. He did not love her for herself, but for what she could and did do for him. David had used her in every way. Had he loved her as he said, Heather thought, he would not have behaved as he had. His motives were much the same as those of the Marquis, except he was more cruel.

Heather studied David carefully. She wondered what he would do next. "Come to bed and leave the babe," he said. Slowly Heather laid her child back on the straw pallet and came to him. As she drew close he reached out and pulled her roughly onto the bed.

After he had finished using her, he said, "Remember what I told you." He then turned on his side and slept.

❧ Chapter Ninteen ❧

As David slowly awoke and stretched, he turned toward Heather and smiled. The smile tore at her heart. He looked like the youth she had loved so dearly but now she knew that he had never been the person she thought him to be.

"Now are you ready to begin work? It is nearly night and that's when the King goes about his business." Heather looked at David with a puzzled expression. "What do you mean?" she asked.

David laughed as he wrapped his hands into the long golden curls of Heather's hair. "You shall see, you will be of much service to us." Then, running his hand quickly down the slim curve of her side, he said, "Yes, my dear, after you are dressed a little more elegantly you will be a great help."

Heather looked into David's face but was unable to find any answer to her questions; then she glanced back to her babe lying on the pallet. "But who will look after my child if I go with you?" she asked.

David rose from the bed saying, "I will send one of

Lizzy's girls down and she will care for the babe. Now feed him and I will escort you upstairs so you can be fitted for your gown."

Heather picked up the child and carried it back to the bed. As she looked at the thatch of black hair that lay soft as down on its small head, she could see the resemblance to another dark head. As she watched the babe suckle, she began to understand many things that she had refused to see in her blind love for David. Even Missy had begged her to see them but she had refused. She had run from the only person who had ever shown her kindness without expecting anything in return. As she looked back she could see that he had wanted her to be happy. Yes, Nicholas had been kind to her, she thought.

She had not named the child and did not know of Nicholas' assumption that he would be called after him. But as she watched the babe at her breast, she called him softly under her breath, "My Nicholas." After he had finished and slept soundly in her arms, she once more placed him on the pallet and turned to see David watching her closely with the now familiar expression playing on his face.

"Come," was all he said as he walked through the doorway.

When they entered the small shop, Lizzy was scurrying about working with different materials for gowns and giving orders to the young girls who worked for her. It was a moment before she noticed that they had come into the room. When she saw them the frown that had creased her forehead a few minutes before disappeared as she awkwardly shuffled toward them.

Holding out her wrinkled hand to David, she said, "Oh, Bagaudae, ye handsome devil, I thought ye were going to sleep yer bloody life away. Now we must rush to have everything ready for tonight."

David took the thin hand into his and raised it to his lips as if she were a queen. "Ah, my dear Lizzy, I know I can depend on you to have everything that will

302

be needed. There isn't anything that you cannot do." And turning to Heather he said, "By looking at her you would think her no more than a simple dressmaker, but we consider her queen of the rogues. She has a hand in every unsavory plot that takes place in London."

Lizzy giggled like a small girl and then slapped David's hand playfully as she said, "You are a devil, Bagaudae, and if I am queen you are surely king, are you not?"

At this David threw back his head and laughed. "Yes, I guess you are right. Now we must hurry and finish her so the king can rule over his throne and let his servants pay homage to him." They both chuckled at this.

Heather did not join in the merriment but stared as they bantered back and forth. She could not keep her mind on what they were saying, for her thoughts kept traveling back to the cellar, where her babe lay on the cold pallet unattended.

David glanced once more at her and said to Lizzy, "Have one of your girls tend the babe while we are out. My beauty here will not be able to do her job to perfection if she is worried over the child."

Lizzy turned to one of the girls and said, "Jenny, go down and see to the babe." As the girl passed them Heather was nearly overcome by the stink of her unwashed body and the sight of festering sores on her hands and arms. She shivered at the thought of the girl touching her child. But she knew that it would do no good to protest, and would only add to David's pleasure to know that she did not approve of Lizzy's choice.

Turning once more to Heather, Lizzy said, "Follow Flossy there and she will help you dress." Heather did as she was told. She and Flossy walked up a short flight of stairs that led to what Heather presumed to be Lizzy's living quarters.

When Flossy opened the door, Heather knew that

she had been right. The room was richly furnished, though cluttered with every sort of object that Lizzy might have thought had value.

Heather surveyed the room, cataloging its contents. On each table several pairs of gold candelabras stood among numerous silver trays. One table alone held three silver tea services, and as Heather walked closer to the dressing table she could see that it was strewn with jewels. Heather reached out to touch a delicate pearl necklace that lay on the edge of the table. As she did so, her hand was violently slapped by Flossy. "Ye are to touch nothing, especially Madam's jewels."

Heather rubbed her hand where an angry red welt had already begun and stepped away from the table. "Come on, girl," Flossy said. "Ye don't have all night and it will be me hide if I don't get ye dressed soon." Heather walked across the room to where Flossy waited with a ruby-red velvet gown and black satin slippers. She helped Heather remove her own garments and then slipped the gown over her head. Flossy then pulled a small stool forward for Heather to sit down; then she proceeded to arrange her golden hair high on her head. After that was done she took one small diamond from a case on a nearby table and fastened it around Heather's neck.

The diamond brought back memories of her first night in Paris and her throat constricted at the thought of what a fool she had been. If she had only known, things might have been different. She now realized that there were worse things that could happen to a girl than being Nicholas Guyon's mistress—perhaps even his wife?

A smile brightened her face as the thought streaked through her mind. Yes, she would like to be Nicholas' wife, to raise his son, who would grow up to be much like his father.

Flossy brought her back from her daydreams abruptly as she said, "Come on, girl, it's time for ye to go." Opening the door for Heather, Flossy said, "The king's made a good choice this time."

Heather looked at her inquisitively and asked, "Have there been others?"

Flossy's expression was one of wonder. "Two before ye, but one got her throat slit trying to lift the wrong bugger's purse and the other was found floating in the river."

Heather felt the room sway and fought to remain conscious. If she did not succeed in David's plan it would mean the death of her child. She leaned against the door for a moment to regain her strength and then said, "Let's go." She walked ahead of Flossy down the stairs to meet Bagaudae.

As she stepped into the shop, Lizzy stopped and stared at her and then looked at David. "Bagaudae, you have made a good choice this time, for she looks the part of a lady. Those rakes will be mad about her and their purses are usually heavy."

David smiled down into the little wrinkled face with eyes that gleamed evilly and said, "I agree with you completely, my chérie, for she could lure the King himself to destruction." They laughed as Heather walked to them.

As she stood meekly waiting for a command from David, he took her pale face between his fingers and looked down into the large frightened eyes. "My dear Heather, I think you are ready to begin your first night's work. But be assured it will not be your last." He laughed. Looking back to Lizzy, David said, "Piggot will be meeting us near the Silver Fox. If all goes well this evening we will have heavier pockets come morn." Taking Heather by the elbow, he led her from the shop and through the same filthy alley through which they had come that morning.

Holding her skirts high so they would not drag in the slops, Heather staggered along under David's firm grip. She was unable to gain any sense of direction as they scurried through the dark alleys of London.

Even if she had the chance to escape she would not be able to find her way back to the child in time to save it from David. Heather choked with fear as she thought of her child.

The warm summer night was brilliant with stars but its loveliness was lost on Heather. Her troubles clouded everything.

After what seemed like hours of walking, David pulled Heather to a stop. Standing in the shadows, Heather could see that they had come to a street which was alive with activity. Elegant coaches passed them and stopped in front of a well-lighted building. A sign reading Silver Fox swayed gently above its door. David scanned the street watching for Piggot.

Shortly he came up behind them and bowed graciously to Heather. "I see that Mademoiselle is ready to work. She looks lovely."

Heather fidgeted nervously under Piggot's gaze. She looked at David, to see that he was enjoying her uneasiness. Smiling, he said, "Yes, she is ready, and I think it is time for us to begin." Turning to Heather he said, "I want you to walk across the street as the next carriage arrives. You will approach the gentleman as he starts to enter the club. You will tell him that you need his assistance. Your aunt fainted as you walked to your carriage." And as he watched Heather's expression he continued, "You must convince him that his help is urgently needed so he will not have time to ask questions about why two females are out unescorted and in this part of town." Taking Heather's face once more between his fingers, he pinched it until she flinched with pain. "Do you understand?"

Just as David released her face another sleek black carriage pulled to a stop in front of the club. Pushing Heather roughly toward the street, he said, "Make sure you succeed. You know the consequences if you don't!"

Heather stumbled but regained her balance just as she reached the street. Straightening her gown as she

306

walked, she hurried toward the club. As the gentleman stepped down from the carriage Heather walked up to him and placed her small hand on his arm.

As Heather spoke the gentleman looked down into her face and drew in a quick breath. It was the girl from Bess's.

Heather did not recognize Count Perier until he spoke. "Heather Cromwell, what on earth are you doing here pretending to have an indisposed aunt? And how did you slip away from that rake Nicholas Guyon?"

Heather released his arm as if she had touched fire, but he clasped her hand firmly with his. "Now, my little dove, tell me the truth. Why are you here?"

Heather could not answer the Count's questions and she glanced about for a means of escape. Finally in desperation she pleaded, "Please release me; if you do not I'll be in danger."

The Count looked down into Heather's pale, frightened face and said, "And am I to believe that also, with the story of an aunt? Now, my girl, I'm not going to let you go before you answer my questions honestly."

Glancing about to see if David was near, Heather said, "Sir, I beg you not to ask questions that I can't answer. However, I would ask a favor of you."

The Count raised a questioning eyebrow and looked at Heather more closely to see if he could see any falsehood in what she was saying. The look on her face was one of fear—no, more terror. He realized that she was speaking the truth. "My chérie, you are frightened and your hand trembles. Tell me what it is. Has Nicholas Guyon abandoned you? If so, you know you are welcome to stay with me."

As Heather spoke the Count could see the glimmering of tears in her eyes as she said, "No, it is not Nicholas Guyon, but please help me to get a message to him. It is a matter of life and death for me and my child."

Shock was apparent in the Count's face. "You and your child? But chérie, how is this so?"

Heather once again glanced nervously in the direction of the dark alley across the street. "I am sorry, sir, but I cannot explain it now. Please, just tell Nicholas Guyon that I am being held at Madam Elizabeth's shop. He will understand. Mention Bagaudae. Please understand. I dare not tell you more." Heather tried to pull her hand from his grasp, but he would not release her. She looked up into his cool blue eyes and said, "Sir, please. I cannot linger or they will kill my babe."

The Count yielded and bowed. "I will do my best, chérie, to be of service to you." He bent and kissed her cheek. "I will go directly to Nicholas Guyon's and give him your message."

Heather watched him go off and then ran back to the alley where David and Piggot waited.

David had watched the scene that had taken place in front of the Silver Fox and was enraged. As Heather walked to them, he lunged at her, catching her around the throat with his hands. "My little bitch, you will die for this, and so will your child. You should have done as we asked. But you and your whorish ways have ruined everything."

Heather nearly lost consciousness before David finally released her. Yet his words had penetrated. "Please," she gasped, "I will not do it again. I will do what you want!"

David shook his head as he jerked her roughly down the dark alley. "No, my love, you have forfeited your right to live and be useful. But before you die you will tell me what you told the old man."

Heather was out of breath and covered in filth by the time they reached Lizzy's. And as David pushed her into the shop, she stumbled, ripping her skirt until it hung in shreds from the waist. Her hair had come loose and was matted to her forehead. "Get up, bitch!" David said as he bent and pulled her to her feet by her hair.

Hearing the commotion, Lizzy scurried in the direction of the noise as fast as her thin old legs would carry her. As she approached the back of the shop, she stopped abruptly. "What in the bloody hell did the girl do to put you in such a temper, Bagaudae?" Lizzy asked as she walked closer.

Tightening his hold on Heather, David looked at Lizzy with eyes of fire. "The wench didn't do as she was told, and now she's going to pay dearly."

Dragging Heather down the steep steps to the cellar, he kicked open the door leading into the bedroom. The girl who had been caring for the child looked at the commotion. Seeing her, David said, "Get out!" He threw Heather down on the bed.

Heather scrambled to her feet, only to be slapped back onto the bed. "Now, Heather, you will tell me," David said evenly, a pulse beating in his cheek.

Tears cascaded down Heather's cheeks as she tried again to get to her feet and to her babe. With another violent slap across the face, she crumpled once more onto the bed. "Shall I give you a little more incentive to talk?" David asked as he walked to the pallet where the small pink bundle lay. As he bent to pick up the babe, Heather screamed, "No, I'll tell you! Please, God, no!"

David turned and came slowly back to Heather. Then dragging her once more to her feet, he said through clenched teeth, "Talk, my love."

Heather swayed unsteadily on her feet and she fought for consciousness. She knew that it would be the end of everything if she slipped into the merciful blackness that threatened to engulf her. "I sent a message to Nicholas."

To Heather's surprise David released her and threw back his head and laughed. "My love, you have done me the greatest service of my life. You have drawn Nicholas Guyon into the lion's den. He will surely try to rescue you. And I shall have the opportunity of killing him."

✑§ *Chapter Twenty* §✑

The sleek black carriage came to a halt in front of Nicholas Guyon's townhouse just as he was leaving. He had received a message from Lurcerne asking that he meet him at a small tavern near the waterfront. Lurcerne's man had seen a young girl with a baby enter it earlier that morning. He did not think anything of it until that evening when Lurcerne happened to question him. It was imperative that Nicholas join him immediately.

As the footman opened the carriage door and the Count descended, a frown creased Nicholas' brow.

Though Nicholas was obviously preoccupied and in a hurry, he smiled amicably at the Count and said, "Good evening, Count. I'm sorry that you caught me as I was leaving."

The Count returned the smile and said, "I am sorry also. However, I would appreciate a moment of your time. I have a message to deliver to you personally."

"Well, sir, shall we go back inside so we may talk in

privacy?" Nicholas said as he turned and led the way back into the house.

"Would you like something to refresh you, sir?" Nicholas said, closing the study door.

The Count shook his head and said, "No thank you, I don't have the time."

Nicholas raised an eyebrow in question to the Count and said curtly, "Well, let us not linger on formalities, sir."

The Count looked at Nicholas speculatively and said, "Do you remember the luscious golden-haired girl that you swept out from under my nose at Bess's?"

The agitation that Nicholas felt at being detained showed on his face as he answered the Count with a nod.

"Well, sir, I had the pleasure of meeting her once more this evening. She asked me to deliver a message to you."

The Count smiled as he watched the expression on Nicholas' face change. When the girl had first asked him to deliver the message to Guyon, he thought it would be a futile gesture on his part. He did not expect Guyon to rush to her rescue. He assumed since she was not with him, he had no more use for her. But as he watched Guyon's face he knew differently.

"And what is the message, sir?" Nicholas questioned.

The Count repeated Heather's words verbatim. Nicholas paled as he listened. As he had suspected, Heather and his child were in grave danger. He moved toward the door, leaving the Count flabbergasted at his rudeness once again.

"I'm sorry, sir, that I have to leave you," Nicholas said, "but I have urgent business. Thank you so much for your trouble, and I will find a way to repay you for your kindness."

Nicholas ran from the house and to his carriage. He instructed the coachman to drive him as quickly as possible to the tavern where Lurcerne waited.

As the carriage traveled through the streets, wild fantasies filled his mind. He could see Heather and his child in the squalor of the gutters with the villainous Bagaudae standing over them. Unconsciously his hands tightened into fists. He longed to have Bagaudae in his grasp—to choke the life from him.

Nicholas did not wait for the footman to open the door, but descended to the street rapidly, scanning it for Lurcerne. It took a few moments for him to see the tall slim man standing in the shadows of the alley next to the tavern. Without slowing his pace, he went over to Lurcerne. "I have the information we need, monsieur." Lurcerne was surprised, and a little disappointed that Guyon evidently had other sources. But what difference would it make if they found the young woman.

"Do you know of a shop called Madam Elizabeth's?"

Lurcerne nodded as the significance of Nicholas' question dawned on him.

"Oui, monsieur, I do and I should have thought of that myself. Lizzy, or Madam Elizabeth, is known for her activities in the criminal world. She is sometimes called the queen of the rogues. Yes, that would be the place where Bagaudae would choose to hide."

"Well, let us not waste time, Lurcerne. I have had a message from Heather. She and the child are being held there."

The two men did not speak again as Lurcerne led the way down the street. Both were absorbed in their own thoughts.

Heather lay on the straw pallet beside her child, her hands and feet bound roughly together. The dampness of the cold floor made her shiver. Her concern was not for herself, but for the babe. David paced the floor as he waited for Nicholas. He knew that he would come and had alerted Piggot to be on guard. Lizzy had already sent the girls away, for the less witnesses to Nicholas' murder, the better. She had also gone to her quarters so there would be no chance of her being involved in the violence that was to come. Lizzy was too old and feeble to enjoy that kind of sport.

David glanced at Heather and smiled evilly at her as she lay protectively close to her child. "It will not be long now," he said. "If the old man does not notify him of your whereabouts I will send him a message personally." He laughed. "Yes, I should have thought of that much sooner. Now I shall be completely free of the past. I shall have my revenge."

After what seemed like an eternity, David stopped pacing and looked toward the door. A slight noise had alerted his keen sense of hearing. With deliberate steps David walked across the room to where his rapier lay on the bed. He picked it up, and casually waited for the door to open.

David knew Nicholas would be alone. He had given strict orders that if he had any companions they were to be shown no mercy. Nicholas was not to be harmed, he was David's alone.

The sound of footsteps brought him back from his reverie and he watched the door intently. Presently it swung open and Nicholas stood there surveying the room.

He glanced in the direction of Heather and then to the child to ascertain that they were still unharmed. As his gaze then rested on the man casually leaning against the wall at the back of the room, he stopped and stared in shock.

It took him a few moments to organize his thoughts. This could not be David, he had been dead now for nearly two years. Yet the man's resemblance to his onetime friend was uncanny. "David, is it you?"

The man at the back of the room spoke as he swaggered to Heather's side. "Yes, it is, but I would prefer that you call me Bagaudae."

314

As David spoke, the odd events of these past months began to take shape in Nicholas' mind. He now knew the reason for Heather's strange behavior. She had fled to her onetime love and been betrayed. He could sense the terror that she felt as she stared at the man of her youthful dreams. He knew that this was the final act of the play that had begun when he arrested the Marquis. And in this final episode there would be death.

"Now that I have acquainted you with my name, I would like for you to meet Mademoiselle Heather Cromwell, your mistress and the mother of your bastard child. You will soon be together, my friend, as you wanted long ago, under an old oak on my estate at Dunhan. Or should I now say, your estate. Am I not right in assuming that it is yours by treachery?" David said as he lurched at Nicholas. The rapier sliced Nicholas' arm before he had time to counter.

David had forgotten one small item and Nicholas soon reminded him. It was Nicholas Guyon, captain of the King's Guard, who had shown his onetime friend how to use the rapier.

As the battle continued, David began to realize that he was fighting for his own life, that he might be the conquered rather than the conqueror.

Heather watched with terror as the two men fought. She stifled a scream as she saw blood seep down Nicholas' sleeve, and as the rapier brought blood across the cheek on which David had already left his mark. David laughed when he saw the blood. "I have already left my mark on you. This time, however, you won't have to make excuses about it. You will be dead."

As David finished speaking, he lunged once more at Nicholas. However, this time it was to find that Nicholas had countered. His rapier pierced David's heart. A stunned expression appeared on David's face as he slowly turned toward Heather and slipped to the floor. Heather screamed and merciful blackness enclosed her in its arms.

* * *

Heather sat under the old oak, as she had years before. Her own child played nearby in the soft clover, while birds sang and the scent of lilac drifted from the garden at Dunhan.

She was thinking of the future, and as she sat and dreamed, she did not hear the soft footsteps that approached. She glanced up at the sound of the voice she so loved.

Nicholas reached down for the child and then lifted it into his strong arms. "Are you thinking of the past, my love?"

Heather shook her head and smiled. "No, my darling, I am dreaming of the day in the near future when our little girl will play here with her brother."

Setting the child down, he walked across to Heather, lifted her into his arms and swung her off her feet jubilantly. "I love you, my darling wife."

NON-FICTION

☐ DR. KUGLER'S SEVEN KEYS TO A LONGER LIFE—Kugler	23811-3	$2.25
☐ NEXT YEAR IN JERUSALEM—Goldston	24103-3	$1.95
☐ METROPOLITAN LIFE—Lebowitz	24169-6	$2.25
☐ ACTRESS: POSTCARDS FROM THE ROAD—Ashley	24104-1	$2.25
☐ THE LIVING TOGETHER KIT —Ihara and Warner	24172-6	$2.50
☐ AND I ALONE SURVIVED—Elder	23864-4	$1.95
☐ BADGE OF MADNESS—Willwerth	23487-8	$1.75
☐ BED/TIME/STORY—Robinson	X2540	$1.75
☐ ...BUT THERE ARE ALWAYS MIRACIES" —J. & M. Willis	23203-4	$1.75
☐ EIGHT IS ENOUGH—Braden	23002-3	$1.75
☐ FELTON & FOWLER'S MORE BEST, & MOST UNUSUAL—Felton & Fowler	23485-1	$1.95
☐ FELTON & FOWLER'S BEST, WORST & MOST UNUSUAL—Felton & Fowler	23020-1	$1.95
☐ HEY, MAN: OPEN UP AND LIVE!—Olson	14038-5	$1.95
☐ HOLLYWOOD TRAGEDY—Carr	22889-4	$1.95
☐ THE INTRUDERS—Montandon	22963-7	$1.95
☐ LOVE—Buscaglia	23452-5	$1.95
☐ SCARLETT O'HARA'S YOUNGER SISTER—Keyes	23656-0	$2.25

If you liked the movie, you'll love the book!

FRENCH POSTCARDS   14297-3 $2.25
by Norma Klein

An utterly charming story of mischief and romance in Paris, written with the same warm sensitivity that Norma Klein has brought to her other bestselling Fawcett novels IT'S OK IF YOU DON'T LOVE ME and LOVE IS ONE OF THE CHOICES.

THE IN-LAWS   14252-3 $1.95
by David Rogers

The hilarious tale of a prime crime and young love in search of a motel. From the Warner Brothers motion picture starring Peter Falk and Alan Arkin.

CAPRICORN ONE   14024-5 $1.75
by Ron Goulart

To all appearances the launching of Capricorn One, the first spaceship to Mars, seemed perfectly normal. But behind the scenes, a NASA director was warning the three astronauts that their spacecraft was faulty. For them, a special fate had been arranged. . . .

ICE CASTLES   14154-3 $1.95
by Leonore Fleischer

Alexis Winston was a beautiful young woman with a dream— to become a champion figure skater. She was also in love with Nick, her childhood sweetheart, who had some dreams of his own. . . . Some dreams are shattered. Some come true.

FREE
Fawcett Books Listing

There is Romance, Mystery, Suspense, and Adventure waiting for you inside the Fawcett Books Order Form. And it's yours to browse through and use to get all the books you've been wanting . . . but possibly couldn't find in your bookstore.

This easy-to-use order form is divided into categories and contains over 1500 titles by your favorite authors.

So don't delay—take advantage of this special opportunity to increase your reading pleasure.

Just send us your name and address and 35¢ (to help defray postage and handling costs).